Goering's War

by

Kim Kerr

Chapter One: April 1942

The Spitfire curved upwards in a gentle arc away from the English coast. Leutnant Kurt Osser eased the stick forward and levelled out. He was heading towards the airfields just north of Paris and a day of partying and fine dining beckoned.

"Delivery aircraft four reporting in flight control."

A cool English voice came through his headset. "Yes aircraft four."

"Crossing the coast now thanks for your hospitality." The last comment dripped with scorn. His brief stay in England had been anything but enjoyable. He had been ignored at the local pub where the beer had been atrocious. The women had shunned him and the official help was cool verging on rude.

"Stay off the air unless it is necessary aircraft four."

Kurt chuckled. The English were poor losers.

This was the fourth Spitfire he had brought back across the channel as part of the war reparations. Kurt had heard that at least two hundred Spitfires and maybe the same number of Hurricanes had made the same journey. They were all flown to airfields around Munich where they were equipped with fifteen millimetre cannon and thirteen millimetre machine guns. The cannon was the same as equipped his old BF109f and was a good gun. He missed the logical layout of his old crate; that of the Spitfire seemed haphazard by comparison. He had to admit it handled like a dream, especially without any guns.

He wondered where this one would end up. Germany wasn't keeping any and had sold most to the Finns and the Hungarians. A few had been taken by the Romanians but mostly that country seemed happy with the old Bf109Es. The Hurricanes were very popular as fighter bombers, especially now they were armed with twin 20mm guns in each wing.

Of course most of the reparation costs had been paid in trucks and Universal Carriers. At least half the German army seemed to be driving them now and it had got to the point where a spare parts factory had been built for them near Berlin. A nearly complete aircraft carrier and a battleship had been taken as reparations as well as a couple of cruisers but it was the trucks that everybody in Germany noticed. There were even a couple of Bedfords being used at his fighter field outside Hamburg. French Citroens were around but not nearly in the same numbers. Kurt supposed that was the price of the light occupation of the British Isles. They had bought themselves a peace deal which meant the only sign of a German presence on their soil was a number of scattered bases around their coast. Most of their fleet had escaped to the Commonwealth nations but that was to be expected.

It was strange that his brother still fought the English. They weren't called that though. The Commonwealth and Rebel English army still held Port Said and the line of the Suez Canal. His brother's panzer division was down there somewhere in Egypt. After rescuing the Italians and eventually chasing Churchill's rebels and the Commonwealth to the Red Sea the offensive had stalled and it didn't look as though Fuhrer Goering could be bothered finishing them off. Maybe he didn't want to upset the Americans, it was hard to know. Sometimes he wished Hitler was still alive. He wouldn't have accepted any half measures. The bomb that killed the great man and some of his entourage on November 8th 1939 was a tragedy for Germany. Himmler's death didn't really trouble him nor did the crippling of Heydrich but coming when it did the decapitation of German's leadership could have lost them the war. Luckily German's enemies were slow to try and take advantage and the attack across France the following year had been a complete success.

As he flew across the channel his thoughts floated to those who had died during the invasion. He supposed that was when Goering had been at his best, when he had let the panzers crash into Dunkirk without waiting. His Father had told him that some of the general staff had called for a delay but Goering had listened to the bold and the British had been crushed before they could escape.

The invasion in mid-August had been a close run thing. It had been when Kurt had cut his teeth as a pilot trying to keep Hurricanes off the Stukas as they fell on the ships of the royal navy. His first kill had been a Spitfire, an earlier model of what he was now flying. He remembered coming in from underneath the aircraft and closing to within 70 metres. His burst had riddled the plane from the nose to the tail. The Spitfire had rolled on its back and dived into the sea pouring smoke. For the two weeks after the landings he had been constantly in action as the Seventh Panzer, the paras and the poor bloody infantry tried to hold on. The trouble had been keeping the troops supplied as the royal navy controlled the channel by night and made things very difficult during the day. If it wasn't for the extensive minefields protecting the landing areas around Dover and the Luftwaffe's efforts to hold the Royal Navy at bay then the invasion of England might have been a disaster. He shuddered as he thought of his aircraft lurching under the hits from the cannons on the British Destroyer. He had strafed the ship length ways and was pulling away when the holes appeared in his wing.

Kurt had just made the coast when he had been forced to bail out. The wind had pushed him inland and he had ended hung up in an old oak tree.

He crossed the French coast and smiled. They had won in the end but had taken every plane in the Luftwaffe and even some help from the Italians. Their transport planes had been very helpful. The big three engine Savoia-Marchetti SM.79 had bravely attacked the Royal Navy with torpedoes and had sunk at least one cruiser and damaged another. He guessed maybe Germany's allies were good for something after all. Their army had turned out to be next to useless and their navy not much better. If Malta hadn't been taken as part of the peace deal and Rommel sent across the Mediterranean then they probably would have been thrown out of North Africa. As it was his brother was still down there. At least he would be getting a sun tan. Kurt wondered if he could get a transfer to North Africa himself. Some action would be good and he might add to his three kills. It would be good to get at least five and become an ace and he had heard that the American P40s the Commonwealth flew were easy to shoot down.

Paris appeared to the south and Kurt contacted the French air controller. He was now out of the thin coastal strip still occupied by the Wehrmacht. He would land and hand the aircraft over before getting a pass from the local authorities and catching a lift to the City of Love.

v

"He still won't believe the evidence," said Kesselring. The head of the Luftwaffe sat in the back seat of the slowly moving staff car heading towards his office in the headquarters on Wilhelmstrasse. Next to him sat Wolfram Von Richthofen.

"The photos don't lie. Stalin is getting ready to strike," said the general. "It is difficult to fly over the Western Polish zone now without getting shot at. Luckily our boys are good enough to escape, most of the time."

"Our glorious leader points out that the deliveries of fuel keep coming and that's good enough for him."

"The Russians have moved massive amounts of armour and troops to the border. Their airfields are crowded with aircraft. Sure they do their best to hide most of it but there is so much it's hard to miss."

"Goering is busy organising the new national park in Bavaria. Either that or planning extensions to Carinhall."

Richthophen scoffed. "Another huge hunting preserve more likely. If the same effort was spent on watching our giant neighbour, or for that matter finishing off Churchill and his lackeys, then Germany would be a lot safer. Is it true he has had wolves and bears moved into the park?"

"And boar as well as bison."

The general shook his head. "Well at least he is not watching what happens behind the scenes. Can't the army move extra divisions into the area?"

"There have been strict orders given that any moves larger than a division need to go through OKW. Goering says he doesn't want to provoke the Russians." Kesselring smiled. "The order doesn't apply to the Waffen SS or the navy. Kaltenbrunner has allowed us to move the 1st, 2nd the new 5th and the 3rd SS divisions to an area just east of Warsaw. The 4th SS is in East Prussia and the Seventh is training in the Hungarian mountains."

"And what is he doing to make Goering listen?"

"The leader of the SS is still trying to get some sort of decision on the Jews."

"Everybody's priorities are screwed."

"The navy has moved its new carriers to Danzig. The Graf Zepplin and the Europa are ready to fight and the Bismarck, Tirpitz and Hipper will join them within the week," said Kesselring.

"Lucky we took that carrier from the British," said Richthophen.

"It was almost finished when we grabbed it. Anyway both ships are now equipped with the BF 109T's. The Me 155 will be ready soon and will replace them."

"Can we move more air units into the area?" asked Richthophen as the car reached the ugly high rise building.

"Yes, but we need to do it carefully and tell base commanders to keep them hidden."

v

Albert Speer walked into Goering's lavish office to find Germany's leader standing at the window. He was dressed in a powder blue uniform with gold trim and looked like a caricature of a nineteenth century general. As he got closer he saw the puffiness around the eyes and the blotchy skin. There were rumours that Goering was taking drugs again and if he was that didn't bode well for the country's future. Speer had received a visit the other day from Wilhelm Canaris head of Army Intelligence. The man had stared down his long nose and fidgeted while Speer ordered coffee.

"I'll get straight to the point," Canaris had said. "The Russians are coming and we aren't ready. Goering doesn't want to listen. He is struggling with his addiction again and has taken his eye off the affairs of the country, unless it's one of his pet projects."

"How long have we got?"

"All the indications are they will attack in May, probably in the second half."

He had listened and wondered what he could do in a month. The path of any attack would almost certainly come across the Polish plains. There would be another smaller offensive against Romania and probably attacks against Hungary as well. There was little industry in East Prussia and not much yet in Poland. If the Russians reached Silesia then Germany would be in trouble. Danzig was also important for ship building and U-Boat construction. He had already ordered the moving of some industry from Warsaw but otherwise all he could do was to try and increase production across the board. He hoped that Romania could be held. Without that country's oil Germany would soon run dry. Speer decided on trying to increase the stockpile in the time he had left, just in case.

Goering turned and sighed. "It is good to see my Minister of Armaments."

"My Fuhrer, I am here to serve."

"Not to bring me tales of doom and gloom?"

"I have heard the reports and believe them to be true, but you are our leader."

"I know one day Germany and Russia will fight it out for control of Europe but has that day come? I don't think so. We are not ready."

"We may have no choice," said Speer.

"Do you think I don't know that? Everybody seems to think me a fool! I still believe the evidence is thin. Canaris has sent report after report but his track record on knowing what the enemy is up to and its strength has often been unreliable to say the least."

Speer didn't comment as there was some truth in the statement. He tried a different track.

"Germany, under your leadership, has built its armed forces to a high peak of efficiency. You led us to victories over France, England, Greece and a host of smaller nations. However Russia is a colossus. They are showing some signs of recovering from their self-induced bloodletting and have a very good tank. We need to keep building so that we are ready, when the day comes."

"We are developing aircraft that will rule the skies," mumbled Goering.

Speer ground his teeth. The jets were still at least a year off and though the Henkel 280 showed promise engine problems plagued the project. Switching to the Jumo 004 engines helped but they were not really matched to the airframe of the Henkel. Goering however was not interested in these technical details.

"The jets are still a long way off, though they are promising. However it is armour and guns that we need now."

"The new Tiger will be ready soon."

"Perhaps in August and we need to work on their reliability."

"So we will have a counter for the T34."

Speer took a deep breath. "The Tigers cost as much as three Bf 109s and often break down. We have a gun that can stop a T34, we just need more of them. The PAK 40 is cheap and a slightly inferior version can be fitted into the Panzer four."

"I was led to believe that was already happening."

"It is, but far too slowly," said Speer.

Goering waved has hand lazily in the air. "I'm tired, do what you need to. Increase production of the guns. I'll sign anything you need."

Speer tried not to grin. He might be able to slip a few other projects through on such a promise.

"There is also the question of workers. Since the return of most of the French prisoners and those from our Scandinavian

16

neighbours we are struggling to increase production. Now that those British soldiers captured at Dunkirk are being slowly returned it's getting more and more difficult to keep the night shifts going."

"I know where you are going with this. German women don't work. They bring up our children and run our families. Use the Poles and the Greeks."

"We are but it is not enough."

"Take more Poles. That country is going to disappear anyway. I'm making a second park there you know. It will be bigger than the one in Bavaria."

Goering had wandered off topic. He did that a lot these days. Gently Speer tried to steer his leader back to the area of production. "All these foreign workers are unreliable. We have to watch them like hawks otherwise they sabotage the machinery. German women are motivated. We could let the unmarried ones join the work force."

"And let them rub shoulders with the Slavs and other lesser races. Never."

Speer sighed internally. At least he had one small win under his belt, though he didn't know how many extra 75mm guns he could get to the army before mid-May. He pondered how he would use the PAK 40 order to increase production of the new panzer fours.

v

Hals stared out over the open stretch of water. Ahead the Timshah Lake glittered in the desert sun. Hot sand pressed against his knee yet he ignored the discomfort. The Suez Canal ran south from here and on the other side New Zealand troops were dug in. Not far to the south the waterway broadened into the Great Bitter lakes where the Australians held the other bank. Or was it the Indians now? It didn't really matter, they were all good troops who fought hard. Even the British who worked for Churchill's government in Exile were competent. It was their training and leadership that had let them down.

"Do you think we will have to cross the Canal?" asked Soldat Mayer.

"I haven't seen any boats or bridging equipment. We have replacement panzers for our division but the 15th has gone back to Europe and still hasn't been replaced. As far as I can tell it's just us and the boys from the 164th and most of our division is partying hard in Cairo."

"Then there are the Italians and Ramke's troops."

"Paratroopers pretending to be motorised infantry," Hals snorted. "And as for our allies, tanks with skins like paper, guns that can't penetrate most of our enemy's armour, machine guns that jam at the slightest sprinkle of dirt and officers appointed on political merit. It's no wonder that their rank and file don't want to fight."

"The Italians are all cowards," snarled Mayer.

"They are brave enough. They just need some decent equipment and a few good leaders."

Suddenly there was a whistle and the two men threw themselves down. The shell burst fifty metres away, followed by another that landed in the water.

"Time to go," said Hals

He and the Mayer ran back to the Sd kfz 231. The eight wheeled vehicle sat parked in a small grove of palm trees near a mud covered hut. Hals cursed the fact his reconnaissance regiment had been ordered here to watch the canal while the rest of the 21st Panzer Division sampled the flesh pots of Cairo. Oh well, he thought, at least I'm not getting a dose of the clap. The car was almost too hot to touch as he pulled himself aboard. Obergrenadier Halder already had the engine going and gunned the vehicle away as he sat.

"Just another day in paradise," Hals muttered as they took off in a cloud of dust.

Chapter Two: May 1942

Corporal Sergi Temkan watched as the small hill and ridge in the distance disappeared in flame and noise. Behind him he could hear the thunder of the guns and the whoosh of rockets. Dust and earth soon obscured the view of the German lines and all that could be made out was the bright flash of flame.

"I almost feel sorry for them," said Junior Sergeant Sokolov.

"They were planning the same for us, never forget that," said Commissar Volkov. "We strike first to save the communist dream."

Sergi nodded. The broadcast last night had made it clear that the Germans were going to attack. Their spies had sabotaged Soviet industrial projects, their army massed and their planes attacked Soviet ships. The Germans had to be stopped. Sergi remembered what his father had said as they stood on the station at Novgorod.

"Germany is our natural enemy. One day there will be a reckoning between the Soviet and the West and you must fight for Stalin and Communism." He had watched his father walk away, back to the ammunition factory where he made shells for the 122mm and 85mm guns.

The noise grew louder as extra batteries joined the bombardment. He could smell the cordite and another odour that reminded him of a ploughed field. The shells fell for another hour and then suddenly the bombardment ended. His company had gathered in a long trench at the edge of wide wield. The captain blew a whistle and the men burst from the earth like hounds released for the hunt. A great yell went up and they sprinted forward. Sergi felt exhilaration as he ran forward expecting the enemy to fire but he didn't care. He would smite them, riddle them with bullets from his 'papasha'. He cradled the PPSh-41 in his arms and felt the bag of grenades bouncing on his back. Today he would kill for the Soviet. The men ran with him lugging light machine guns and mortars. The Captain sprinted towards the low hill waving his TT-30 pistol. Still a shot hadn't been fired in their direction.

They reached the German positions to discover they were empty. Sand bags were shredded and trenches collapsed but there were no Germans. Sergi noted the worried look on his captain's face. He turned to the runner and sent the man sprinting back the way the company had just come. A squad was sent to the top of the rise and soon returned to say that there was no sign of the enemy.

"We should keep moving," said Junior Lieutenant Morozov.

"Not without orders," said Commissar Volkov.

The Captain chewed on his moustache and stared at the empty trenches.

"I don't like this," said Junior Sergeant Sokolov.

"Why?" asked Sergi. He knew the young Sergeant had risen through the ranks after serving in the Far East. He had fought the Japanese and had one of their bayonets as a souvenir.

"Because it shows they knew we were coming. Not only that, they knew when."

"Shut up sergeant," snarled the Commissar. "Or I'll have you arrested for undermining the morale of the men."

The tall sergeant shrugged and moved towards the ridge.

The company sat there most of the morning until the runner returned with written orders. Captain Lebedev read through them and then nodded. "We are to move to the village of Orchowek. There is a woodland about a kilometre wide and then open ground. It's about 3 to 4 kilometres in all."

The company picked up its gear and advanced over the small rise and past a burning farm house toward the distant forest. Ahead the woodlands were dark. Sergi could see that they hadn't been hit by the dawn bombardment.

"Follow the folds in the ground," said Sergeant Sokolov quietly. Sergi passed the order and his squad drifted into a number of small dips and furrows to the south of the company. To the north Sergi could make out another company moving west. The chatter of a machine gun surprised him and he stood watching as men nearby jerked and twitched. Two men fell and Volkov screamed at him to hit the ground. Sergi followed instructions and then rolled into one of the hollows. Ahead there were bursts of light from the tree line. Men were falling and others firing back. One of the company's Degtyaryov light machine guns was firing at the woods with short bursts. The rest of the company had hit the ground as well. Sergi wriggled over to Sokolov. "What happens now?" he yelled over the noise.

"We will probably be told to charge and then get chopped to pieces. However we will do it differently. One squad will provide suppressive fire and the other two will charge. When the Germans switch their fire we will change rolls."

"The company hasn't trained for that!"

"Then they better learn fast," snarled the sergeant. "Order your men to target the machine guns."

Sergi did as he was told and watched as the rest of his platoon jumped to their feet and ran forward. The rest of the company was up and charging as one. He could see the ground being chewed up and soldiers falling yet his men seemed to be making progress. Then some of them fell screaming and Sokolov yelled for them to drop. He signalled with his hand for Sergi to get up and move forward. The young corporal felt his bladder tighten. The rest of the company was still charging but men were dropping everywhere. He screamed and sprang to his feet running forward. They had only moved a dozen paces when there was a soft whistle. The first mortar shell landed in the hollow where the light machine gun was firing from. Both men disappeared in an explosion of fire and blood. Sergi threw himself back to the ground as shells exploded around him. He heard screaming and realised it was his own voice. Then the sergeant was yelling in his ear and hauling him to his feet.

"We have to fall back. Get the men to the ridge."

Sergi nodded and gathered his squad. He felt moisture in his crutch and running down his leg and realised he had pissed himself. Somehow his platoon made its way back to the reverse of the sloop and flopped down. Sergi looked around and saw that at least four men were missing. The rest of the company soon joined them and it was obvious that his platoon had got off lightly. The captain was dead and at least half of the unit was lying back in the field. The sergeant told him some of them were probably just staying very still and would re-join them latter but he wasn't so sure.

Junior Lieutenant Morozov grabbed a runner and looked at a map. Then he wrote quickly and handed the man a note. Half an hour later the woods that had caused them so much trouble erupted in flames.

The company advanced again and men did spring from the ground to join them, but not all. They had taken about twenty percent casualties. As they moved forward a German machine gun fired on them but the Russians soon smothered it with small arms fire and then rushed the position. Sergi walked through the shattered and burning trees and stared down at his first dead Germans. Some were terribly torn up missing limbs or heads. Others looked as though they were sleeping. He thought one of them had a striking resemblance to his older brother Ivan who served in the navy.

"Just like us eh," said the Sergeant in a whisper. "It was different in the east. I found it easy to hate the yellow men. What they did to prisoners beggared belief. Here, I just don't know."

"They are fascists," said Sergi.

"Just looks like a man to me."

The whistle was loud and it took everybody by surprise. Sergi was pushed into a German trench and found himself face to face with his brother's look alike. Shells dropped on the woodland rolling in the same pattern as the previous bombardment.

"They're our own bloody guns," yelled Sokolov in his ear.

The shells rolled over the forest from east to west and then back again before falling silent. Men screamed as hot splinters tore at their bodies and others howled with fear. When it finally stopped the company was in a state of shock.

Junior Lieutenant Morozov came raging from his foxhole. "Our own guns! Who ordered a repeat bombardment? This is lunacy!"

"Calm yourself Lieutenant," snapped Commissar Volkov. "I will get to the bottom of this and someone will pay."

v

The Spitfire curved through the air above the airfield. To the east the mountains hid behind the clouds. The valley below where the small airfield had been built was a hive of activity. Second

29

Lieutenant Gyorgy Debrody continued to climb with his squadron into the growing light. Soviet Bombers were on the way. He gloried in the power of the British aircraft and thanked the Germans for forcing them to sell the aircraft to the Hungarian air force. The Re2000 were long gone, relegated to training and ground attack. Spotters placed in the mountains had warned his unit that the enemy were on the way. Puma squadron were ready. They had been training for this day for months. The Soviets were attacking across Romanian territory to hit this and other Hungarian airstrips. Early report suggested that the air force of the Romanians was also under attack. He wondered how their Bf 109Es and Hurricanes would go against the Russian Yaks and Laggs. His friend Miklos Kenyeres had said the Romanians had received some earlier marks of Spitfires but most of the newer models had gone to the Finns and a few to the Bulgarians.

His wing man Senior Aircraftman Sandor Tanacs spoke over the radio. "Bombers three o'clock, same altitude. Fighters same but higher, look like Laggs."

Debrody didn't know how his wing man could be sure at this range but it made sense. From what they knew of the Yak 1 that had accidently landed at a German Airfield in April was the new Russian fighter lacked the range to reach his air strip for which he was grateful. The latest Soviet fighter was said to be a vast improvement over the Lagg.

"Bombers are Pe2's," his wingman added.

The Finns had told them all about this tough durable twin engine machine. As a light bomber there wasn't very many planes that could match it.

Captain Jozsef Kovacs ordered Debrody's flight to be top cover while the rest of the squadron attacked the bombers so he continued to climb. The rest of the Spitfires turned and tried to angle behind the PE 2's. The sky was bright blue so there was no cloud to interfere with the attack. Debrody watched as the Lagg3s started to dive towards his friends.

"Time to help out," he ordered. His flight turned and followed the rest of the Spitfires. It was going to be the case of who reached who first. Unfortunately the Laggs had built up speed in the dive and the Captain had to order his eight aircraft to turn to face their pursuers. The two groups flashed through each other. From the confrontation one Spitfire fell away trailing white smoke while a Lagg fell towards the ground in flames. Debrody put the number of the enemy at fourteen fighters and perhaps slightly fewer bombers. This attack was probably a side show as far as the Soviets were concerned. Debrody watched as four Laggs formed up and turned towards the fray. He took his flight around behind them and dived. As they closed the range the Laggs must have spotted them but the Russians all broke in the same direction, straight across Debrody's sights. He held down the gun button and watched as the 13mm bullets and 15mm cannons walked down the length of the first Lagg. The plane burst into flame and the cockpit disintegrated. The second aircraft veered slightly and the cannon shells tore through the wing root and outer panels. There was a massive explosion as the fuel tank ruptured sending the plane spinning away in pieces. The other two Laggs turned viciously one skidding sideways, its wing buckling and then shearing off.

"You didn't even hit it!" exclaimed Sandor.

Debrody switched positions with his wing man as they followed the last Lagg3 out of its turn. Sandor moved smoothly in behind the Soviet aircraft and fired two quick bursts from one hundred metres. Debrody saw hits on the tail and fuselage and then the pilot threw open his canopy and jumped. His parachute opened just before he hit the ground.

When he landed Debrody noticed the fires around the air strip. A Caproni bomber was smouldering as was a nearby British truck. One of the hangers had been hit destroying a Spitfire that had been under repair and an AA pit had been wiped out by a direct hit. At the end of the runway a PE 2 burned. He landed his aircraft and taxied it to a sandbagged wall that provided some protection from air attack. Walking across the tarmac he joined his Captain who had just dismounted from his own plane.

"Three kills, Lieutenant! Well done."

"I shouldn't really count one of them. He just tore his own wing off."

"It counts. I got a PE 2 and Janos got another Lagg. Our damaged plane landed safely but unfortunately most of their bombers got away."

Debrody looked around at the damage the attack had caused and realised that it could have been much worse.

"They'll probably move us after this," said the captain.

"Why?" asked Debrody.

"They'll want us closer to the front. Most of the fighting will be in Poland or Romania and they won't move us onto the soil of our old enemy.'

Obersturmfuerer Wolfgang Fischer stared out from the commander's hatch of the new panzer four. He looked out along the 75mm L43 cannon and tried to imagine it sending an anti-tank round at a T34. That day was coming. The Leibstandarte Adolf Hitler 1st SS Panzer Grenadier Division was on the march and he was leading a zug of four of the most powerful panzers available to the German armed forces. The single battalion of tanks had been formed in January and attached to the division. It had trained on panzer twos. The battalion had put up with these old panzers until the start of this month. On May 1st the new unit had received the panzer fours. This morning May 16th the Russians had attacked and the 1st SS along with the 2nd SS were moving to attack. He felt sorry for their sister division as they only had panzer threes and a few of the new Marder ones.

The long 50mm guns on the older panzers wouldn't penetrate the frontal armour on a T34 unless they got lucky. It was fortunate that they even knew about the Soviet tank. If the Ukrainian crew hadn't driven one across the border to seek asylum in November of the previous year then the Army would have remained in the dark about the tank's potential. The rumours about an even heavier panzer called the KV1 were even more disturbing.

He led his tanks with the rest of the battalion and two companies of infantry mounted in French P107's half-tracks. Four 222 four wheeled armoured cars led the way. They spent the evening west of Ostroleka listening to the sound of artillery in the distance. Later Wolfgang Fischer sat with his crew around a small campfire in the evening light.

"We'll have to put this out boys when it gets dark. Even now the Soviet Air Force could use it to find us."

"It's alright Obersturmfuerer. The weather is fine and once we have had our coffee we will do so."

"You remember when we couldn't get real coffee," said Sturmmann Kruger.

"Yes, for that short period before the British and the French surrendered," said Oberschutze Braun. "My brother was wounded fighting those scum."

"The French?" asked Kruger.

"No the British near Dover. He was with the Seventh Panzer when it landed on the second day."

"We almost lost that battle," added Fischer. "I've an uncle in the high command. Just a clerk really but he heard things. The navy was next to useless except for the U boats and if it wasn't for the minefields and the efforts of the Luftwaffe we would have lost. They threw every plane into the battle. Even the Italians helped. We only controlled the air over the very bottom corner of England but it was enough. After all the men the British lost at Dunkirk they just couldn't maintain the effort."

"Yes, but that war criminal Churchill still fights on," said Braun. "I don't know why the Canadians fight for him?"

Fischer shrugged.

"We should have finished them in the desert," said Oberschutze Kohler.

Fischer shook his head. "I think our leader didn't want to provoke the Americans."

"Do you think Goering also lost interest? After all, Africa was supposed to be the Italians area."

Fischer bristled. "Our leader showed amazing energy and led us into crushing the French and destroying the British on the beaches of Dunkirk. Again my uncle told me that various generals were saying to hold off, to wait for the infantry. Kesselring wouldn't guarantee that the Luftwaffe could do the job of destroying the English on the beaches and Manstein said attack so we did. It was a brilliant victory and he followed it with the invasion of Britain in late August."

His crew exchanged glances so he softened. "Granted, since we took Greece Herr Goering has been quiet."

They drank their coffee in silence and then checked the panzer one more time. Fischer visited the company leader Stumbanfuerer Hersh before returning to his crew.

"The Russians have broken through," he told them. "Catch a little shut eye. We refuel in four hours and then we are off."

The panzers moved along the main road towards the thunder of guns through the last hours of darkness. At dawn the company commander ordered Fischer to take his zug into a small patch of woodland. "I want you to watch our flank. From all reports there's a lot of armour coming this way and I don't want to get hit in the side. If things get tough call for help. The battalion is keeping a few panzers in reserve."

He could hear the sound of branches snapping and the odd sapling fallings as they pushed along the narrow dirt track in their panzers. Ahead some infantry had taken a position at the other side of the wood. An officer carrying an MP 40 came running up waving.

"Lieutenant Maulder 65th infantry division. Boy are we glad to see you guys. My company has been falling back for most of the night. We have dropped trees across roads and laid mines but our anti-tank guns can't stop their tanks."

"Do you only have PAK 38's?" asked Fischer.

"Yes Herr Obersturmfuerer. We need to hit them in the side to have any chance and they aren't always that obliging."

Fischer nodded. "Can your boys shield us against any Soviets on foot? I don't want to get caught in these woods without support."

"We would be glad to help Obersturmfuerer."

Fischer smiled, he liked the man's spirit. "Good, then let's go and give the Russians a bloody eye."

They stopped at the tree line in another small patch of wood and listened. Ahead they could hear the roar of engines.

"Sir, those can't be our panzers. I aint ever heard an engine so noisy in my life."

Fischer grunted. Braun was right. The man had driven just about every type of German tank and knew their strengths and weaknesses. He had been complaining for the last few days about the steering of their new mount. The extra weight of the gun made the panzer four heavy at the front. Fischer didn't care, the new gun was worth the problem.

Two BA 11 Soviet armoured cars sat in the middle of a ploughed field, one with a hole in its chassis just below the turret. Two men lay unmoving on the earth beside it. The second car had greasy black smoke pouring from two open hatches. In thick scrub three PAK 38's lay hidden protected by a machine gun and a couple of squads of infantry. Fischer conferred with the commander of the guns and discovered that except for a few mortar shells the Russians had made little attempt to push through. On the radio he heard the rest of the company was locked in combat around some small Polish village called Skrzypek. This concerned him as he knew the crossroads the village sat astride was a kilometre behind him. "Ostroleka must have fallen," he muttered. That meant that this particular thrust from the old boarder had made fifteen kilometres in two days. He knew that the 1st Panzer Grenadier regiment was moving on Nowa Weis to the north to block another important road juncture but didn't know where the other two regiments of the division were heading.

He stared at the forest in front of him and decided to wait. The clearing was only 400 metres wide and a fast attack could cross it in no time. The sound of enemy armour grew louder and then suddenly four tanks burst from the forest. A PAK 38 fired at the one furthest to the north and sparks shot from the location of the hit. The other guns started firing and more shells bounced from the armour of the T34's. The enemy stopped and fired back, gouts of flame and earth erupting near the hidden guns. A man popped up from one of the T34s and started waving flags and more tanks appeared.

"Take that one," said Fischer to Gunner Huber. The small man answered with a yes sir and the electric traverse moved the turret slightly. With a roar the shell was away. A small hole appeared on the front of the T34 followed by an internal explosion that lifted the individual with the flag clear of his machine. Smoke and flame poured from the top hatch followed by more explosions.

"New target," called Fischer.   Huber missed with the next shell but the third sheared off the track of a stationary tank before the next one put a hole in the turret. The other four panzers were all firing now as well as the Pak 38's. Soon twelve tanks were burning or knocked out. Russian Infantry tried to push across the open ground but was mown down by machine gun fire. Mortar shells started falling near Fischer's panzer and he was forced to close his hatch, his view now reduced to the slits in the cupola. He felt a moment of sympathy for the German troops outside. The Russians tried a second armoured attack but four more T34s were destroyed for no loss. It was then that Oberscharfueher Otto Weber radioed in.

"The Russians are trying to push infantry and panzers through the woods to the north of us."

Fischer didn't want to split his forces but he realised he couldn't leave the anti-tank guns to cover the open ground alone.

"You and I will stop them Otto. Grab what you can of the infantry and we will push through the wood for 400 metres. Then they can dismount and move forward by foot with us," he radioed.

The lieutenant from the 65th pulled together a platoon and the combined force pushed through the open woods, the panzers knocking down small trees as they went until they had gone half a kilometre. Ahead the woods had been recently harvested. There were piles of timber and open areas. Soviet tanks and infantry were firing in a north westerly direction, unaware of the German forces approach. Fischer guessed that the boys from the 1st regiment were somewhere up there. Nowa Wies was probably a kilometre further on. Stopping at the edge of the track that ran north-south Fischer ordered his panzers to open fire. Two T34s burst into flame immediately but the others just kept firing at Nowa Wies. The infantry set up a couple of mg 34s and took the Russian foot soldiers down with short bursts and the hull machine gun on Otto Weber's tank joined in. Soon all eight enemy tanks were destroyed and the Soviets were running back towards the forest.

Fischer ordered his panzers into the open and quickly joined up with the halftracks of the 1st regiment. These were German 251s, some of them carrying mortars. The Russians were thrown back past the village of Zebry Chudek. By the end of the day Fischer and the 1st regiment had advanced almost as far as the outskirts of Ostroleka. To the south the rest of the panzers had been almost as successful. However the news from the rest of the front wasn't as good.

v

Speer sat at his desk looking across at Ernst Kaltenbrunner. The leader of the SS was looking dishevelled. His usually immaculate side part in his hair was ruffled and his jacket unbuttoned.

"After two weeks of hiding on his estate our glorious leader seems to be returning to us," said Kaltenbrunner.

"I hear he is off the drugs and on a diet," said Speer.

"And taking an active interest in the war."

"Manstein's plan brought him out of his depression?" asked Speer.

Kaltenbrunner raised an eye brow. "You shouldn't know about that."

"I have to supply the tanks and guns to make sure it succeeds. I believe we have to hold East Prussia and The Carpathians to make it work."

Kaltenbrunner smiled. "The Hungarians hold the passes and even some of the plains and my SS have thrown the Russians back on the northern shoulder of their attack. Memel is under siege but the navy with planes from the carriers support the city. The Soviets have pushed hard towards Warsaw and the old Polish capital is in trouble."

"But that is part of the plan," said Speer.

"Indeed," said Kaltenbrunner. "Our only concern is Romania. The Russians have advanced about eighty kilometres across the border."

"What's Rommel doing to stop them?"

"Well he doesn't command remember."

"Yes, but he has the only German army in the area. I sent him the very first StuGs with L48 75mm guns and one hundred panzer fours. The Tenth and Fifteenth panzer divisions are at full strength. He also has the Sixteenth Motorized as well as three infantry divisions," said Speer.

"Yet he is supposed to follow the orders of the Romanian high command."

"Like he followed Italian orders in the desert?" Speer's smile pushed at one side of his mouth.

"You have to understand that the Romanians have only French Char B's with the long 47mm gun. They have little that can stop a T34," said Kaltenbrunner.

"Well I'm about to send them a small number of PAK 40s."

"Ah, about that. The reason that I'm really here is to talk to you about the new SS division. The 9th Panzer Grenadier Herman

Goering division is almost ready for battle. However it has only six panzer 3s and the same number of panzer 2s."

"PAK 40's aren't tanks," said Speer.

"Yes but we have Geschützwagen Lorraine available to us and we plan to mount the guns on them," said Kaltenbrunner.

"It's already being done on other half-tracks I don't see why the SS can't do it. I'll need to find guns to replace them to send to the Romanians something. Maybe those 57mm guns I got from the British will do. They will match the 25 pounders we took from them and sold to the Romanians nicely."

Kaltenbrunner laughed. "It will go with their British trucks and cars as well as the aircraft but will a 57mm gun stop a T34?"

'Tests show that at 200 metres it is possible. They are about 30 percent more powerful than a PAK 38."

"That's pretty close," said Kaltenbrunner.

Speer shrugged. "They are Romanians. Our boys need to get the best stuff first."

Chapter Three: June 1942

The Romanian countryside was flat but it was not featureless. Geifreiter Paul Becker cursed the British Bren carrier in the foulest language and received a hard stare from Sergeant Fuchs.

"Is that really necessary Becker?"

"Well if they gave us decent German equipment then I wouldn't get so angry, sir."

"Sir? You only give me honorifics when you swear. If Wolf didn't throw the vehicle around like it was a racing car then maybe we wouldn't have lost the track."

"Sorry Sergeant," said Max Wolf

The grizzled non-com grunted and then pointed at the crow bar and wrench. "Just fix it. Hofmann you can help him. Becker you man the 38 and I'll take a little stroll to that clump of trees over yonder. Pass me the toilet paper."

The sergeant picked up his MP 40 and a roll of old paper and jumped from the side of the small vehicle.

"Why the British couldn't make a proper sized half-track is beyond me," grumbled Becker.

"Technically it's not a halftrack," said Wolf.

"What is it then?" asked Hofmann.

"I'm not really sure," said Wolf scratching his head.

Becker looked around. They had been sent out here to scout for the 1st battalion of the 104th Motorized Regiment. Most of their transportation was the small tracked carriers, though a few larger French vehicles had joined them recently.

"Do you think the Ruskis will come this way?" he asked.

Wolf shrugged and started working on the track.

Hofmann glanced up. "Who knows? One thing is for certain, we will be moving soon."

"Why do you say that?" asked Becker.

"The 10th Panzer and 16th Motorized have joined us. I was talking to a truck driver who was delivering fuel and he said that Rommel had pulled everything into one location. One big armoured fist if you like. You know the boss. We fought with him in Africa. He won't wait too long to throw the punch."

Becker frowned. He didn't particularly like being shot at. It was alright for the SS and the other glory seekers but he wanted to make it through the war alive.

Presently Sergeant Fuchs returned smiling. "Don't go down there. The stench has burnt some of the leaves."

"Too much information," said Wolf.

The track didn't prove difficult to fix and they were about to leave when Fuchs stood a little straighter. "Company," he said.

"Ours or theirs?" asked Becker.

"Let's not take a chance. Move the carrier down into the scrub slowly. I don't want us to kick up any dust," said Fuchs.

They parked in the low scrub and the Sergeant told them to rip off some large branches and place them on the carrier. They then took positions lying down amongst tall grass as the engine noise got closer. A small armoured car soon bumped over the ridge line and rattled in their direction.

"It's a BA 20," said Fuchs. "I'm surprised it's off road as the intelligence on them is that they can't cope cross country."

"Well it looks like it barely is," said Becker. "They are heading straight for us Sarge."

"I know," said Fuchs.

The PzB39 anti-tank rifle was brought from the carrier by Wolf and handed to the Sergeant who loaded the weapon and aimed at the approaching vehicle. Becker looked at the long barrelled rifle and wondered if it would have the hitting power to stop the armoured car.

"Maybe we should just let it pass," he said.

"Shut up Becker and get some stick grenades ready," said Fuchs.

The armoured car stopped about forty metres from the scrub side on to the German's position. A man opened the hatch on the small turret and looked around before bending down to say something to the men inside. That was when Fuchs fired. The bullet hit the side of the vehicle just back from the driver's window. Three stick grenades arched through the air and exploded around the armoured car and Hofmann fired at it with the MG 34. Becker almost felt sorry for the men inside as the noise must have been deafening. Bullets bounced from the steel sides and shrapnel pelted the wheels and the front of the car. A man stuck his hand through the top hatch and waved a dirty rag around while yelling in Russian.

"Stop firing," yelled Fuchs.

The Russian scrambled clear of the armoured car and kept his hands in the air. A second man soon followed him. Becker noticed both were young, probably no more than twenty and were rather dirty.

"Keep 'em covered Hofmann," said the Sergeant.

"Where's the rest of the crew? There must be at least three of them," added Neumann.

Becker was ordered to go forward and check while Wolf made sure the other two Russians were unarmed. He opened the side door with the old British Enfield pistol, a souvenir from Africa, in his right hand. What he saw caused him to turn and empty his stomach contents onto the dust. The heavy calibre anti-tank round had penetrated the armour of the car next to the man's head. The lead had probably flattened and distorted before hitting the unfortunate Russian in the side of his skull. Most of the head above the jaw was missing. No wonder the other crew members had been in a hurry to surrender.

Wolf came up next to him. "Jesus, what a mess."

"Drag him out," yelled Fuchs. "And check his pockets."

Becker left the disgusting job to others and rinsed his mouth out with water. He noticed that the reason the Russians were so dirty was that they were covered with blood and brains.

"What will we do with the car?" asked Neumann.

"You and Becker can drive it back."

"No, no, no," said Becker. "I'm not getting in there."

"When did you get so squeamish? We've seen worse in Africa," said Wolf scratching the end of his flat nose.

"Yes but I always got to walk away. Besides, this would measure up to anything we witnessed down there."

"You help the Ruskis bury their mate and I'll let you off," said Fuchs. "Lange can manage the gun in the armoured car's turret."

Becker thanked his sergeant and signalled the two Russians to get the dead man. He then collected the MP 40 and a couple of shovels. He tossed the shovels to the men and then pointed at the ground. It was a hot day and the Russians were soon sweating. Becker kept them covered with the sub machine gun. He tossed the younger of the two a canteen of water before telling him to drink. The man nodded his thanks before passing the canteen to the other soldier. Becker reassessed his age and now believed the younger of the two to be no more than eighteen. Not really a man at all. Becker shook his head, everyone had to grow up fast once they pulled on a uniform.

v

"Rommel's attack has thrown the Russians back towards the border," said Keitel. He stood with Goering in a huge ballroom at Carinhall. Large maps were strewn across tables or pinned to the walls. The only other men present were Speer and Kaltenbrunner. Goering didn't like meeting a large group of generals at one time. Speer guessed he found the experience intimidating.

"He gathered the Fifteenth Panzer, Tenth Panzer and the Sixteenth Motorized and punched through the side of the advancing Russians who had become badly strung out. The Romanians attacked the other flank with an armoured division and a motorised one. About forty thousand prisoners, 200 guns, many trucks and at least eighty tanks have been captured. Suffice to say the Romanian oil fields are safe for the moment. It seems that the attack on the Balkans was relatively weak, compared to that coming through Poland."

"And what is Rommel doing now?" asked Goering.

"He is forging across the rivers on the frontier. We have told him to halt when he has secured bridge heads," said Field Marshal Keitel.

"Why?" asked Goering.

"We have no troops to spare to support him. Everything is needed for Poland."

"My new division is ready isn't it Kaltenbrunner? The Ninth SS Herman Goering is equipped and ready to fight."

"That is true my Fuhrer."

"Then send it to him and tell him to continue his advance."

"My Fuhrer,' said Keitel "we need that division for Poland. That is where the final decision will be made."

"I know that,' snapped Goering. "But we need to distract the Russians. If we can threaten Odessa then it will force them to pull units away from their thrust on Berlin. I want to reinforce success."

Keitel tried to argue but Goering cut him off.

"I don't interfere often with the running of the war! I sanctioned Manstein's plan! Most of you Generals have little imagination and I have to support those who do! Rommel is one of those men and I will give him his head and see how far he can run. Now draw up the orders and have them before me by dinner."

Goering drew a breath. Speer could see that his skin was still pale yet he did seem a little thinner.

"What is the latest from Poland?" asked their leader calmly.

"The flanks are holding thanks to the counter attacks by the SS and the border defences in East Prussia. Memel is cut off but is being supplied by sea. Since the Kriegsmarine defeated the Soviet Baltic Fleet at the Battle of Riga Gulf they have been free to support operations from off the coast. The Graff Zeppelin was slightly damaged and so was the Scharnhorst but both will be back on station within a month. Soviet marine aircraft were decimated and no longer pose a threat."

"A great victory," muttered Goering.

"The line in Poland runs from Krakow to Radom. From there it goes to Warsaw before gradually curving back towards the East Prussian border. To the south, from Krakow the line curves east back along the Czech border. We expect Warsaw to fall any day now."

"And this is all part of Manstein's plan?"

"The one you approved," said Keitel.

"By God it's a risk," said Goering.

"To describe the line as such is also a bit of a stretch. It has many holes and the Russians are pushing forward everywhere. There are signs they are going to thrust into East Prussia soon, to tidy their flanks. We will need to give some ground in the north, otherwise the central thrust might slow."

"You plan to use some of the panzer divisions in an attack near Warsaw soon?" asked Goering.

"Yes," said Keitel. "We need the Russians to believe we are using everything to hold them. We don't want them to expect a massive counter strike. We will also do the same in the south where the enemy has made even better progress. That's where the French and Spanish divisions will make their first appearance."

"The British should send us some troops too! I will squeeze them for more equipment if they won't help," said Goering.

"We were too soft on them," said Kaltenbrunner.

Goering pursed his lips. "You are probably right, yet I was feeling in a generous mood and once Churchill had fled to create his rebel government I just wanted some peace and quiet. I didn't think the Commonwealth would continue the war."

"They are waiting for the Americans to join them," said Speer.

"Well, one thing at a time. First we need to beat the Russians. Now, how are negotiations with the Finns going?" asked Goering.

v

Second Lieutenant Debrody walked the shells down the road and over the truck. The bonnet exploded upwards as the vehicle disappeared in dust and fire. His Spitfire eased away from the ground as he pulled back on the stick. Ahead he could see at least a dozen other burning cars and trucks. Hurricanes pulled away from the remains of the burning fuel vehicles having dropped their 250 kilo bombs. Some still raked the Soviet traffic with twin twenty millimetre cannons. Debrody's flight of Spitfires had been sent down to join the attack leaving the rest of the squadron at five thousand metres elevation as top cover. He continued his climb eventually levelling off at three thousand metres and surveyed the southern Polish plains. Krakow blazed in the distance having just fallen to Soviet armoured columns. Debrody wondered if his squadron would be forced to relocate again. Their current airfield was just outside Rybnik, about eighty kilometres from the current front line. He knew the Russian advance had been at its most successful in the south of Poland but units of the 4th and 5th panzer divisions were now counterattacking from Oswiecim toward the north east and a French armoured division was attacking from the north. The group of supply trucks they had just attacked had come out of the town of Skawina and would have been destined for the Soviet forces fighting this thrust.

A call from Captain Jozsef brought him out of his musings. "Enemy fighters nine o'clock. It looks as though there are at least twenty of them."

Debrody chastised himself for not being more alert. He scanned the area indicated by his squadron leader and saw the approaching planes. The Hurricanes began to climb to the west but Debrody could see that they had no chance of escaping. It was up to the Spitfires to protect the Hungarian fighter bombers. He realised that the Hurricanes could probably look after themselves, but until they gained altitude they were very vulnerable. He thanked the Germans for getting these planes off the British. With them at least they had decent equipment and a better chance of winning than they would have with the older Italian planes.

He led his flight to the north and continued to climb while the other eight aircraft of the squadron dived at the enemy. He saw the two formations flash through each other in head on attacks. One Soviet plane burned brightly and a Spitfire fell away trailing smoke. Debrody continued upwards and then rolled his plane around and dived towards the rolling melee. Two Yak Ones were turning towards the still climbing Hurricanes and he chose the trailing aircraft as his target. "Watch my tail," he ordered his wing man before opening fire. Flames appeared in his gunports as the fifteen millimetre cannons and heavy machine guns spat shells at the Yak. The pilot had no chance as the first burst shattered his cockpit and then shredded the fuselage. The plane rolled over trailing smoke and went into a spin. The other Yak dived towards the ground and Debrody followed after ordering half of his flight to separate. All he needed was a wing man for protection he decided. The Yak turned at the bottom of the dive but the Spitfire had stayed with the enemy plane and actually closed the distance. The Yak turned tightly and Debrody tried to go with it but found he was going too quickly. "Take it Sandor," he ordered.

His wingman was at least five hundred metres behind him and cut inside the enemy plane's turn. Debrody dropped behind his wingman, the two planes basically swapping place with his plane now covering the other. They were now very low. Sandor fired a burst that cut through a hay stack and some trees in front of the low flying Yak causing it to turn left. Debrody noted that they had pinned the enemy plane to the ground. It was out of room and out of options. The next burst hit the enemy planes tail section causing the aircraft to drop suddenly. The pilot tried to correct the dip and managed to level the plane out but the altitude must have been about ten metres. The Yak couldn't avoid the oak trees that appeared before it. The wing caught the branches near the top of the tree causing the plane to stagger and dip again. The Yak hit the ground on its belly and skidded through a ploughed field, smashing a stone wall and crashing into a line of low shrubs before coming to rest. Debrody noted the pilot clambering from the wreck and running just before the Yak exploded.

"Lucky man," he muttered as he began to climb once more. The air combat still swirled above them and he could hear Spanish in his ears. It seemed a group of Bf 109fs had joined the fray. This was the Spanish Blue Squadron and it had only arrived at the front three days ago and had painted the noses of their aircraft to match their name. Debrody hoped they had studied their aircraft recognition and didn't shoot any Spitfires or Hurricanes down. He took his aircraft up to three thousand metres when he noted some

Mig 3's diving in and decided to go after the new comers. He was surprised to see these aircraft as intelligence said they were being phased out.

Their performance at the lower altitudes was poor and he thought they would be easy targets. The air battle was growing by the minute and while Debrody turned back towards the fighting he watched as two aircraft spiralled towards the ground. He couldn't tell if they were friend or foe but one did look like it had the lines of a Hurricane. Debrody hoped the fighter bombers would flee as soon as they got the chance as many would be low on ammunition. The Migs were diving towards two Bf 109s and he slipped in behind them and opened fire at two hundred metres. He was directly behind the last plane and his burst went high. The plane didn't take evasive action and the next burst caused the Mig to fly apart. The rest of the flight continued on and he started to line up another plane when Senior Aircraftsman Tanacs yelled a warning. "Yak on your six."

"Get him off me," said Debrody as he turned sharply.

"Skipper, I've got my own problems."

Debrody tuned his head and saw his wingman throwing his plane into a tight turn followed by a dive. At least four yaks were attacking them and Debrody pulled the stick into his chest almost blacking out. He then half rolled and dived. As he reached one thousand metres he looked around frantically finding that only one Yak had followed him. Tracers flashed past his wing and he turned again but the Yak followed him. Debrody then tightened the turn and climbed slightly. He knew that the Spitfire would climb better than the Yak but wasn't sure that he could out turn the enemy plane. The problem was that the Russian was too close. More tracers flashed past and he was forced to turn again.

"Wait there brother," said a voice. "Just hang on."

Debrody didn't recognise the voice and continued his turn.

"Break left now!"

He knew there wouldn't be any Russians speaking Hungarian here so he obeyed. The Yak must have turned to follow him, probably thinking he had an easy kill. Debrody heard the explosion and then the whoop of triumph before seeing a Hurricane fly past his wing tip. It seemed the enemy pilot was so fixed on his destruction he hadn't seen his compatriot diving to help. The four twenty millimetre cannons had ripped the Yak to pieces. "I owe you a bottle," said Debrody. As he levelled out next to the Hurricane he noticed they were alone. The sky seemed to be empty. He realised with his two extra kills he was now the highest scoring pilot in Puma squadron. He could add two more stars to the five already painted on his tail. Looking across he noticed that the Hurricane had seven stars on it. His saviour had shot down more Russians than he had while flying an inferior aircraft. He would have to see if this pilot was interested in moving to his squadron.

v

Obersturmfuhrer Fischer stood looking at the bodies with Obersturmbannfuhrer Peiper. What had happened to the nurses was the most shocking. They had been pack raped and then had their throats cut. The wounded who had been captured had been drenched in petrol then set alight.

"This proves what sub humans we fight," said Peiper. The tall handsome man's eyes blazed. "We need to send Ivan a message. All the prisoners we take will be executed, the officers and commissars hung. These animals need to be wiped out."

Fischer was shocked at the orders but when he thought about it he agreed with them. Strong action needed to be taken. What had happened to the Germans captured in the East Prussian villages that had fallen was equally disgusting. He had twelve prisoners marched out immediately and cocked his MP 40. Braun, who was from East Prussia joined him and they both stood next to each other with machine pistols ready. The Russians looked at them in horror before they both opened up. The small wall that was behind the Soviets puffed as bullets chipped off pieces of timber. Three short bursts each and it was over. Braun then walked up and riddled anybody that still seemed as though it might harbour a spark of life.

Huber, their gunner stood back white faced and Fischer turned on him. "This is what they deserve!"

"But they surrendered sir," the man stammered.

"They are Russian! You saw the nurses!"

The man nodded and then walked towards the panzer four. The rest of the tanks were warming up, some revving engines. Peiper mounted his vehicle and shouted, "Well done Fischer. We'll hang those junior officers when the attack is over."

The First SS Division was moving again. They had surged across the Wkra River and retaken the small town of Glinojeck. Now they were going to drive down the main road in the direction of the village of Nowa Garwarz with the intention of reaching the road junction At Huta. About four hundred metres of field lay before them until they reached the woodlands where the Russians had dug in. Houses screened the approach of the panzers until they were close to the trees but the armour would need infantry support if they were to push the enemy out of the way. Artillery came down

70

on the forest landing on all of the positions that were suspected of containing enemy anti-tank guns. The 105's fired for half an hour before the panzers moved forward. Fischer was concerned about the attack as the battalion was only at two thirds of its strength. Only forty tanks were available and the infantry was in even worse shape. Yet to a man the division was determined to keep the Russian horde away from the German border for they knew what had happened in those few areas where the Soviets had crossed into East Prussia.

To the south the news was that the enemy had penetrated into the suburbs of Warsaw. Fischer was concerned at the course of the war. He felt that the German army was holding something back but he wasn't sure what. He had seen infantry divisions being driven south to plug holes in the line in the ubiquitous British trucks yet no armour had gone with them. The 5th SS Wiking was now in East Prussia and the 2nd SS Motorised Division somewhere slightly to the south west of the Fifth's position. He had no idea where the 3rd SS was.

Ahead of him the 1st zug moved from the road through the gaps between the houses into the fields. The five tanks fanned out and then one stopped to cover the others as they drove towards the woods. Infantry went with them. Fischer took his panzer next to a small shed and scanned the edge of the forest with his binoculars. As he watched he saw a flash near some bushes. One of the panzer fours stopped suddenly and smoke started pouring from the hatches. Three men staggered clear before a machine gun fire chopped one of them down. The other two immediately hugged the ground.

"Huber, do you see that small tree near the fallen logs," said Fischer.

"Yes, skipper."

"There's a gun hidden next to it. Hit it with a high explosive shell."

"Got it sir."

"And Kruger, the machine gun near the hedge, make sure they keep their heads down."

Both the main gun and then the hull machine gun fired. The enemy gun disintegrated but it was impossible to see what had happened to the light machine gun. Another panzer four stopped, its crew abandoning the vehicle and hiding in a dip in the ground. Fischer searched for the source of the fire. Buildings and smoke obscured some of his vision so he ordered Braun to take the tank along the main road to where the houses ended. He crouched low in his cupola as bullets zipped and tinged from the armour. It would be safer inside but a lot harder to see the anti-tank guns. Another panzer four was immobile in front of them and Fischer wondered if the attack should be called off. Artillery hit the woodland briefly and infantry rushed past making their way to the final house and the long hedge that ran along its driveway to the main road. Trees lined the way and Fischer ordered more speed. The panzer four took off on the hard surface and passed the hedge. There was a small side road ahead where another group of buildings clustered.

It was only one hundred metres away. German troops were already

there hiding amongst the bushes and sheds. A flash came from next

to the farm house that sat near the edge of the woods and the track

on the front of his tank came apart. The tank slewed sideways

chopping through scrubby bushes and coming to a halt amongst a

line of rowan trees.

"Everyone out," he yelled. Grabbing his MP40 he didn't wait

to see who followed. It was forty metres across the road and over a

gravel driveway to someone's vegetable garden. The tall corn would

screen him until he reached the more substantial shelter of the

house. He found Huber and Kohler with him and pointed. "Let's go,"

he said.

They raced across the open ground as the puffs of dirt

around them showed that at least some Soviets were interested in

them. Enemy rifle men were firing at them from at least four

hundred metres away and probably through trees and smoke. Once

in the corn Fischer made his way into the house. German soldiers

lay hidden in different positions and he spotted an Oberscharfuhrer next to a new MG 42. He ordered the man and his squad to follow him to an upper story window. When he got there Fischer stayed away from the light coming through the curtains.

"Oberscharfuhrer you will only get one crack at this. There is an anti-tank gun tucked up against the farm house just out from the woods. It is on the southern side and camouflaged with branches. You will get one chance to cut down the crew before your position is spotted. Be fast, be efficient, and then move."

"Yes sir," said the blond man. Fischer thought he looked like the type that would appear on a recruiting poster. The MG 42 moved to a position just back from the window. After the squad had located the gun they opened fire. Fischer thought the machine gun sounded like a buzz saw. He couldn't hear the noise of the individual bullets. The short bursts kicked up dirt around the anti-tank gun shredding the branches that hid it. The shield would provide some protection but if the gun was angled then enough bullets would hit the crew members and that would help the remaining panzer fours. Then the machine gun stopped firing and

Fischer knew the squad was on the move. From his position behind an oak tree he saw the soldiers run from a side door just as the upper storey of the house was hit by a salvo of mortar shells.

In the end Standartenfuhrer Kurt Meyer took the reconnaissance battalion across the river further to the north with two companies of infantry in half-tracks. The Soviets were outflanked and fell back towards the small hamlet of Huta where another patch of woodland offered them more cover. The Division advanced approximately three kilometres and recovered its damaged tanks. Fischer stood by his crew as they worked on the track watching a dog fight above the river. Bf 109s duelled with Soviet planes and at least two had so far fallen. A parachute drifted down towards the fields next to the forest where two burnt out panzers lay. Fischer picked up his machine pistol and took Huber with him to greet the pilot when he landed.

The figure hit the ground hard and was dragged for a few metres before Huber ran in to help. The chute was collapsed and the pilot staggered upright. It was a Russian and Fischer brought his

MP 40 up ready to fire. Huber cut the chute free and the figure

raised its hands. A helmet was pulled from the pilot's head and long

blond hair spilled free. A woman! And she looked just like his sister

Helga. He lowered the gun slightly his mouth hanging open.

"She's an officer sir. Aren't we supposed to hang her," said

Huber.

"Do you want to string up such a creature?" said Fischer.

Huber stared. "I can't say that I do sir but they were the

orders."

"They didn't say anything about beautiful women."

Huber shrugged. "Those German nurses were probably

pretty as well." A hard edge crept into the man's voice.

"We are not animals like them."

The woman's face had gone white. "You understand us?"

said Fischer.

"Yes, I heard what you said and find it hard to believe that the glorious Russian army would abuse nurses. Perhaps you have been lied to?"

Huber struck her in the stomach and she doubled over. He took the pistol from her holster and then grabbed her by the hair.

"We were there bitch! We saw what those animals did!"

"Enough," barked Fischer. "This pilot wasn't part of that and as far as I'm concerned Peiper's orders only relate to ground troops."

He took the woman back to one of the undamaged houses and sat her on a couch. She looked just like his sister except for the figure. This woman was well rounded and he found himself staring. She sighed and started unbuttoning her jacket. After she had removed it the pilot started to take off her shirt.

"What are you doing?" asked Fischer.

"Isn't this the price for keeping me alive? You stare at me as though you want me," she said.

"No!" said Fischer. "You remind me of my sister. I find you attractive but I am a German officer."

"You are SS," said the pilot. "You shoot prisoners."

"And your men rape nurses," he snarled.

The woman looked at the ground and chewed on her lip. "What's to become of me?"

"We talk and then I send you back to the camps. Being a woman you will probably end up somewhere more comfortable than any other prisoner of war."

"I won't tell you anything and I don't want any favours."

"Too bad, you're going to get them anyway. The questions I'm going to ask aren't military. I was wondering where you learned German and what your name is?"

"My name is Junior Lieutenant Litvyak."

"I'm Wolfgang," Fischer held out his hand.

The woman seemed to relax a little. "Lydia," she whispered.

"Where did you learn my language Lydia?"

"The regimental commander taught it to me. I knew one day we would fight you and so I studied hard."

"You are, what twenty one years old?"

"Twenty," said Lydia. Her eyes grew cold. "I think I've told you enough."

Fischer spread his hands. "Alright. I will arrange some food for you and something to drink, then I'll organise transport back to a holding area. I hope you won't mind if I write a note offering you some protection on your journey west."

The woman shook her head and looked away. "There's something you should know. I'm Jewish."

Fischer glanced around and noted that they were alone. Part of him was disgusted that she was a Jew and he thought of shooting her. Then he stared at her again and his sister's face swam before him. She had been so beautiful before the cancer took her.

"Why are you telling me this?"

She shrugged. "A test perhaps or maybe I realise that someone will look at my papers and then you will get in trouble for protecting me. You have been kind, for a German, and I would not dishonour that."

Fischer made a quick decision. "Give me your paper work and anything that might mark you as a Jew. She reached inside her top pocket and pulled out a small book. Then she got out another few sheets of paper.

"No identity tags?" Fischer asked.

"No," said Lydia.

"Why am I doing this?" he muttered to himself.

"Because you are a decent man?" answered Lydia. "It's a pity you're German."

Fischer's mouth twitched in the beginning of a smile. "I hope you make it through this war in one piece Lydia."

"I never thought I'd say this but I wish you luck German. Try not to die."

81

Fischer promised he would give it his best effort.

V

Corporal Sergi Temkan couldn't believe that they were putting the poor runner in front of a firing squad. The young man had been held responsible for the repeat bombardment on the first day of the attack and now he was to line up with the rest of his squad and shoot the man. Junior Lieutenant Morozov had raged against the decision until Commissar Volkov had warned him to shut his mouth. It seemed the commander of the guns had contacts in the NKVD. The captain commanding the 122mm guns had covered his tracks and his father had ordered the arrest of the unfortunate private. Volkov had refused to go up against a colonel in the infamous security troops. And so they shot him.

The truck took his regiment through the ruins of Warsaw and headed southwest down dusty roads. The front line was now somewhere just to the west of Lodz and his division had been ordered to reinforce the drive towards the German border. The road was littered with wrecked trucks and dead horses. Overhead the odd air battle occurred and at one stage the trucks hid in a small forest while Heinkel medium bombers pounded a small town a few kilometres down the road. The Soviet Air Force was nowhere in sight and some of the men cursed their absence until Commissar Volkov told them to shut up.

Eventually they passed through Szadek where they were told to get out of their transportation. They walked until they reached a very small wood on the outskirts of the town where tents had been set up. Of course there wasn't enough shelter and some of the men slept under the stars. When Serge asked why his sergeant told him that they didn't want the men to scatter. "Too hard to find us all in the morning. Also the town is more likely to be hit by a raid or artillery. We are only eight kilometres from the front here."

That made Sergi think the battalion was probably going into action in the next day or two. He gathered what food he could, which wasn't much and then wandered into some of the surrounding fields where he managed to steal some tomatoes and half ripe corn before a farmer yelled at him. He shook his gun at the man but left anyway. Mixing the stolen food with his own supplies he managed to make his squad a half decent dinner. He had just finished eating when the first shells whistled into the town. It was just harassing fire but it caused a large fire and knocked down the local church.

"See, better off here," said Sergeant Sokolov.

In the morning officers led the men south west into a forest where the battalion followed narrow tracks until they reached an open area. The thoroughfare ran through the woodland they were in. Along the road sat a number of houses. The buildings were clustered more thickly at an intersection where another track ran into the main highway from the south. They managed to get to within three hundred metres of a village before the officers told them to lie down. Then rockets crashed down. Long streaks of fire fell from the sky churning up the earth with fire and steel. The houses disappeared and the battalion advanced. Mortars kept falling after the rockets finished and the battalion moved under the protection of the barrage.

Sergi could see shattered barbed wire and scattered sand bags. A zig zagging line of a trench cut the earth moving north. He ran quickly for the first building. This outlying farm house was burning fiercely but the Germans hadn't been stupid enough to be inside. A machine gun and some rifles started firing from amongst the sand bags and men fell. A Russian light machine gun began to fire back and other members of the company were close enough to throw grenades. At least a dozen of the explosives arched into the trench and exploded with flat crumping sounds. A man started screaming and then he saw some Russian soldiers jump into the trench. There was a burst of gun fire then silence. It was probably one hundred and fifty metres to the road but before Serge lay a shattered orchard of pear and apple trees.

He ran along a German communication trench before reaching an area where rockets had collapsed the earth. A hand stuck from the fresh dirt as though reaching for something. Sergi left the wrecked trench and ran on hearing rifle and machine gun fire. There was the buzz saw sound of the German MG 42 and screams as some of his friends fell. He ran at the German gun position from the left firing from the hip and saw the gunner jerk and fall over the weapon. He sprinted closer and watched as a German tried to pull his dead comrade off the gun so that he could turn it. Another German shot at him with a pistol. He fired a burst at both men and noticed the man with the pistol grab at his stomach and fall. The loader dropped into the trench and disappeared. Sergi emptied the rest of his magazine into the wounded German and watched as his body twitched and jerked. He then reloaded and jumped into the trench. As he landed the hidden German swung at him with a shovel. Sergi just managed to block the blow with the butt of his PPsh41. The man swung at him hard again and this time he was hit on the helmet, the blow stunning him. He groaned and held his head as the German pulled a Walther pistol from his holster and took deliberate aim. A bayonet came through the man's chest and his arms arched outwards. Sergi just stared at the silver metal smeared with the blood of the man who had been about to kill him. Sokolov pushed the man clear and then snatched up an abandoned MP 40 that lay nearby.

"Close one eh. Always wanted one of these German guns. Handy at close quarters don't you think."

Sergi could only stare. Sokolov pulled him to his feet and pointed at the buildings by the road. "We're not finished yet Corporal. A few more Germans to kill before the day is done, eh."

The next house was only forty metres away but already Russians could be seen storming across the fields. Grenades rained down into the trenches and the Germans put their hands in the air.

Soon a line of prisoners formed before the shattered orchard. The firing died down and Commissar Volkov wandered over. He started yelling at the Germans but they didn't seem to hear him. Sergi thought they looked like they were in shock. Volkov then drew his pistol and shot the nearest man in the head. He jerked once and fell. That woke the other Germans up. They stood and stared wildly around before a man with some insignia on his shoulder yelled something at Volkov. The commissars eyes narrowed and he shot this man as well. A moan went through the prisoners as they all realised how great a danger they were in. "You will tell me where the rest of your unit is, its strength and your commanders name," Volkov yelled.

Sergi hoped he would shoot them all. He could see friends lying dead in the ruins of the orchard and felt a great hatred flow through him. Then the shells started to fall. Everyone ran to jump into the trenches but some didn't make it. Both German and Russian were hurled into the air, their bodies ragged and bloody. When they landed Sergi could no longer tell one man from the other.

Chapter Four: July 1942

"The British supplied the tanks we requested and some more Spitfires but they are demanding payment in gold for any further military supplies. They say they have now paid all their war reparations, my Fuhrer."

"Our credit isn't good enough for them?" said Goering quietly.

Speer could see the man's eyes glittering and knew he wasn't pleased.

"Apparently not. We did manage to get one hundred and twenty of their crusader tanks with 57mm guns for the Romanians and one hundred Cavalier tanks for the Hungarians though we had a fight over the later vehicles. They tried to give us the early model with poor engines. They squealed and fought us all the way saying that all the panzers for their only tank division would be lost to us."

Goering snorted, "I bet they have panzers squirrelled away in barns and garages all over England."

"Anyway our allies are retiring the older French panzers and re-equipping their front line divisions," said Speer.

"These 57mm guns will stop a T34?" asked Goering.

"They are better than our 50mm guns, so the short answer is we think so. However the range has to be close."

"An improvement then."

"Yes," agreed Speer.

"And they will be with the Hungarians and Romanians before our great offensive?"

"I believe so," said Speer.

Goering walked over and stared at a large map of Poland, East Prussia and Eastern Germany. "This is an enormous risk for the German nation. The Russians are close to the pre-war borders."

"We cannot let them in Silesia," said Speer. "We need the region's industries too much."

"I don't want to let them walk on German soil! The fact that they crossed into East Prussia is bad enough and now we have the British behaving badly. I need to send them a message as well"

"I thought every unit was allocated to the Eastern fight," said Speer.

"No, we still have the equivalent of three divisions in Egypt and one division in England based around Dover. I was forced to strip all the other bases and they now only contain naval defensive troops and Luftwaffe personnel. There are two divisions in Norway, another four occupying Belgium and Holland and two holding the thin Atlantic coastal corridor we still occupy in France."

"What can we send to the English bases then?" asked Speer.

"I was visiting a parachute division the other day. They are ready to fight. I'll send them. We also have the 22 Air Landing Division in reserve in Germany. I'll move them to Belgium. Maybe that will make the British more cooperative."

"What about the Commonwealth forces and Churchill my Fuhrer? They won't sit by while we are distracted in the east."

"The Italians will have to hold them. All I have asked for from Mussolini is a few wings of his most modern fighters. Africa and the Mediterranean are his responsibility for now. The French have sent two divisions to help us, the Spanish the same. We are forming the Europa Division from Dutch and Belgium anti-communist troops but it will be a year before its ready. Most of Europe is with us, except for the stubborn English."

"And then there is America," whispered Speer.

"What they plan to do is in the lap of the Gods," said

Goering.

v

The Spitfire came down through the clouds and turned

slightly towards the Russian bombers. Lieutenant Debrody

recognised them immediately as Ilyushin Il4's. His flight came at the

enemy planes head on. Debrody realised that he would only have

time for a quick burst before he would need to lift his plane's nose

or collide. Then he decided he would climb, half roll and dive again

on the bombers from the rear.

His first burst fell under the lead plane and he knew he had

opened fire too soon. He counted to three and then fired again. His

shells hammered home around the cockpit and nose of the plane

with pieces flying off. Then he was flashing above the bombers and

climbed away. Machine gun bullets arched after his plane but the

Spitfire was moving too quickly to be hit. He didn't see the havoc

his burst had done to the enemy bomber. The co-pilot was dead, his

chest shattered by a fifteen millimetre shell, the pilot had lost an arm when two heavy calibre bullets had hit him just below the shoulder. The forward gunner had been hit in the throat and killed instantly and the cockpit area had started to burn. The plane immediately fell into a dive as the blaze grew around the pilot and streamed back into the fuselage. The navigator tried to reach the extinguisher but found that his legs wouldn't work. He had been hit in the spine and could do nothing but watch as the flames grew. The dorsal gunner could see the fire spreading and fled for the hatch. He managed to open the small door and threw himself out just as the plane started to spin.

Debrody came down with his flight for another attack and saw his victim fall out of the formation. Another bomber had smoke pouring from it port engine. Lieutenant Miklos Kenyerys who had joined them from the Hurricane squadron had obviously been on target as well. The man had become Debrody's good friend and rival ever since coming to Puma Squadron. Both pilots had nineteen kills and were the top scorers in the Hungarian Air Force. In the past few days Soviet planes had been harder to find and their rate of scoring had slowed so when the unescorted bombers had appeared they had pounced. The Iluyshins had missed their Yak escort that had been sent to shepherd them to the target and now were going to pay.

"Watch out for the dorsal gunners," said Kenyeres. "They are heavy calibre weapons."

Debrody could see the bullets coming at him from the rear gunners of a number of planes but the formation had broken up somewhat after the frontal attack and many of the gunners were out of range. He opened fire at two hundred metres walking his burst down the fuselage and over the dorsal turret and down towards the port wing. The Ilushin shuddered and a sheet of fire came from the wing root enveloping the side of the plane. There was an explosion and the port wing folded back over the aircraft before tearing free. The bomber then fell like a burning rock.

His wing man was firing at another plane and this burst hit the tail and then the starboard wing. Senior aircraftsman Sandor then screamed and dived through the enemy formation. Debrody was just about to ask his wingman what had happened when he saw Kenyeres' wing man collide with a bomber. His friend had finished off the plane he had damaged early and the other pilot had followed him in. The man was new and Debrody hadn't even remembered his name, just some dark haired kid who was keen to attack the Russians. He saw the Spitfire's propeller chew into the bomber's fuselage just behind the gunner's position before bouncing free and curving into the starboard engine. The Spitfire's wing disintegrated as it hit the prop and then rolled end over end through the sky pulling itself to pieces. Debrody watched fascinated. He heard the pilot scream briefly but the sight was unlike anything he had ever seen. The bomber's tail started to tear loose and figures started to jump from the stricken plane. Four parachutes opened and he realised somehow even the pilot had got clear. The tail then tore off and the bomber went into a spin.

"More planes, and there ours," said Kenyeres.

French Dewointines 551's dived from the clouds and started to attack the bombers. Debrody had heard the French had improved

96

their old 520's with better engines. They were supposed to be at least seventy kilometres faster than the original though they still had only rifle calibre machine guns in the wing. At least the twenty millimetre cannon firing through the propeller would hurt the bombers. He waggled his wings so they wouldn't mistake his plane for a Yak and turned towards his wingman.

"Are you alright Sandor?" he radioed.

"I'm hit skipper."

"How bad is it?"

"I'm losing oil pressure and my leg is numb. I think I took a bullet."

Debrody realised they were over the front line and his wing man would soon be able to bail out if necessary. He dropped his aircraft below Sandor's and took a look at the damage. There was a stream of thin black fluid running along the cowling and white smoke was coming in a line from a dark hole.

"Looks like at least two slugs hit your engine," he said.

97

Kenyeres flew in from above. "The French are ripping into the bombers. I'll fly top cover in case any Soviets coming sniffing about." With that he climbed to about one thousand metres above them.

Debrody noticed that the white smoke had turned black and was growing in volume. He looked below and realised they had crossed the front line. The French and Spanish had finally stopped the Russian advance on the far south of the line near Zory, just short of the old border with Germany.

"Alright Sandor, I think you should bail out now," he said.

"I can't feel my legs," said his wing man. "I can open the canopy but can't push myself up."

Debrody felt his heart sink. "We'll put you down near a column of infantry. You will ease her in with the wheels up."

Sandor didn't answer for a moment and then whispered. "I don't think I can sir."

"You have no choice, now I see some armoured cars and trucks ahead and there's a long stretch of clear road so slowly lose altitude."

Sandor did so and then brought the nose up as he neared the ground. The smoke from the engine was thicker and the plane was wobbling as it moved through the sky.

"Easy Sandor, keep her steady."

Flames appeared when the plane was only fifty metres from the ground. "I'm on fire," screamed his wingman.

"It's not in the cockpit. Put her down gently and you still can get out of this," yelled Debrody.

The wingman panicked and dropped the plane down onto the field hard. The Spitfire bounced and came down unevenly, a wing digging into the ground. The plane flipped and the cartwheeled before disintegrating. Two armoured cars were driving fast in the aircraft's direction but Debrody knew that his compatriot had no chance. The plane burned fiercely near the edge of a small wood. He sighed

deeply and started to climb away from the conflagration.

v

The new panzer four sat with four others at the edge of the

forest. More tanks could be seen through the foliage.

Obersturmfuhrer Wolfgang Fischer sat in the vehicle with the rest

of his crew glad of the transfer to the new panzer battalion. Kurt

Meyer led the 2nd battalion that had joined the division making the

1st SS a full sized panzer division. He heard the same had happened

with the 2nd and 3rd SS with plans for the same to occur with the 5th

when there was the available equipment. He was happy to be away

from the first battalion as Standartenfuhrer Peiper had not been

impressed when he found out about the Russian female pilot he

had spared.

"You need to be merciless in war," he had been told. Fischer

had been concerned that his old commander might try and track

the woman down and have her shot but the expansion of the

division and preparations for the upcoming offensive had distracted him. Not enough though that Peiper hadn't spoken to Meyer.

"I'm my own man so you have a chance to start fresh here," his new commander had said. "Though if I say shoot all prisoners you better do as ordered." Fischer did note he had been passed over when a raft of promotions had come through. He shrugged; his time would come. Either that or he'd be dead.

The bombardment came before dawn and lasted an hour. It was heavy and intense. Then waves of Luftwaffe planes flew over to pound the Russian positions. When the panzers started to move on July 12th there was enough light to see clearly. The first Russian line was breached easily with only a few anti-tank having survived the bombardment. The enemy flanks were stretched thin and though reserves came at the Germans it was in uncoordinated groups that were defeated in detail. By the late afternoon the battalion had advanced twelve kilometres and had taken Ostroleka. The large town sat on roads that ran south west towards Warsaw and North East to Bailystok. During the night the Soviets sent bombers over but the bombs fell in the open country to the north. In the morning, after a few hours sleep the panzers attacked the town of Rozan while the first battalion pushed in the same direction but along the other bank of the river. In the distance Stukas bombed targets, probably artillery concentrations but it was impossible to know for sure.

Fischer watched as the lead panzers motored past positions that the motorized infantry had destroyed earlier. His battalion drove along with woodlands to the west and fields to the east. An armoured car stopped them at a group of houses. Ahead there was a small patch of forest with a larger one a little further on.

"Russian heavy tanks are driving towards us from the south, strength unknown," said Panzer Meyer from the armoured car. Half of the battalion's tanks were ordered to drive cross country around the eastern side of the small wood and into another group of houses. Fischer manoeuvred his panzer four next to a farmhouse. He could see a track leading west through open fields from the small village to the main highway. A part of the view was blocked by a single farm and barn.

The KV 1's came slowly from the forest in a line heading across the company's line of sight. Fischer picked out one tank with a higher profile than the others which he thought might be a KV 2.

The lead tank suddenly stopped and veered off the road into the field. Men jumped from its hatches as smoke poured from the openings and then Fischer heard the flat crack of 75mm cannons. He ordered Huber to fire and watched as the shell hit the turret leaving a neat hole near the top of the high structure. A second shell hit just below the first a moment later and the KV 2 burst into flame. Nobody escaped. The heavy Russian tanks tried to scatter but the lead vehicles were quickly destroyed. The survivors fled back to the forest from which they had emerged losing more of their numbers as they did.

Fischer waited for orders while scanning the edge of the forest through powerful Dopplefernrorh binoculars. He noted a small road just back from the edge of the wood that ran to the south and wondered where it went. Panzer fours started moving from the north firing at unseen targets. From somewhere in the woods the Russians struck back. Two Panzers stopped suddenly with one belching flame. Meyer ordered the battalion back into cover and brought down smoke to cover the withdrawal.

Fischer decided to follow the track to the south as it offered the promise of flanking the Soviet position. He led his zug out of the small village through another wood until he hit a forest track running east west. He turned at the dusty crossroad and edged towards the sound of the firing. Fischer stopped every two hundred metres and scanned the forest with his binoculars, he also listened carefully for engine noises. The platoon had gone about six hundred metres when two BA 10 armoured cars came flying down the road towards them. The panzer fours were in single file so only the front two could fire. The lead BA 10 was hit through the driver's vision slot with the shell taking of the man's head before ploughing on into the engine after spraying most of the survivors with metal shards. The force of the heavy AP shell hitting the engine block caused an explosion that sent the vehicle spinning off the road in flames. The following armoured car hit the brakes and skidded to a halt. It had just started to reverse when a shell tore off its turret. Two crew members bailed out but were cut down by a hull machine gun before they had run more than a dozen paces.

The Panzer fours continued to move cautiously as Fischer was aware they had no infantry support and would be vulnerable to Soviets on foot or to hidden anti-tank guns. Another four hundred metres later they approached the main road. Ahead four trucks were unhitching 76 mm guns and teams of men were starting to move them. Fischer's Panzer four burst upon them firing in all directions. Men scattered as trucks exploded. Some men were cut down while others fled into the woods. The other panzers burst from the forest chasing the panicking Soviets. Two of the panzer fours fired into the rear of a KV1 which sat close by, its gun pointing out over the open fields where the rest of the German company had tried to attack not long ago.

The Russians were totally confused by the appearance of the platoon of panzers in their rear and most of the KV1s remained unaware of their existence as they were buttoned up with their attention focused to the front. A T34 did notice Fischer's tank and turned to face it but was destroyed before it could train its gun. The lack of radios meant that the Russians couldn't warn each other and tank after tank was destroyed. In the end some crews, so disorientated, simply abandoned their vehicles and ran.

When Meyer arrived he was impressed. "Four guns and a truck plus three tanks captured as well as the position taken, well done Fischer."

He couldn't help but grin. "I took a risk sir, and it paid off."

"We all make our own luck Fischer. Now get your panzers fuelled up. We need to push as far south as we can while we have light."

By the end of the day the battalion had made it as far as the large village of Mlyarze and captured the bridge over a small river named the Roz. They had advanced another fifteen kilometres and were only eight from their first objective of Rozan.

v

Lieutenant Gyorgy Debrody took his flight down on the column of trucks ignoring the line of traces that came arching up from a double heavy machine gun mounted on a jeep.

"I'll take out the flak first," he radioed.

The car disappeared as he watched his guns chew up the road and then the vehicle. He skimmed over the open fields and the climbed to one thousand metres. They were attacking Soviet supply convoys about forty kilometres north of Krakow. The large southern city had fallen two days ago and the sixteenth panzer division was pushing up Highway Seven in a northwards direction. The German plan was obvious to everyone now. Rumours abounded of an equally powerful thrust out of East Prussia. The Russians had advanced over the Polish plains to the old pre-war German border but they hadn't secured their flanks. The only thing that remained in doubt was where the jaws of the trap would snap shut and if the Russians would be able to escape. There was always the chance the Soviets would hold the Germans at bay and perhaps even throw them back but from what Debrody was seeing from the air that looked unlikely.

He didn't like ground attack missions. Flak was unpredictable and could snatch a plane from the air regardless of the pilot's skill or experience but with there being less and less Soviet aircraft in the area the Spitfires of Puma squadron were being called on more often to support the ground offensive.

He had climbed to one and a half thousand metres when he heard the warning yell from Kenyeres. "Break right Red Section."

Debrody didn't hesitate and hauled the stick of the Spitfire over while kicking the rudder. He heard a scream and saw an explosion out of the corner of his eye. Then he felt the G-forces build and his vision blur. Debrody started to refocus two hundred metres from the ground. He looked around wildly and saw two planes curving around trying to get on his tail. There was the sound of his

comrades on the radio yelling warnings and calling out the enemies'
position.

"These are a new type," said one of the Puma squadron
pilots. The Hungarians had been bounced by eight LA 5s. It was later
to be discovered that the Russians had decided to replace the Lagg
3s and had taken away the formers engine, replacing it with a big
radial model. These eight were the first to reach the front and each
had been assigned to an experienced Soviet pilot. The first pass of
the powerful new planes had shot two Hungarians from the sky
leaving the opposing forces almost even in numbers.

Debrody waited until his attackers were within about three
hundred metres before turning his plane hard to the left. He
continued through the turn with the Soviets trying to follow him.
The heavy radial fighters had picked up a lot of speed in their dive
and couldn't stay with his turn and Debrody quickly realised this.
Both planes started to climb, probably intending to try a second
attack but Debrody climbed with them. To start with the Russians
moved away from him but then he began to close the gap. It

seemed the Spitfire had a better rate of climb than the new Soviet machines. Both aircraft noted that he was gaining on them so half rolled upside down before looping over and diving towards him.

Tracers flashed passed him from the lead plane but Debrody held his fire until his sights settled on the enemy pilot's cockpit. He heard a clang and saw some holes appear in the Spitfire's wing but kept his nerve. The closing speed was over seven hundred kilometres per hour and the LA5 filled his windscreen as he held down the firing button. He saw the strikes on the wing root and around the Soviet plane's engine.

"You got him," yelled Kenyeres.

The Spitfire shuddered and Debrody noted the oil splashing his windscreen. "The old girl is badly hit. I'm going to have to put her down."

"Not here," radioed Kenyeres. "Just keep her in the air a little longer so we are clear of the convoy."

Debrody didn't have much altitude to play with and was worried about a fire but he could see the sense in what his good friend was saying. If he came down near troops he had just been spraying with cannon fire and was captured he wouldn't last very long. He flew south nursing the Spitfire along, easing the throttle back and slowly losing height. The canopy was becoming covered with oil so he opened it and tried to use the side view to help. Then there was a bang from the engine and it stopped.

"I'm going to have to glide down," he said.

"There's a field about a kilometre ahead, you just need to make it over the woods," said Kenyeres.

Compared to most modern fighters the gliding qualities of the Spitfire weren't too bad, but it was still losing altitude quickly. The trees loomed up and Debrody braced for impact but the plane cleared the woods with metres to spare before coming down in a field of wheat. The Spitfire ploughed through the yellowing crop towards a low wooden wall. Debrody heard the wood splinter as the plane crashed through and onto a dirt road before continuing on to the other side into a crop of sun flowers. The large plants pelted the plane covering it with petals before it skidded to a stop. Debrody immediately jumped out and ran back along the cleared track his Spitfire had carved as it started to burn.

As he reached the road he saw Kenyeres' Spitfire approaching with its wheels down.

"He isn't going to land is he?" Debrody said to himself.

He had heard of other pilots in Hurricanes landing to rescue their comrades but orders were not to attempt the manoeuvre in the Spitfire due to the narrow and fragile undercarriage. The plane lined up on the track and came down perfectly further down the road where the wooden fence stopped. Debrody ran towards the taxiing plane, his heart pounding in his chest. On the other side of the woods two other Spitfires dived on an unseen target and fired.

Kenyeres smiled at him and gestured at the cockpit. Debrody climbed on the wing and sat on the older man's lap.

"This is going to be cosy," said his friend.

112

"What are our comrades shooting at?" asked Debrody as he tried to sit.

"Russian trucks. It seems the enemy haven't given up on capturing you. Now you handle the stick and I'll do the rudder and flaps. Follow my instructions."

They flew back to the airstrip at low altitude with the cockpit open. The rest of the squadron flew top cover as they skimmed above the Polish countryside. As they passed over the front line a few Germans shot at them but then the other Spitfires fired recognition flares and the firing stopped. They landed and were immediately greeted by the squadron commander.

"Kenyeres, I don't know whether to court martial you or put you up for a medal," he said.

"Just buy me a stiff drink and I'll be happy sir."

v

Geifreiter Paul Becker cradled the MG 34 to his shoulder and scanned the town in front of him. Nearby a PAK 38 was wheeled into position and logs placed in front of it. The crew of the gun then cut some limbs from the surrounding oak trees and arranged them around the metal shield. After that they started to dig fox holes. The Bren carrier was hidden in a fold of ground and covered with the camouflage net and the rest of his squad were hidden amongst the houses near the edge of a large cemetery.

He cursed the fact that they were out here on point with the rest of the company at the furthest point of Rommel's advance. The Fifteenth Panzer Division had taken Chisinam four days ago before crossing the mighty Dniester River yesterday. They had taken the road bridge at Bender as the Soviets had failed to blow it and pushed eight kilometres from the river to another town named Tiraspol. The Fifteenth now held a bridge head at a bend in the river that was ten kilometres deep and about the same wide. The 104th motorized regiment was pushing towards the airfield to the north of the town with the second battalion (to which Becker belonged) to the south of that thrust.

The Romanian and German armies had advanced quickly to the 1940 borders of the former country after the defeat of the Soviet offensive in June and had spent the first ten days of July pushing to the old borders, pre 1939. Resistance had become stiffer at first but then the 9th SS had joined them and the lavishly equipped formation had prised a hole. Then the armour had rampaged across open countryside allowing the Fifteenth Panzer to bounce the river. The Romanians with their crusader tanks had done well guarding the German's flank and Goering had reinforced the whole enterprise with two motorized divisions and an infantry corps. But now the offensive had been told to consolidate its gains. The Germans held two bridgeheads and had closed up to the Dniester. Rumours abounded that Rommel had his heart set on taking Odessa which was now only sixty kilometres from the closest German formation and about one hundred from the position of the Fifteenth Panzer. Yet all eyes were on the conflagration in Poland and that front was sucking in men and supplies like a whirlpool.

"I can hear tanks," said Feldwebel Fuchs.

Becker strained and heard the unmistakable sound of heavy engines and the grinding of tracks. Just great he though. So far any armour they had come across had been dealt with by the 88's or the Marders mounting PAK 40's. The open topped French tanks carried powerful 75mm guns that could defeat the armour of any Soviet tank. Otherwise they had faced old Russian T26's and they had been easily defeated. Fuchs was tying the heads of a number of stick grenades to a central grenade to make a very large explosive and Private Neuman was scrambling around looking for a satchel charge. Mortar shells stared to land around their position and men jumped into fox holes or took shelter in basements in nearby houses. The bombardment continued for ten minutes getting progressively heavier but most of the shells were overshooting and landing in the cemetery where they knocked over grave stones.

Then the armour moved from the houses to the south with swarms of infantry. There was about two hundred metres of open ground covered with a little scattered scrub before the Soviets reached the company's position which sat between destroyed warehouses and the grave stones. The odd tree had been blown up

or stood stripped of most leaves on the battle field, some being

splintered wrecks. Becker had based himself at the base of one of

the large tree stumps and now opened fire. He used short bursts to

cut down Russian soldiers as they ran forward. The tanks fired their

main guns at the Germans knocking out two PAK 38's though losing

eight of their own vehicles.

The Soviet machines were a varied lot with T26s being

mixed with T22s and there was even a pair of KV 1s. The multi

turreted T22 broke down after it had gone fifty metres and its crew

abandoned it and fled, with its twin losing a track to an anti-tank

round. The T26s were all knocked out but the KV1s came on. They

were the older model with the shorter main gun but their armour

was thick. The one PAK 38 was destroyed after a hit on to the

leading tank but the shell just broke up.

The Soviet infantry started to cluster behind the two

remaining KV1s as they approached Paul Becker's position. One of

the tanks suddenly accelerated and rose over an anti-tank gun's location grinding over branches and sand bags before crushing the PAK 38's shield. The crew scrambled to get away and Becker saw a white faced soldier moving crab like away from the destruction.

The Soviet infantry came around the KV1 firing sub machine guns and cut the crew down. A grenade exploded near Becker throwing him backwards and wrenching the machine gun from his hands His loader Hofmann took most of the blast and fell dead over the roots of the tree they had been using as cover. Becker crawled and ran alongside the trunk using it as cover. Ahead he saw Fuchs and Neuman signalling him. They were hiding amongst the rubble of the Warehouse and firing with an MP40 and a Czech ZBvs 30. Neuman was firing the light machine gun from the hip but it didn't seem to diminish his accuracy, or maybe it was just because the Russians were so close that they fell. The KV 1 ground onwards and Soldat Wolf threw the lashed up heavy grenade at the tank. The missile landed on the engine cover but slid off and detonated behind the vehicle with a crump killing a small group of Soviets huddling behind the tank. Becker snatched up an MP 35 from next to a fallen German and opened fire. He finished the magazine and then searched the dead man for more ammunition. As he looked up he saw Fuchs run past him with a heavy satchel. A burning fuse could be seen trailing from the package. The Feldwebel hurled the charge onto the back of the KV1 and then dived into an empty fox hole. For a second nothing happened and the tank moved on. Then there was a huge explosion on the decking covering the engine and the whole vehicle disappeared.

"How much explosive was in the sack?" he asked Wolf.

'Five kilos.'

Becker whistled. The manual said two would be enough to disable a T34. He guessed Fuchs was making sure.

There was a grinding noise from the tank and then the vehicle shuddered to a halt. Men poured from the hatches and smoke with them. Becker shot one with the submachine gun and the others raised their hands. The second tank had disappeared into the cemetery and Becker would later find out that it made it half way to the river before running out of fuel. The Soviets fell back

into Tiraspol as German artillery arched overhead. One hundred

and five millimetre shells tore into the houses where the Russians

had fled. From the west Panzer threes and fours advanced driving

into the town with infantry, pushing the now disorganised

defenders from the ruins. By the end of the day the whole town

was in German hands.

v

Corporal Sergi Tempkan lay against the side of the trench

looking at the small jar. He had filled the container with German soil

the day they had crossed the border. He remembered two hours

later Stukas had hit their position. The sounds of his comrades

screaming, the dust and the fire had almost sent him mad in those

horrible ten minutes but he had survived. The division had been

withdrawn as it was now at thirty percent of its pre-war strength.

His company had twenty six men still standing when they had been

driven east. Six wounded men and thirty others had joined them

since then but Sergi had not been impressed with the quality of the replacements. Half trained boys and older men weeded from transport arm had arrived armed with old rifles. Luckily there were plenty of spare weapons to rearm them with. They had been told they would be made up to strength and rested but then the Germans had broken through and everything had gone to Hell.

The SS had taken Rozan and had then split their formation with some units heading for Warsaw and others going east for Ostrow Mazowiecka. His Lieutenant had said another German attack was moving towards Wyszkow and only Stalin knew what was going on further to the north east. Other powerful German divisions were attacking towards Brest but were still one hundred kilometres north of that city.

So the Forty Seventh Rifle Regiment had been moved into Ostrow Mazowiecka to halt the advance of the Third SS division. Motorized infantry were said to be heading their way supported by StuGs and armoured cars. These troops were brutal veterans and Sergi didn't know if his division had the strength to stop them. Even if they did he wasn't sure it would matter. The front seemed to be coming apart. At least this would be street fighting and that might even the odds.

The industrial area where they had dug in was in the northern part of the town and bordered to the west by a small patch of woodland. The main road to Brok and the bridge over the Bug River ran right through their position with more factories on the other side of the thoroughfare. They had dug in near the corner of a cement factory with a pair of 45 mm guns hidden nearby. Hot food had been acquired and eggs had been taken from a local farm including a goat which was spited and shared among the company. For once Sergi had a full stomach and all that was missing was some vodka or wine. Lieutenant Morozov was playing his violin and some of the men were singing along.

"You should play something patriotic," said Commissar Volkov. "These old ballads are from a time before Stalin."

That's what makes them more interesting thought Sergi but he kept his mouth shut. The Lieutenant, who had recently been promoted ignored the commissar and played until Sergi dozed off. He slept

122

well with a full belly lying on an old mattress next to the factory until dawn crept into the sky. He went to the toilet and grabbed some left over goat meat before drinking some tea.

The sound of onrushing shells sent him diving into the trench and he landed face first in the earth. The howitzer shells exploded around their position before moving back to hit the centre of town. Mortars followed and then Nebelwerfer rocket artillery exploded near the trench. Somewhere a man screamed briefly. Another soldier was whimpering and calling for his mother. The pounding continued for another ten minutes before slowly easing.

The sound of tracks came from the other side of the road and three StuGs with short 75mm guns clanked into sight. Grey clad figures ran behind them with other groups running a short distance before flopping to the ground. Then a different group would repeat the move. Soviet snipers fired and two Germans fell. Then light machine guns joined cutting down more of the enemy. The StuGs stopped and fired and the Russians shooting disappeared in an explosion of flesh and earth. The 45mm guns were the newer type with the longer barrel and Sergi was pleased to see one of their

shells put a neat whole in the front of the nearest German vehicle.

The StuG stopped and its crew scrambled away. A volley of 20mm

cannon shells from a hidden 222 armoured car sprayed across the

trenches with another car spraying the anti-tank gun position. The

shells smashed through the gun shield killing the crew and the

other machine gunners took cover. Some of the German soldiers

had reached the woods one hundred metres to the west of Sergi's

position and he could hear the crump of grenades and bursts of

machine gun fire as the two squads placed there fought back. The

second anti-tank gun destroyed another StuG causing the vehicle to

burst into flames. Crew members covered in flames threw

themselves from hatches and rolled around on the ground until

other soldiers threw dirt on them and dragged them into cover. The

snipers picked off two of the rescuers in the process.   The

armoured cars kept up their withering fire until the antitank gun

picked one of them off. The final StuG disappeared into the

woodland to the west but the Germans were across the road with some of them hiding amongst the wrecked cars and broken down trucks that sat in a scrap metal yard next to the cement factory. To the west Germans appeared at the edge of the small woodlands firing with submachine guns and rifles. Squads of SS troops broke cover and charged the Russian positions near the cement factory. Sergi started firing back with his PPSh 41, using short bursts. Near him a figure rose out of the rubble firing single shots from a rifle with a scope. He hadn't even known the sniper was there. A German fell with every shot from the figure. Blond hair fell from a cap which had been dislodged. Sergi realised the sniper was a woman and she was driving the enemy back with her own rifle. He saw Germans appearing from the metal yard and started throwing grenades in that direction. An explosion blew two SS troopers off their feet and others took cover amongst the wrecked trucks and cars. Lieutenant Morozov appeared with a group of soldiers firing sub machine guns and throwing grenades. A DShK 12.7 heavy machine gun lashed the Germans cutting down more soldiers. The

SS turned and started to melt away covered by the 20mm cannon in the light armoured car which forced the Russians to take cover.

The enemy were able to retire across the road and into the wood taking their wounded with them. The woman turned and smiled at Sergi slowly looking up from the trench where they had both taken shelter when 20mm shells had lashed the area.

That night orders came through to abandon the town. Sergi listened impassively. He stood next to the two female snipers and spat. The SS had flanked their positon to the west and had taken the bridge at Brok twelve kilometres to the south. To the south east the 3rd Panzer division had reached the Bug River at Nur. The Lieutenant said they had to withdraw quickly or they would be cut off.

v

Sergeant Tom Derrick sat near the rear of the troop ship watching the Canadian shore line slowly disappear behind him.

"I like Canada," said Private Snowy Hobson.

"Yeh so did I," said Tom." It reminded me of home but colder. Big cities on the coast and lots of space inland."

"Yeh but forests instead of desert in the interior," said Lieutenant Harry Breman. "It's even nicer on the west coast. The winters aren't as bad on the Pacific side."

"Still don't know what we are doing here though," said Snowy. "They pull us out of the Sinai three months ago, give us an armoured regiment and a whole lot of Yankee halftracks and say we are now motorised and even give us bloody American rifles."

"Don't rag on the Garand," growled Private Freddy Peterson. "Or the Browning."

"I'm not, I just don't get why all the changes."

"Cause Australia is so busy creating divisions to keep the fight goin' we can't make our own stuff," said Turner.

"That's right, we can't even keep up with supplying the Sentinels. Two of the regiment's companies are equipped with Grants," said Tom. "And our air force is all yank planes."

127

He thought of the Thompson submachine gun he favoured and realised that only the Owen and Bren were home grown weapons. The artillery still used twenty five pounders and the anti-tank crews 57mm guns but nearly everything else was from the States.

"Why are the Americans giving us all this stuff?" asked Snowy.

"They want us to stop Goering," said Peterson.

"Well why don't they join us?" said Snowy.

Tom shared a look with his lieutenant.

"That might be happening sooner than you think," said Harry.

Private Charlie Gaunt walked over and handed his Sergeant a mug of tea. "The story is we're going to Iceland."

"I heard Norway," said Snowy.

The lieutenant laughed. "You really think they would waste a veteran division that is newly equipped on occupying an island in the middle of the Atlantic? Didn't you see the preparations at the docks? Our Canadian friends were loading up transports and there were Yanks everywhere in Quebec City. No this is an invasion force."

"Then where are we going?" asked Freddy Peterson.

"We are going back to Old Blighty. Churchill has decided that while the Germans are distracted fighting the Russians it would be a good time to go home and throw out the collaborationist government. That's what I reckon anyway, not that anybody has confided in me," said Harry.

The men fell silent for a minute before Tom spoke up. "Oh well, killin' Germans in Britain is as good as killin' them anywhere else."

"Yes, and I think the good old USA will be along for the ride," said Harry Breman.

Chapter Five: September 1942

Goering was smiling from ear to ear. "A great day gentlemen. The jaws have snapped shut and we have over six hundred thousand prisoners already. Odessa has fallen to Rommel in the south and the Russians in Poland cannot escape."

"There is still a lot of mopping up to do my Fuhrer," said Speer.

"We predict another half a million prisoners at least and the Soviets have suffered almost a million casualties already," said Generaloberst Keitel. "And as they flee our motorised troop will capture more. It is the greatest victory of German arms in our history!"

"But we must move fast," said Goering. "Soon the rains will arrive and forward movement will become difficult. General Keitel, do you think we can make Moscow before winter hits?"

Keitel rubbed at his chin. "I doubt it my Fuhrer. The further north we go the sooner winter will arrive. Then, as you mentioned, there are the rains of October. Roads in Russia are as bad as those in Poland; maybe worse. This may be a long war."

Speer noticed that Goering's elation was draining away.

"We will need to increase production," said Speer. "The British and French need to be pulled in behind us and we must have winter uniforms."

"And anti-freeze," added Keitel. "Russian winters can be brutal."

"I've managed to increase the output of armoured vehicles by about a third. The supplies coming in via South America and France have been very helpful. The Commonwealth blockade doesn't apply to Spain and though it costs a bit more to work through a number of middlemen it's worth it," said Speer.

"We are lucky Churchill and his cronies don't want to aggravate the Spanish or the South Americans," added Keitel.

"That will all change if the USA enters the war," said Goering. "I'm concerned about the attacks on the Canadian convoys to Murmansk. US destroyers are now escorting them as far as Iceland. We sank one recently and the American press screamed about it."

"We cannot let those convoys through Mein Fuhrer. They are delivering aircraft and transport as well as aluminium."

"I know, I have ordered the Kriegsmarine to move elements of the fleet to Narvik. We need to force a battle. The carriers, Tirpitz and Bismarck are on their way as well as the Hipper, Scharnhorst and Prince Eugene. Ten destroyers will screen them. Doenitz has sent a dozen U boats to the area. I have also asked Kesselring to reinforce the northern route with a Gruppe of JU 290's as well as some Heinkel torpedo aircraft."

"That sounds impressive Mein Fuhrer. On the Central front I've ordered that we march on Minsk as quickly as possible. Estimates are that it will be ours in a week. On the northern sector we should be at the Estonian border in six days. I have ordered that

Rommel halt. He just doesn't have the forces to push any further without substantial reinforcements and as there are signs of an impending Commonwealth attack on Egypt we have nothing to give him. As it is we are transferring the Sixteenth Motorized to Africa and sending some of the captured Russian armour to the Italians. Maybe it will improve the quality of their panzer divisions."

"I would like to keep Rommel moving forward but I can see that is not practical at the moment," said Goering. "He doesn't like it but needs to understand the priorities. This fight with Russia will be to the death."

"With that in mind we need more allies Mein Fuhrer," said Speer.

"The Finns are going to join us though they have stated they won't advance past their old borders," said Keitel.

"We need more," said Goering. "Our losses have been heavy."

"The Russian prisoners can be used as labour on our farms, on road building and other projects," said Speer.

"That will free up some manpower for the army and SS but is it enough?" said Goering.

"What about some of the occupied Eastern European nations? The Latvians and Estonians are supposed to hate the Russians," said Speer.

"Slavs," sneered Keitel dismissively.

"They are subhuman," said Goering.

Speer was never sure of these arguments. The Jews he understood to be the enemy of his people. He had heard all the stories and knew of their perfidy but he wasn't so clear on why the Slavs were less than men. "The Teutonic Knights held the Baltic Coast for centuries. Their blood must still be present in the local population. We could promise them semi autonomy and recruit their best men for the SS as a crusading force against communism. I'm sure Kaltenbruner would welcome the extra recruits."

"The SS is supposed to be the most pure of our forces," said Keitel.

"These would be crusaders. We could check the recruit's family background for German blood," offered Speer. He knew that this last suggestion would never occur. Once the SS had access to a man power pool they wouldn't care that much if a tall young man had any German blood or not.

Keitel scoffed but Speer could see Goering was thinking about it.

"Look into it Speer and see how many possible divisions it might be worth."

"I ran it past Kaltenbrunner a couple of days ago and he got back to me saying that somewhere between four to six divisions are possible. Since we have just won a great victory men of these small nations will flock to our banner, but we need to rule them with a careful hand. If we use a fist of iron then recruit numbers will fall."

"We cannot be too soft on these people," said Keitel.

"I'm just saying we take a gentler approach than their former masters."

"Six divisions is not to be waved away," said Goering.

"It will take time to train and equip them. They probably wouldn't be ready for eighteen months," said Keitel.

"Then we better start now," said Goering.

Speer didn't have enough hours in the day. He knew everything that was going on in the Reich and was pleased with many of the changes. Since Hitler's death the fracturing of Germany's manufacturing into many different fiefdoms had been broken down with most of it coming under his control. Only the SS remained aloof. The problem of the profusion of different types of aircraft and other vehicles remained unsolved but even that was better than before. Speer had squashed a number of different proposals, like the one for the Heinkel 177. The overly complicated bomber was a strain on resources as was the new Tiger tank, however he had lost the battle on the panzer. A transport plane with a series of wheels running down the middle of the aircraft was also canned, with the emphasis being placed on the Junker 290 which could be used as an ocean recon platform, a transport plane, and even, at a pinch, a long range bomber.

The jet was still Goering's pet project but the engines were proving difficult to perfect. The high temperatures of the turbines caused all sorts of problems but at least the metals they needed to resist the flame outs were available. Speer had stockpiled nickel, cobalt and molybdenum metals from South America in case the USA entered the war and the supplies from across the sea were blocked. In the meantime the Bf109 and the FW 190 would have to serve. A new version of the Bf 110 was being developed as was the Junkers 188 but neither would be ready until 1943.

The pilots that would fly these machines were being trained at flying schools that had started to double in size the day the Russians had attacked. This had been a hard decision to take as nearly every pilot was needed at the front, but Kesselring had insisted. He had seen that the attack by Russians meant that the war might be a long one and Smiling Albert was still nervous about the uncommitted Americans. Speer signed orders for an increase in the production of the Tiger tanks with a frown knowing that the first ten were undergoing trails in France. When the phone rang he jumped involuntarily.

'Speer here,' he answered.

"Kaltunbrunner," said the caller. "I thought you might want to know the US ambassador delivered a declaration of war to our glorious leader an hour ago. Our bases in Britain are under attack and the Luftwaffe has reported troops landing at Glasgow, Bristol, Belfast, Liverpool and Exeter."

"How did the Recon planes fail to see them coming?" asked Speer.

"Apparently all our efforts were directed at finding convoys to Murmansk and they were all watching the area around Iceland. The invasion force came across the south central Atlantic by the look of things. A plane did disappear out that way about three days ago but we thought it was pilot error or mechanical failure. It was probably shot down. American carriers are covering the convoys. We have reports of Canadian and Australian troop as well as US divisions. Goering is furious at the 'stab in the back.'

"This changes everything," said Speer.

"A war on two fronts, not something that favours our nation. Luckily we have the Russians on the run, for now."

Speer thought of how the supply of British aircraft, tanks and trucks would dry up. It was unlikely that the collaborationist government would be able to put up much of a fight. He was glad that he had stockpiled certain important metals though he knew they wouldn't last long. The spare parts factory for the English vehicles would be more important than ever and he patted himself on the back that he had insisted on its development. At least he had a huge stockpile of Nickel and Cobalt for the jet engines.

"Goering wants to see you. He is trying to scratch together enough forces to hold on to London and the southeast of the country."

"Is that wise?" said Speer.

"I'm not sure," said Kaltenbrunner. "But I know he wants to make the English bleed."

v

Sergeant Tom Derrick stared across the fields towards the Manor house. The building was a solid two storey white washed house with a slate roof. A low barn was attached. Low hedges ran from the barn to the north before turning at a right angle along the narrow road. The ground dipped where he lay into a shallow depression. There was little cover between his small hollow and the house but he knew he could fall back to a patch of woodland where the rest of the platoon waited. A brisk autumn wind scattered thin cloud over head. The occasional shower of rain ran ahead of the breeze pattering the ground with rain drops for a few minutes before moving on. Derrick found the land gentle and green. He could appreciate the soft English country side but part of him missed the yellows and browns of the South Australian countryside on a summer's day.

There was no movement near the house or at the windows.

"Looks empty," said Private Arthur Gurney.

"I don't believe it. The last two days the Jerries have put up a fight. This house has a good view of the surrounding countryside for a number of miles. They'll be in there," said Tom

"So why don't we call up the arty boys to blast it?"

"They're still catchin' up. We charged across the country so quickly that they got left behind. It's just us and the armour for the next few days. Even the fly boys are still getting organised."

The advance across England had taken the Australian Ninth Motorised division from Bristol down the Thames valley before they had swerved south to Portsmouth. The British collaborationist army had not opposed them joining the attacks on the German bases and over throwing the hated government in London. The Canadians had taken Glasgow and advanced across Scotland while the Americans had advanced from Liverpool across the Midlands. There had been brief resistance at the scattered German bases but where they could the enemy withdrew. Some got away by air, others on the coast escaped by sea, but not without loss. Those in the interior tried to fight their way to the coast but the English army blocked the German's way and these groups, never more than regimental in size, were forced to surrender.

In the South East the story was different. The Germans had recently reinforced this area with elite paratroopers and a whole infantry division was dug in around Dover and Folkston. From somewhere the Germans had found more divisions and even some armour. Now the story was that Goering had put Rommel in charge of the Army of England. Derrick didn't like the idea of facing the Desert Fox in battle again. Until two days ago they had fought adhoc groups of Germans who manned road blocks with MG 42's and the odd PAK 38. Even Luftwaffe flak guns had been pressed into service with the quad 20 mm guns proving very dangerous.

Yesterday that had changed when the 2/4th attached commando battalion who were leading the advance had run into forward units of the German 22 Air Landing Division. Converted French tanks carrying short 75mm guns or 50mm anti-tank guns had attacked the 2/4th causing many casualties. Then six pounder guns mounted on the back of trucks had ambushed the German armour knocking out five vehicles. The commandos had counter attacked throwing back the accompanying infantry.

"We need to get closer," said Gurney. "What about if we crawl along the road using the hedge as cover. The road is sunken any way."

Tom Derrick surveyed the area and thought it might be possible.

"We'll try it even though we are going to be dragging our stomachs in the mud for a fair distance."

They back tracked to the forest and told the lieutenant what they had seen.

"Right, too many will be spotted. I'll take you Tom, Snowy with his Bren, Stan, Freddy and Charlie. Bring plenty of grenades."

They left the forest almost a mile from the house. The small group of Australians moved slowly staying very low and hugging the hedge. Lieutenant Breman had left orders that if there was any firing then the rest of the platoon was to target the upper windows of the house from the small rise where Tom had watched the dwelling previously.

Tom didn't look at the house until they were very close. He knew how the human face stood out. They were now only twenty paces from the front door. Ahead the driveway created a gap in the hedge before running up around to the back of the house and then to the barn. He thanked God that the Germans hadn't had time to put down any mines or the hedge line would have been the first place they would have placed them. He had been watching for any signs of disturbance in the soil for most of the way but it had been clear.

The 30 calibre machine gun suddenly fired at the upper windows from the platoon's position seven hundred yards away. An MG 42 ripped off a burst at the distant target as Breman yelled, "Now."

Snowy fired with his Bren at the same window while the rest of the squad dashed the twenty paces to the building. A German appeared at a lower window in front of them and the Lieutenant sprayed him with fire from his Owen gun. Tom hurled a grenade through the shattered window like a cricket ball. There was a dull crump inside followed by dust and glass flying from the area of the explosion. Harry leapt through the window at the run while Tom sprayed the back door with his Tommy gun before kicking it open. He found himself in a narrow kitchen looking past a doorway into another room. The Lieutenant lay at the bottom of some stairs where a stick grenade bounced down towards him. Harry caught the projectile in his right hand and then quickly flicked it sideways and out of the window where it exploded harmlessly. He started for the stairs when a German opened a side door and started firing with a pistol. Freddy was wounded in the shoulder but miraculously the lieutenant who was standing right in front of the man wasn't hit. He threw himself to the ground and Tom fired a burst into the man's chest. Harry stepped over the body and a German voice cried out, whether in fear or surrender Tom never knew. He saw the Lieutenant hesitate for a second before firing a short burst. The voice stopped.

Stan was with them now and he pointed up the stairs. Tom counted to three with his fingers before firing the rest of his clip through the door at the top of the landing and then reloaded quickly. This was followed by two grenades. The sound of the explosions in the confined spaces echoed in Tom's ears but he ignored the smoke, dust and buzzing in his head and ran up the stairs. He went right and Harry went left. Behind the door a German lay moaning holding his stomach. Beyond him through an open door two others manned an MG42. One of them was cocking an MP 40 and turning in his direction. Tom cut them both down with a single burst. Behind him his lieutenant was firing. There were three spurts of fire from the end of the Owen and then it was quiet.

Tom walked over to where the German lay dead around the MG and signalled from the window to the men across the field. The 30 calibre had stopped firing soon after the first grenade had gone off but he didn't want the platoon to open up again on them. He turned and saw a ladder running up into a man hole in the ceiling. There was another German in the roof, probably a spotter with binoculars.

"Come down Fritz. All your friends are dead. Throw down your gun first," said Tom.

"Name not Fritz. It Hals."

Harry grinned at Tom before calling up. "Alright Hals. There's been enough killin'. Just toss down your gun and come down nice and slow."

A rifle came clattering down followed by a stick grenade that sent Harry and Tom diving for cover. When nothing happened they both stood laughing. A white face appeared at the man hole. "That all weapons," said the German.

"You might have warned us about the potato masher," said Tom.

A young blond man climbed to the floor where Harry Breman took the man's bayonet from a scabbard.

"Sorry, forgot," said Hals.

Tom just smiled. "Sure there's nothing else now?"

The German nodded. Then looked at the bodies. "All dead?" he whispered.

"There's one in the next room Hals who is alive. I'm not sure how bad he is," said Harry.

"Me look, please?" said the German.

Harry Breman frowned and then nodded. "Show him Tom."

One older man in the next room wasn't moving and stared from the floor with eyes of glass. Near him a dark haired man of no more than twenty years of age groaned gently.

Tom moved the man onto his back and noticed a bullet hole in his arm, upper thigh, and just above the hip.

"We might be able to save him Hals," said Tom.

The German gave him a small smile and nodded.

"Why should we?" said a voice from the door. Snowy stood leaning against the door frame cradling the MG 42.

"You got a new toy so why not be happy with that?" said Tom.

"He's a Jerry. We should kill him."

"Been enough of that for the time being so give me your field kit," said Tom.

"Just let me shoot them both and we can move along," said Snowy.

"Do as he says Snowy," growled the Lieutenant.

Frowning, Snowy put down the German gun and fished around in his pack. "Don't know why we are bothering," he mumbled.

"Because my mother said I've a soft heart," said Harry Breman.

Peterson lay on a couch down stairs, his shoulder swathed in bandages.

"You lucky bastard," said Snowy. "That wound will give you two months of white sheets and soft nurses."

"Bloody hurts," said Peterson.

"Don't be a baby," said Snowy. "Think of the food and the smooth hands washing away your cares."

Tom laughed and nodded at the MG42. "What are you going to do with the Bren?"

"Jacko said he would take it. There were a number of boxes of ammo for the German gun."

"Yeh, but they'll rip through the bullets with their rate of fire," said Tom. "And you'll have to carry all those spare barrels."

"Then 'I'll get more, or go and get my Bren. Harry thinks it's a good idea. I'll get others to carry the different bits and pieces."

"It will certainly increase our fire power, just make sure the company knows and tell The Hammer so no one shoots at you by mistake."

The Battalion commander Heathcote Hammer had been with them since the division had fought in Syria with the Free French. The capture of the two Vichy colonies had been tough work but German lack of support had allowed the Commonwealth to secure their Middle Eastern flank.

That night the battalion had pushed to within a few miles of Hayward Heath. Ahead lay the small village of Bolney. Lieutenant Breman pulled out an old road map of south eastern England and pointed to a rough pencil line on the map.

"Right, the division has taken Crawely to the north. The Yanks have got Tunbridge and the Canadians are fighting in Maidstone. The Brits themselves are in Faversham and are clearing the Isle of Sheppey. We have taken Brighton but the Germans are rapidly reinforcing and it looks as though they mean to make a fight of it. The aim is to take Burgess Hill and Hayward Heath before pushing on to Uckfield, with the eventual target being Hastings, though we could be asked to change direction before then as that is probably the Big Red One's target as well. Sir Leslie our esteemed divisional commander wants us to beat the Yank division to the coast."

"That's twenty miles for us and probably fifteen for the Americans," said Tom.

"We'll beat 'em," said Snowy confidently.

"First we take Bolney. The armour is here as are some of the supporting units. The RAAF is going to hit the village at dawn then we move in."

The Sentinel tanks with their single cast hulls and turrets clanked by. All were now equipped with 57mm guns, though a few had the shorter 25 pound guns which fired useful high explosive rounds. Tom knew that the First Australian Armoured Division in the desert was using Grants supplied from America with Honeys as the light recon tank but he was glad that the 9th used a home grown vehicle. Nearby an M3 half-track covered the advance with its 75mm gun. This was an example of why he preferred the old equipment. The Bren carrier might not be able to carry the heavy load but it was easier to hide and being fully tracked could go places the half-track couldn't. He was stunned to hear from the British that they had been forced to sell the little carrier to the Germans for the last two years.

He watched the RAAF attack the town with Kittyhawks dropping bombs until some German planes dived on them. One Australian fighter bomber ploughed into the ground exploding behind the village.

Tom's company started to follow the tanks. They advanced

down a road and across a field of short grass towards the back of a

number of houses. They were only fifty yards from the woods when

the first tank exploded. The whole vehicle erupted in flames and

then the turret flew from a second tank with such force that two

men directly behind it were killed. Machine guns opened up slicing

down some of the leading soldiers and Tom immediately realised

attacking from this direction wasn't an option. The officers came to

the same conclusion and signalled that the battalion retire. The

men fell back covered by heavy machine gun fire and mortars.

Snowy was firing short bursts from the MG 42 before sprinting to a

new location to repeat the process. Three more tanks were

destroyed in quick succession all of them exploding and losing their

turrets. A battery of six pound guns started firing from the woods at

the German positions as the surviving tank and the infantry

regained the woods. The Sentential had pushed only a dozen yards

through the trees when its track came flying off as an AT round

smashed through the bogies. The crew quickly abandoned the

vehicle before a second round put a neat hole in the frontal armour. The Tank started to smoulder and then burst into flame.

"What the hell are shooting at us," said the Sergeant from the burning tank. "The armour on my tank can usually ward off a 50 mm shell but these have to be 88's."

Tom glanced back towards the village and saw two panzers emerge. These tanks were unlike anything he had seen before. They were huge with guns like telegraph poles. They turned and fired and one of the six pounders disappeared in a flash of fire and steel. The other guns fired back but the shells just broke up on the monster's frontal armour. Machine guns racked the woodland and more Australians fell. He saw Lieutenant Breman signal the company to fall back. The captain lay dead near the mangled anti-tank gun. The half-track fired at the panzers but even its shell had no effect. Then it just disappeared as a heavy shell tore it apart.

All of the six pounders had been knocked out except one. Their crews had been cut down by machine guns or high explosive. German infantry were cautiously moving forward behind the monsters as Tom helped the crew of the remaining gun drag it away. As he looked back one of the tanks suddenly stopped. There was a grinding noise from its engine and its commander had thrown open his hatch and seemed to be very unhappy. The other tank kept going. The Australians pulled the six pounder through the forest while groups of men ran passed them. To their south was a large open field probably two hundred yards wide by six hundred long. He could see the crew was tiring and thought of abandoning the weapon when the huge panzer burst from a line of trees onto the field's eastern edge.

He stopped the corporal in charge of the gun and pointed. "How many rounds do you have?"

"Only one box of six shells, but you saw it's useless. Our rounds just bounce off that monster."

"From the front yes, but from the side? We know that the armour on our own tanks are always thinner on their flanks."

The corporal looked doubtful so Tom persisted. "He won't even know where we are and if after a couple shots it doesn't work we dump the gun and move back."

The man nodded and helped push the gun to the edge of the trees. "We've got German infantry coming from the east Sarge so we better do this fast. Still it would be good to get some payback after what these panzers have done to the rest of the battery."

The tank clanked across the field while its hull machine gun sprayed the woods to the west. Tom and the six pounder were seventy yards to the north of the panzer. He marvelled at the size of the gun and its bulk this close up. The crew went about its business while he watched the woods to the west for approaching German infantry. The first shell broke up on the side of the huge tank's turret but the second punched a small hole in the hull near the engine, with the next hitting the track and shearing it away. The panzer ground to a halt with the track flipping free if the sprocket. The corporal put the final three rounds into the hull near the engine with two breaking up but the other creating another hole the size of a cricket ball. The last shell hit next to the driver's position but didn't penetrate. The black clad crew quickly abandoned the massive panzer. Tom fired a burst at them but bullets started to spark from the six pounder's shield and he was forced to take cover. German infantry were firing at them from the east and he was forced to crawl away into the woods with the six pounder's crew.

"We got the bugger Sarge, you were right," the corporal kept saying as they made their way back through the woods away from the firing.

v

Leutnant Kurt Osser was very happy that his transfer had come through. He knew the crisis over England was the reason but didn't care. The training school he had been working at since late April was an important task, and one he took seriously, but he hungered for action again. Now he was leading a flight of FW190 A4's from the British airstrip at Hawkinge to attack the enemy. The landing ground had been attacked by US Mitchell B 25 medium bombers and later by a strange twin engine fighter the Americans called a Lightning or P38. Captured pilots had stated that the bombers had been flown across the Atlantic via Greenland and Iceland while the fighters had been rapidly assembled at Liverpool after having been unloaded from freighters. As a result of the attacks only six of his aircraft could fly. His base was now well protected by Flak and the planes dispersed and protected by sandbags or blast walls.

So far he had only shot down a British Spitfire V and that had felt strange. He knew the enemy plane extremely well and understood that the FW Shrike could out climb it, out dive it and was faster. The Spitfire had a better turning circle but this was offset, to a degree, by the Shrike's rate of roll. What he really loved was the firepower of his new mount. Four twenty millimetre guns packed a punch and the twin centre line rifle calibre machine guns made up for the fact that the heavy guns were wing mounted.

Today they were to sweep to the north where the Canadians had advanced to Lenham. The Germans held the high ground to each flank and were pouring artillery onto the exposed enemy spear head and the Allied air force was trying to hit back. The distance to the front was only forty kilometres and they needed to spend most of that climbing. A scattering of low cloud was the only obstruction with the air above one thousand metres being clear.

They were over Stalisfield Green when they spotted Kittyhawks below. Osser gave the order and rolled his plane onto its back before diving towards the enemy. The aircraft were American as shown by the stars on their side and they quickly dropped their bombs and then their noses. That was a mistake he thought. They should have turned into us and taken us on head on.

"Watch my tail Keller," he ordered his wingman.

They closed quickly with the last machine and Kurt opened fire at one hundred metres. He saw hits on the tail and wing and then a flash from the wing root. The pilot threw open his canopy and jumped flying past Kurt's aircraft and missing by very little. The other planes dropped down to a few hundred metres and turned back towards their own lines. He half rolled and followed them around losing speed but forcing them to fly across his nose. The

161

deflection shot would be tricky but it looked like the range would

be close. The trailing plane was his target and he fired ahead of it by

about its own length. The Kittyhawk flew right through the burst

and exploded, its port wing coming off and the plane hitting the

ground next to a small church. He noticed German armour nearby

on the heights and wondered if Rommel was readying an offensive.

There was no time to think about that now though and he

turned hard to chase another Kittyhawk that had become separated

from it companions. The pilot didn't seem to be aware of his

presence and was climbing away from the ground. He started to

ease up behind it when his wingman yelled a warning. Kurt snapped

off a quick bust before rolling away. He had the distinct impression

that his shells had hit home but was now dodging a stream of

tracers that raced passed his own plane. "Keep turning Leutnant,

it's one of those twin engine jobs."

The burst seemed to be getting closer as he rolled his

aircraft around the sky. Then his wing man yelled. He looked over to see a twin engine plane falling towards the ground with a man floating towards the ground.

"Was he the only one Keller?"

"Yah skipper, just a lone wolf but now a very unhappy one."

"I'll shout you one of those warm English beers for that."

"Make it a snapps and you're on. He is drifting towards his own line skipper and you know what the orders are."

"I'm not shooting someone hanging in their chute. Those orders are from Berlin. If we start doing it so will they."

"I won't say anything if you don't sir."

v

They were probably one of the few groups of Soviet soldiers yet to have surrendered. Corporal Sergi Temkan was with the remains of his company and an assortment of other survivors outside Zabuze near the river Bug. They had been heading for the ferry crossing but the Germans held the river in front of them in force. There were about one thousand men and women hiding in the woods. It was a large patch of forest but the Germans knew they were there. Mortars had been firing off and on all day forcing the Soviets deeper into the trees. They had received no food or other supplies for days and had stripped the countryside bare. Sergi was luckier than most as he and the female snipers that travelled with them had shot a pig two days ago. They had managed to cook it and take a few mouthfuls before the rest of the company descended and stripped the animal bare. Sergi had filled his stomach that day but since then it had only been berries and a mangy ear of corn which he had shared with Zoya.

The young woman had become his friend since he had stood up for her and Irina when a group of soldiers had tried to rape them. He had been disgusted at the time. These women were heroes who had killed many Nazis. He had brought the Lieutenant in to threaten the offending men with shooting.

Now they hid in rough shelters as a thunderstorm drenched them.

Sergeant Sokolov returned from a scouting expedition looking grim.

"The Lieutenant has hung himself."

"What! Why?" exclaimed Sergi.

"Because he heard that German armour has taken Minsk. Even that might be old news."

"Then we are screwed," said Irina. "That puts us almost three hundred kilometres behind the front line."

Sergi was shocked. He knew that the Russian army had been heavily defeated but this was catastrophic.

He lay in the mud until morning numb until he heard yelling. There was no shelling and over two hundred soldiers had gathered.

"We must surrender," said Sokolov.

"Never," said Commissar Volkov. "We will gather every available body and charge the Germans. Then we shall take the ferry and cross the river."

Sokolov shook his head. "We have little ammunition and we are exhausted. There is no food and we have wounded. Baring our way is a regular German infantry regiment. They have been taking prisoners all night. At least one hundred of our number slipped over to them during the storm."

"Traitors," screamed Volkov. "I command here and I order all able bodied soldiers to be ready to attack in half an hour."

No one moved. The Commissar drew his pistol and waved it around.

"You will follow me or I will start shooting. All cowards deserve to die."

Sokolov started to move backwards as did the other soldiers. Volkov pulled his gun up and fired twice randomly into the crowd. There was a groan but all of the men stopped moving.

"Now comrade, where does this get us," said Sokolov.

Sergi could hear sobbing behind him and then what sounded like a growl. Volkov's eyes narrowed and he aimed at the Sergeant. There was a shot but it was the Commissar who reeled backwards with the top of his skull missing. Zoya stood with her face covered in tears, a smoking rifle in her hands. Behind her Irina lay still with a bloody hole in her chest.

"I guess that means we surrender," said Sokolov.

As they marched passed the Germans they held their heads high. The enemy had treated them well so far and had even given them a little food. The wounded were taken away to a field hospital and the captured arms piled near the side of the road. The snipers rifles had been hidden and Zoya had changed into the uniform of the signals unit. The Germans were not known for their mercy to the crack shots who killed from hidden locations. Zoya was allowed to stay with them until they reached the railway station where she was separated and placed with a number of captured Russian nurses. He never saw her until after the war. She was to be mistaken as a nurse by the Germans and used to care for the sick of all nationalities until the war ended. Sergi wasn't to be so lucky.

Chapter Six: October 1942

Goering had calmed somewhat but was still frowning. The naval battle had been a draw with both sides losing a carrier and a battle ship. Grand Admiral Raeder sat next to the table where he had placed a map of the Norwegian coast.

"The enemy had two carriers, one Canadian and one American. The Wasp was finished off yesterday by U 136. The enemy were attempting to tow it clear of the battle area," said the Admiral.

"We lost the Bismarck and the Graff Zeppelin. The Europa is damaged but can be repaired in a few months."

"They lost the Hood as well as a heavy cruiser?" asked Goering.

"We believe so. Aircraft losses were heavy on both sides but the new ME 155's did very well completely out classing the American fighters. However our Stukas suffered heavily from Flak."

"So a draw at best?" said Goering.

"The convoy to Murmansk turned back after losing five ships so we believe it was a victory," said Raeder.

"But the Tirpitz is damaged as is our remaining carrier and our newest carrier is at least three months from being ready," said Goering.

Speer interjected, "I think we could knock a month off that if you want me to."

Goering grunted. He was uncommitted, probably thinking where sacrifices would need to be made if the carrier was pushed up the list of priorities.

"We have nothing to stop them next time and the convoys will start again as soon as the weather deteriorates."

"There have been lessons learned," said Raeder. "We need better attack aircraft with longer range. The Americans got the first punch in because we were too far away. It was only the quality of our fighters that prevented a defeat."

"And the battleships never even saw each other?" asked Goering.

"No. naval warfare has changed, probably forever," said Raeder.

Goering turned to Rommel and Kesselring, both who had been sitting quietly waiting their turn.

"What about the situation in England?"

The leader of Germany grew red in the face. Whenever Goering considered the entry of USA into the war and the failure of German intelligence to warn him of the move he seemed to grow angry. The fact that the British army had changed sides on mass and facilitated the landings just made him more furious. Now it seemed that they had hidden enough Cavalier and Crusader tanks to equip an armoured division and had even developed a new variety of Spitfire in secret. At least the updated model was only present in very small numbers at the moment.

"The line is holding but I am making a few changes to our forces. The First Airborne Division are wasted as regular infantry. I am withdrawing them," said Goering. He turned to Rommel. "You have the 71st infantry division as a replacement. It is rested and almost at full strength."

"It has no mobile capacity," grumbled Rommel. "All its trucks were left in Poland."

"You won't need them in Britain," said Kesselring.

Rommel shrugged. "And the other troops?" he asked.

"The new 65th division is crossing the channel at the moment and the 46th division is already in Dover. You have the 22nd Air Landing Division and the StuG 3s have arrived to reequip it. The 25th Motorised is already fighting on the Kent Downs and the 20th division is to its west. The experimental Tiger unit has been brought to full strength."

"Twelve tanks"' said Rommel.

"The 11th Panzer is on the way. It is collecting fresh tanks in Germany and should arrive in England in a week. With the 3rd Mountain Division you will have eight divisions."

"In the meantime I have seven divisions with sixty tanks and assault guns," said Rommel.

"He has a point," said Goering. "The Army of England is probably facing five hundred enemy tanks at least."

Kesselring looked at the table top before meeting his leader's gaze.

"Keitel told me we can scrape together an independent brigade from the training schools. They will be instructors mixed with recruits. If we do this it must not become a habit and it will only allow another fifty tanks to cross. They will be a mixed force of panzer fours and threes.'

"It's better than nothing," said Rommel. "I'll attach them to one of the motorised divisions."

"I want the Gross Deutschland division's training accelerated," said Goering. "We need a reserve in Germany."

Later Speer sat down with Kesselring for a drink. The head of the Luftwaffe was far from happy.

"He wants us to bomb London by night. I sent one hundred and twenty medium bombers and thirty JU 290 heavy bombers over. At the moment the English air defence is dislocated. No radar and few night fighters, but that won't last and it all robs from the effort in Russia."

"Then there's Africa," said Speer.

"Exactly!" exclaimed Kesselring. "The Commonwealth have crossed the Suez in force and it is extremely doubtful if we can hold Cairo. The Italians are doing better than expected thanks to the Russian equipment we gave them but they won't hold. We have three divisions in Egypt and one brigade. JG 27 is at full strength but one hundred fighters won't last long."

"What about the stukas?"

"Forty of them plus a similar number of JU88s."

"The Italians?'

"They have another fifty stukas. They bought almost one hundred and twenty in 1941 but most of them are for anti-naval strikes. Their fighter strength has improved with the introduction of the Macchi 205 but these are few in number, perhaps eighty in all. Some of the poor sods still have to fly Macchi 200's!"

"Their new Fiat G55 sounds promising and they have another type under development that is even better," said Speer.

"True but that development is so slow and they should stick to one type."

"Something I keep telling you," said Speer waggling his finger at Kesselring.

"I'm doing my best! Our strength is up to five thousand serviceable aircraft. The pilot schools are running well but now fuel is starting to become an issue."

"I'm working on that. Hopefully there will be a jump of eight percent by the end of the year. Two more synthetic oil plants are about to open."

"We'll need every drop," said Kesselring.

V

The SD Kfz 232 sat under its camouflage netting just north of Cairo. Hals Osser wondered how his brother was going. Last he had heard his older sibling had a cushy job training pilots near Berlin. He wished he was back in Germany. Things weren't going so well here. Behind him the outskirts of Cairo began. There were a couple of 88's hidden in the buildings with a battery of 105's further into the city hidden in an area of ruined houses. A battered company of infantry held a rough perimeter in front of the 88's. Everything was hidden from air attack as the Commonwealth Air Force dominated the sky.

For the first few days of the offensive the Luftwaffe and the Regia Aeronautica had fought back bravely shooting down a number of Kittyhawks and even a few of the new American Lightings but relentless attacks on their airbases had worn them down.

The Australian First Armoured, with the Sixth and Seventh Australian divisions had crossed the canal just south of Port Said and hooked north, trying to cut off the 164 German Infantry Division. The Fourth Canadian Armoured and the 2nd New Zealand division had crossed just south of that covering the flank of the Australian Force. Two Indian divisions and the South Africans had followed these forces into the bridge head and moved south west.

Hals remembered scouting for the 21st Panzer division as it tried to stop the attack. They had met the Australian Grants and fought them to a bloody stop, allowing the 164th to escape. Then the Canadians had hit the panzer division in the flank throwing them back. The 21st would have been destroyed except the Ariete division attacked. It was the first time Hals could think of where the Italians had saved a German formation. He supposed it was the captured Russian equipment that made the difference. The T34's clearly outclassed the Ram tanks with the six pounders on the Canadian tanks not becoming effective until almost point blank range. In the desert that was a real problem. But the Italians only had fifty of the ex-Russian tanks and the Australians turned south with their armour. The guns on the Grants could knock out a T34 at ranges up to a thousand metres and the other Italian excuses for tanks were wiped out easily. Now the Italian and German survivors were fleeing to the Nile.

The Commonwealth had fed reinforcements into the fight and the British 7th armoured now faced them outside Cairo with the South Africans approaching the city from the south. General Von Arnim had decided they would fight for the city. German troops were pulling back to defend the line of the Nile but even with Ramke's paratroopers it was doubtful that they had the necessary troops.

A group of Honey tanks moved cautiously into view followed by some M3 half-tracks. British infantry dismounted and crept forward towards a small house. Hals radioed their position to the artillery and the 105's opened fire. He walked the shells on to the British position and then over the half-tracks seeing one of them burst into flame. Then a group of the new Shermans moved forward. It was the first time Hals had got a good look at the tank and he was impressed. It had a useful gun and was probably a match for the latest panzer fours. The profile was higher than he would have liked but it looked as though the tank had fair manoeuvrability and speed. He warned the 88's by radio and then watched from the turret of his armoured car. The anti-aircraft guns had proven to be very effective tank killers though they were hard to hide.

The first hit smashed the frontal plates of a British tank. The Sherman burst into flames immediately and Hals was glad he was too far away to hear any screaming. There was another hit with the same result. It seemed the enemy tanks burned easily. That wouldn't be good for moral he thought. One of the tanks started to fire back and an 88 was knocked out but then another Sherman erupted and the British drew back. The enemy infantry had also gone to ground and Hals knew what would happen next. Ten minutes later a formation of Kittyhawks appeared. The enemy aircraft came in shallow dives dropping their bombs on the edge of the suburbs as the Shermans started to edge forward again. British infantry appeared in small groups rushing from one piece of cover to another. To Hals they seemed to move like scuttling crabs he had watched on the beaches near Rugen where his family had gone on holidays when he was a child. One of the tanks had its turret torn off by a direct hit but then a number of aircraft attacked the gun that had made the kill quickly putting it out of action.

"They must have someone on the ground in contact with the planes," Hals muttered to himself. Just as he was thinking this two planes swooped down and flew towards his position.

"We've been spotted," he said. "Halder, get us into the city now."

The engine fired up immediately and Obergrenadier Halder accelerated out from under the camouflage net. Hals stuck his head out and watched the planes diving ready to order a sudden change in direction. When he judged the range optimal he yelled, "right now!"

The SD Kfz 232 changed direction and Hals ducked inside the vehicle. Two bombs hit the ground one hundred metres to the left exploding with a roar. The next plane didn't drop its bombs but sprayed the armoured car with bullets. The armour wasn't thick enough but the jinking of the driver meant that only a few rounds hit the engine. It was enough. The car rolled to a halt as oil spewed from the engine block. Luckily the car hadn't been moving for a while meaning the engine was relatively cool so there was no immediate fire. Hals ordered his crew out and they started to run for the building in front of them. He led the three others and had just dived through the door way of a two storey building when he heard the chatter of machine guns. The bullets smashed through the walls around him filling the room with dust and fragments of brick. Then there was the roar of bombs exploding. Sound and dirt cascaded into the house and the old wooden door flew passed his head.

Slowly he crawled to his feet and shook the dust from his clothing. Peering out of the doorway he looked for his crew. There was little left of them. The point five bullets had torn some of them apart and then the bombs had finished the job. He stepped back into the shade of the room and threw up. Shock hit him. He had been with these men since France when they had served with the 1st Panzer Division. Together they had accepted the surrender of British troops at Dunkirk. They had celebrated long and hard after the great victory. He could still remember the long lines of English troops marching away from the town. Now his friends were dead.

The sound of battle and the sight of advancing Tommies brought him back to the present. He had only his Walther pistol with a single clip of ammunition so he ran. He went through the building and out the back door before running down the street into the city. The Kitty hawks were leaving but the flat crack of 75mm guns could be heard as well as bursts of automatic fire. Before long he found a German patrol. The Oberfeldwebel in charge directed him to the remaining guns of the artillery battery. A Hauptman with a bandaged arm took his salute and then passed him a canteen of water.

"You look as though you have had a rough time," said the officer. The man was in his early forties and had probably fought in the last war.

"Lost my crew sir. We had been together since 1940. Damm fighter bombers. Almost didn't make it myself."

"You are with the recon battalion?"

"Yes sir."

"Good, I need a spotter. Clean yourself up and grab a gun. There's a few captured weapons over in the car."

Hals drank deeply and then took off his shirt and shook it clean. He then wiped his face with a little water. Glancing around he saw that the 105's were hidden in the rubble with netting covering their positions. The kublerwagon was actually inside a building with the trucks that were used to tow the guns also hidden.

Walking to the back of the car he noted that there was a Bren, two lee Enfield rifles and a sub machine gun. He believed the British and Australians called it a Tommy gun. Picking it up he checked it for damage and dirt. It was clean and there were four clips for the weapon so he claimed it. A soft cough caused Hals to turn. Two men stood in front of him, one with a radio on his back. Both of them looked to be no more than twenty years old.

"Sir, the Captain said you would lead us to somewhere we could spot from."

"Your names?"

"I'm Felix and this is Max," said the shorter of the two.

Hals raised an eyebrow. First names, this must be a casual unit but time in the desert seemed to promote this sort of informal attitude.

"I'm Hals Osser."

The men glanced at each before the one carrying the radio shrugged. "Where should we go sir?"

Hals looked around shielding his eyes against the glare of the Egyptian sun. He noted a three storey building that was higher than most of the other structures. "There," he pointed.

The lines in South Eastern England had solidified. German troops had flooded across the channel. Tom Derrick rested in his slit trench on the high ground just outside of Plumpton.

In this area there was a small bulge into the German lines. The view to the north was impressive with the ground falling away towards Barcombe.

He had talked with Harry about the fate of the German prisoner he had taken. In the end the prisoner's companion had been patched up and sent to the Hospital at Birmingham. Peterson had gone with him after having his shoulder bandaged and the German had gone on a truck to the cage at Bath. Everything was quiet except for the occasional burst of shells or the odd crack of a rifle.

They now faced a mountain division and some of those boys were good shots. At first the Americans had tried to give the Australians some Springfield snipers rifles but the scopes were poor and Heathcote Hammer, their battalion commander had complained. The commanding general of the division, Leslie Morshead had intervened and the good old 303 Lee Enfield with no. 32 x 5 telescopic sights had been issued. Charlie Gaunt was there best shot and he had taken on the task of combating the German snipers.

Tom slept through the day eating a healthy meal of eggs and potatoes taken from a local farm before being woken in the morning with orders to move.

"Rommel's attacked either side of Tunbridge Wells. The thrusts seem to be aimed at the High Ground around Seven Oaks but they could go as far as Croydon if things go well for them," said Lieutenant Breman. "Or Rommel could cut the Yanks off if the two pincers meet."

They grabbed all their gear and mounted the half-tracks. Further down the road armour started to join them. Tom could see the tanks on side roads that ran parallel to theirs. They had just passed through Horsham when FW 190's dove through high grey cloud to attack. Everyone jumped out and ran for cover as the planes swooped in. A number of men stayed with the .5 machine guns and opened up. A few Aussies with Brens joined them and soon a German fighter bomber turned to the southeast trailing smoke. Bombs landed among the vehicles causing one to explode and another to smoulder. Cannon shells raked the road and men screamed but there was no panic. The Australians had been attacked by Stukas and knew what to do. They laced the sky with return fire and the American .5 calibre machine guns gave them the fire power to do so effectively. Yet there had been casualties and the column had been stopped. Officers yelled orders and the men remounted the undamaged vehicles. Within half an hour the winding convoy of men and material was moving again.

They reached Turner's Hill after passing south of Crowely. To the south Haward's Heath was still in enemy hands. Lieutenant Harry Breman crouched around a map and pointed with a small branch. "We are up here on the high ground and the boss wants us to attack along the ridge line with the hope of taking Witches Cross.

This is one of the highest points of the hills and if we are successful we should threaten the German flank. Of course they will be aware of this. We know the 11th panzer is pushing up on either side of Tunbridge Wells supported by battle groups from a German motorised unit. We don't know who is guarding the flank."

"So where are the Germans now?" asked Snowy.

"Here at the twin villages of West Hoathly and Sharpthorne. We will move with the armour through Selsfield Common. The enemy are about a mile down the road from there. We will use the woods on the northern side of the road for cover," said the Lieutenant. "The armour and the 2/23rd will move across the fields after a bombing raid and the commandos and 2/4th pioneers are with us. We will have artillery support."

The battalion advanced in loose formation through the woods until they reached a stretch of open ground one hundred yards wide. On the other side the trees started again. Slowly the Australians went to ground and called in the artillery. Soon shells rained down on the other side of the clearing ploughing the earth and turning timber to match wood. Overhead Tom noticed aircraft flying low over the village. Bombs tumbled from the bottom of the Mitchells and the ground rumbled. He noticed some sticks of bombs tumbling short and yelled to take cover. Three bombs fell into the field that separated the two patches of forest with two more landing amongst the artillery fire. Tom realised how close they had been to being hit by their own side and hoped none of the bombs had dropped too far to the west.

As soon as the shelling stopped the men were up and sprinting in a wave across the field to the shattered wood. An MG42 opened up cutting down a group of men but the position was immediately smothered in fire from Brens covering the advance. Snowy's gun joined the fire spraying German trenches as surviving troops shook off the dust and shock and stood to fire. The Australians were on top of them before they could respond effectively. Grenades and then automatic fire blasted the German troops and soon hands were being thrown in the air. The Australians cut some of the surrendering men down before officers ordered them to cease fire. The prisoners were herded to the rear as the battalion surged on.

The battalion swung to the south to hit the first village of West Hoathly. Ahead lay a small track running east west. A German company came out of the trees on the other side of the road and crashed into the Australians. The commandos were immediately caught up in a swirling hand to hand battle where men shot each other at point blank range or clubbed their enemy with rifle butts. Tom stopped and fired short bursts at Germans no more than five paces away. He saw an officer with a pistol shoot Joey Towmey and avenged his comrade by shooting the man in the chest. The Germans were swamped by the Australian numbers and what was left of their company fled back to the south.

Tom stopped by the dead officer and snatched up the Walther P 38. He ripped the iron cross from the man's pocket and then searched quickly for an extra clip. Finding ammunition he saw the blood on his hands and held them up in shock.

"What am I doing?" he said out loud.

190

"Come on Tom,' yelled Charlie Gaunt from the other side of the track.

The rest of the battalion was attacking into the rear of a number of houses which lined the main road. When he pushed through the thin line of trees he saw that long back yards led to the rear of a group of two storey buildings. Some Germans were firing from upper windows but as he watched Australian supporting fire either killed them or forced them back. He noticed Harry kick open a door and hurl a grenade inside. There was a flat crump sound and then the officer was inside firing his Owen gun as he went. Snowy and Stan were both with the Lieutenant so Tom ran to catch up. Some pioneers joined him in the dash and he saw what remained of the commandos assaulting other houses. He found his friends inside what used to be a lounge room crouched by a door to an adjoining room. Harry signalled him forward and Tom fired a number of rounds with his gun through the door creating a large hole. Charlie put a grenade through the opening and then they all ducked. Tom was first into the room and shot a wounded German holding a MP

40. The two men behind him put their hands in the air. Both were covered in dust and one had bloody legs from shrapnel. He held his fire and then glanced at the stairs. There was noise coming from the upper floors. He gestured that the Germans move and both stared at him. Harry stepped past him and killed both of the prisoners with short bursts. He then glared at Tom before throwing another grenade up the stairs. Snowy fired up through the floor boards with his captured MG 42 before surging upstairs with his officer. There was more firing and then silence. Tom looked at the dead Germans and again glanced at the blood on his hands.

"What are you doing Tom? We are in the middle of a fire fight!" said Stan.

"They surrendered," said Tom slowly.

"So?" said Stan. The Wiry man then gave him a frown before stomping up to the next floor.

The pioneers went past him until they reached what was a master bedroom. It over looked the main road at the front of the house. A hedge with another road running north south formed a T intersection in front of the window. There were more houses down the road interspersed by thick scrub. Then Tom heard firing from the next house. Three Australians in the front yard fell and fire spurted from the upper window of the building. One of the men tried to crawl away but another burst cut across his back killing him.

"Germans next door," said Stan.

Harry looked at the wall that separated the two houses. The two dwellings were joined by a central triple brick barrier that cut out noise and kept the neighbours apart. Where those civilians were at the moment was anyone's guess.

"You," said Tom pointing at the pioneer. "Got any charges?"

The man shook his head but his mate answered. "I do."

The tall red head dropped his pack and pulled out a lump of green putty. He scraped out a brick with his bayonet before stuffing the lump in the hole. Then he fixed the blasting wire and a small detonating plunger. He let the wire off a small spool and then signalled everyone downstairs.

"This was for land mines or other obstructions but it will do the job," said the pioneer.

The blast left Tom's ears ringing but he charged up to a door sized hole and tossed through a grenade before throwing himself to one side. After the smaller explosion Snowy jumped into the room and sprayed everything that moved with his machine gun. The Germans were dead but bullets came up through the floor clipping the butt of Snowy's weapon and sending it spinning from his hand. He jumped towards the wall while Tom and Harry shot back into the floor boards. Part of the room collapsed downwards as beams were severed. As this happened the pioneers tossed more grenades.

"No," yelled Harry. It was too late. The explosions killed the Germans downstairs but also collapsed the rest of the floor sending Snowy tumbling into a shattered dining room. The white haired man had also been hit by some of the shrapnel. There was no way to get to him so they ran out the back door and into the adjoining house. Snowy lay unconscious in the wreckage near four dead Germans. He was breathing but wounded. Stan called for a medic and then carried the injured man back towards the forest. Tom caught his breath and checked his weapon. His submachine gun was damaged the barrel having been hit by either a stray bullet or some shrapnel. He picked up an MP 40 and scavenged six magazines.

"No prisoners unless I say Tom. I don't know what you were trying to prove before but a firefight is no time to show mercy," said the Lieutenant.

Tom nodded glumly. "Got it Harry."

From the front room came a yell. "Tank."

A StuG was rumbling up the street from the south, the crew seemingly unaware that the houses along the main road were all occupied by Australians. It was buttoned up and unaccompanied by German troops.

"Must be trying to hit our armour from the flank," said one of the pioneers.

"How do we stop it," said a blond commando who had just joined them.

"Do you have any C4 left?" Harry Breman asked the red head.

The man nodded grimly.

The assault gun clanked up the street and then turned west at the intersection. It then stopped with the engine idling. Tom spied German infantry running up the road to support it.

"This will be our only chance," said Harry.

Tom grabbed the lump of plastic explosive and ran to the side of the StuG. The wire played out behind him back to the plunger. Once it got caught on a bush and he had to stop and untangle it. The assault gun's bulk screened him from the approaching Germans and the men inside the vehicle had no idea he was there. His heart was thumping in his chest as he placed the C3 half way along the tracks before running back. He had just reached the gate when a rifle bullet cracked past him. At the same time the StuG started to move.

He threw himself flat and yelled for the Pioneer to set off the charge. The blast lifted him off his feet and spun him into the bushes. Behind him was dust and smoke. He saw hands reach for him and then he was picked up and dragged into the house. The debris and haze cleared as the assault gun reversed. Its track came off and it skidded to a halt facing north south. Tom saw the gun drop and fire. The shell was an anti-tank round and it smashed through the wall and continued through the house before clipping a tree in the back yard.

"Move, move, move," bellowed the Lieutenant.

Somehow they bundled Tom out of the back door just as the high explosive round blew out the front of the building. The small group of Australian continued to run up the backyard as two more shells demolished the building. Tom lay on the ground at the edge of the track. Nearby dead Germans were scattered. More troops ran passed him towards the firing.

Later he was told that the German crew abandoned the assault gun. The other attack had come across the fields with the

197

armour and crashed into the enemy defences. Hit from two sides the Germans tried to retreat into the other half of the village. The Victorians from the 2/23rd battalion looped back around through the forest and drove the enemy from Chapel Row before pushing along The Hollow to Church Hill. The Germans left in West Hoathly were cut off. The 2/24th then advanced into the woods north east of Sharpthorne while Kittyhawks bombed and strafed the town. By night fall Australian infantry was fighting the Germans in the streets of the large village. The fighting was fierce and Tom's unit was fed back into the conflagration around midnight. His platoon mainly took a defensive roll protecting against German counter attacks but were lucky that none came their way.

As the sun rose the exhausted Australians held both villages and the 2/9th cavalry had driven their Honey's as far as the woods outside Wych Cross. Here the Germans blocked their way with PAK 40's and infantry from a motorised division. Other Australian units took Forest Row, and, reinforced with armour, held against determined counter attacks. Rommel was forced to slow his drive against the Americans and reroute units to defend his threatened flank. Tom heard some of this as he ate. He leaned the MP 40 against a stone and chewed half-heartedly on his bully beef. Snowy, he was told would be fine, given time.

He looked at the blood on his hand and remembered looting the dead German officer. Maybe robbing the dead was what made him try and spare the prisoners. He wasn't sure. Standing Tom went to a nearby pump and started to clean his hands. The blood under the finger nails proved stubborn.

v

Haumptsturmfuhrer Wolfgang Fischer stood fingering the new rank on his shoulder and wondered at the cost. His panzer four was waiting for parts with three others at Glinka fifty kilometres south east of Smolensk. The front line ran north east from here to the Estonian border, then south to an area near Kiev. The capital of the Ukraine had fallen a week ago after a pincer movement. The line then continued south to an area one hundred kilometres east of Odessa. Most of the bend of the mighty Dnieper River had yet to be cleared and the Romanians were struggling to reach the neck of the Crimean Peninsula.

The advance to Minsk had been almost free of Russian front line soldiers with the service troops fleeing as fast as they could. The First SS division had moved very quickly for the first two weeks of September before the Soviets started to recover from their crushing defeat. Many weapons and a few factories had been captured intact during the advance. Once they had come across a whole train of brand new T34s just sitting in a siding. He had heard of the 5th SS capturing a tanker train in a similar state. Thousands of 76mm guns had been taken as well as many trucks. Most of the prisoners were captured in Poland but another one hundred and fifty thousand were rounded up as the army approached Minsk. About half way to Smolensk things started to change. The Soviet Air Force put in an appearance strafing a column of trucks and then Russian units mounted small scale counter attacks.

Then the rains came turning the ground into mud. Roads were impassable, airstrips unusable. Everywhere the advance had gone from being measured in kilometres to metres. In the south there was still movement and some panzer divisions had been sent to help the push towards Rostov and the Crimea but eventually that front would shut down as well. They probably only had days left.

At least the winter uniforms and anti-freeze were starting to arrive. He had been told by unsympathetic locals that soon the ground would freeze, and then, a few weeks later their blood would too. The truth was that since they had crossed the border into Belarus the attitude of the population went from indifferent to hostile. He wished he was with the 1st or 3rd panzer division advancing through the Baltic States. There men were flocking to the banner of the SS. The word in SS circles was that Latvia, Lithuania and Estonia were to be treated softly. Germanic blood had left traces amongst these people and they were to be accepted into the SS brotherhood. Kaltunbruner had even decreed that Galicia on the Ukrainian Polish border be afforded special status. Scuttlebutt was that the SS was looking to create an extra six to seven divisions from these recruits. Fischer wasn't sure how he felt about that. The

Scandinavians and the Dutch sure, hell even the French at a stretch, but Slavs?

He didn't buy the story that the Teutonic knights had left traces of their noble blood in the present population. The real story was power and troops. Losses had been heavy amongst the German Army and the war looked like it wasn't going to be over anytime soon. Moscow was still at least three hundred kilometres away and winter was fast approaching.

The line of broken down trucks, cars, panzers and half-tracks also slowed the advance. Spares for the British trucks had arrived but the French equipment hadn't done as well. Indeed without the trucks from England it was hard to know how they would have gotten as far as they had. The trucks had allowed the infantry to keep pace and had kept the army supplied but now there were the beginnings of a new problem. Partisan attacks were small scale but troubling. His commander Standartenfuhrer Kurt Meyer believed the best response was swift retribution.

Fischer could still see the questioning look in the young boy's eyes before they shot him. They had lined up a whole family and mown them down. The mother had held her daughter before the bullets had torn into them. He knew his willingness to participate was being watched. Meyer had told them these people were vermin, and the Slavs were not to be pitied. Yet just across the border Estonians were being invited into the Sacred Brotherhood of the SS. It was confusing. He remembered the Russian pilot who had looked just like his sister. She was Jewish but he wouldn't have been able to tell the two women apart at twenty metres.

Now there were the dreams. His sister came to him at night and asked why he was shooting women and children. He tried to explain that they weren't really human, more like animals. She would frown and say how they looked just like Germans. Then she would tell him it was time for him to shoot her. Panzer Meyer would hand him a pistol and he would put the gun at her temple. Then he would wake up. He didn't want to kill anymore civilians but didn't think he would have the option of opting out.

Chapter Seven: November

1942

All of the generals were there. Goering sat at the head of the long wooden table in the drawing room of Carinhall looking uncomfortable. Keitel, Halder, Kesselring and Rommel were there. Guderian was still at the front but Kluge and Rundstedt had flown in from Russia. Speer was allowed to sit in to discuss production issues.

"We have reached the outskirts of Leningrad though we haven't reached Lake Lagoda. The Finns have advanced to the old borders and stopped. In the central front we have just taken Kaluga and Vyazma one hundred twenty kilometres from Moscow," said Halder.

"What about in the south?" asked Goering.

"The line then runs to Orel before moving south west to the Dniester River. We cleared the bend of the river and have taken Melitopol. The Crimea is cut off from the north."

"So a bulge has developed?" asked Kluge.

"Yes, around Orel and the Eastern Ukraine," said Halder. "Basically the southern sector of Russia."

"The line has solidified my Fuhrer," said Keitel. "We need to decide where our next effort should be. Splitting our resources is no longer an option. The Russians have shown remarkable powers of recovery."

"Suggestions?" asked Goering.

"We could put Leningrad under siege by advancing around the western side of Lake Ladoga or we could strike for Moscow," said Kluge.

"Then there is the bulge," said Halder. We could strike south from it and protect our flanks while aiming at Rostov and a big pocket of Russian troops."

"Too far at this time of year," said Rundstedt. "Winter is about to hit in its full fury. It's already freezing in the east."

"Or we can reinforce the drive from the south and take Rostov that way," said Kluge.

"To what purpose?" asked Rommel who had stayed quiet up until now.

Kluge frowned at him. "It would open the gate way to the Caucuses."

"A doorway we couldn't use until next summer," said Goering. "No I'm looking for a success now."

"Then its Leningrad or Moscow," said Halder.

"I would take the northern city," said Rommel. "If we do then that sector becomes dead, especially if we push the front to Tikhvin and cut the rail links. It's an achievable objective."

"With respects to the Field Marshal, Moscow is their capital. If it falls we will probably win the war."

"That didn't work for Napoleon," said Rommel. "It's also where the strongest defence lines are and most of their troops, and it's further from the front lines than Leningrad."

Halder looked as though he was preparing a retort when Goering stepped in. "What is the latest from England Herr Field Marshal?"

Rommel rolled out a map of Kent and East Sussex. "We pushed the Americans back towards Croydon and took four thousand prisoners but the Australian counter attack allowed most of the American 1st division to escape. The line is now quiet but the enemy's strength grows daily. It is now only possible to transport supplies at night across the channel. The Luftwaffe needs reinforcements."

Kesselring bristled. "So does everywhere. We are stretched thin! The night time blitz ate into our strength and in the end we were forced to move aircraft to the Mediterranean as well as fighters with the collapse of the Nile front. Despite this *you* are still supported by over three hundred and fifty fighters and fighter bombers."

"The British and Americans have twice as many and then there are their medium bombers," said Rommel.

Kesselring threw his hands in the air.

"You need to make do," said Goering. "The situation in Africa is dire. We are back at El-Alamein and our army is a shell. I have thought of abandoning the whole theatre but that would free up over ten enemy divisions to be deployed elsewhere."

"What about the French?" asked Kluge.

"They may help this time. After what the British rebels under Churchill did in Syria and the attack on their fleet by the Allies they may send troops to help us from Algeria. The signs are promising but I wouldn't say certain," said Goering.

"Well, in England we are also in trouble. I need more armour."

"The new 23rd panzer division is ready. It has a mix of

Marders, panzer fours and threes. It will be the last division I will

give you and it will replace one of the infantry divisions, probably

the one that has sustained the most casualties, I haven't decided

which one yet," said Goering.

For a second it looked as though Rommel would argue but then his

shoulders slumped forward and he nodded.

"I will send more T34's to the Italians. It sounds as though

they have used them well so far. Also the 21st panzer division will be

brought up to strength and the 29th motorized along with a

battalion of assault guns will be sent to Africa. All these fronts have

to understand that will be the last reinforcements they will get

except for equipment replacement. Russia is the key gentlemen."

Speer noticed a soldier at the door. The man saluted and

then handed Goering a note. The big man read it and a smile spread

across his face. "Gentlemen, we now have a chance. Japan has just

attacked Pearl Harbour. The Americans are reported to have lost six

battleships and two carriers. The Japanese took loses as well, losing two carriers as well. A large number of US submarines were hit as well as the oil storage plant. There was a massive air battle but American air power in the area is supposed to be severely degraded. Many brave Japanese airmen were shot down but it sounds as though the cost was worth it. The Americans will have three carriers left if our intelligence is correct, the Japanese six."

"Are they attacking elsewhere?" asked an excited Kluge.

"Those Panzer fours we made for Japan are currently rolling onto beaches in Malaysia and In the Philippines. The tank factory we helped them build in 1941 may just start paying off. As will the U boats and Bf 109 Fs we sold them. Maybe they will make their own copies of those too, eventually," said Goering clapping his hands.

Speer thought he hadn't seen his leader look this happy in a long time.

v

The new aircraft were Italian but they were painted in winter camouflage and sported Hungarian markings. The Fiat G55 was brand new and replaced Gyorgy's aged Spitfire Five. Such was the price of Hungarian oil that the Italians were prepared to sell some of their newest fighters for the precious liquid. Gyorgy Debrody was pleased with the different aircraft. It was faster than the Spitfire, handled well, had a good turning circle and decent fire power. They had replaced the twenty millimetre cannons in the wings with the fast firing fifteen mm guns. The twenty millimetre gun firing through the engine block and the two 13mm machine guns firing above the engine increasing the hitting power of the fighter and provided centre line sighting that didn't rely on the shells converging at a certain point.

The aircraft engines had been warmed that morning by lighting small wood fires in portable stoves. This provided enough warmth that the planes started easily. Only six aircraft were serviceable and all taxied through the snow and took off a minute apart allowing the air to clear and visibility to improve before the next one began to taxi.

The understrength squadron climbed to three thousand metres enjoying one of the few late autumn days of good weather. Scattered clouds below them travelled east on a stiff breeze.

Gyorgy Debrody now had forty two kills and was the second highest scoring Hungarian fighter pilot in the air force with only his friend Miklos Kenyeres ranking above him with forty five. His rival however was on leave and this was his chance to close the gap. He knew there were Germans who had made more kills. He had heard of a Heinz Bar who had over sixty kills and then there was Adolf Galland who had eighty five kills but had been promoted to run the training schools. The great Werner Molders however had reached one hundred and five victories before being made the Inspector General of German Fighters.

"Russians at 3.00 o'clock low," said his wing man.

Glancing to his right he saw a dozen twin engine bombers about ten kilometres away. They appeared as blurred specks but as they dived towards them he realised they were TU 2's. The twin engine Russian plane had a good reputation, being fast and well-armed.

212

"Watch these guys, they have a good turning circle and are tough," he said.

They closed the distance quickly and noticed the Soviets dump their bombs and turn for home.

"No escort in sight," he said into his radio.

The Russians tightened their formation and a storm of fire came from the rear gunners. He tried to ignore it and aimed at a trailing aircraft. Gygorgy fired and saw his bullets impact the first gunner's position. His cannon shells chewed into the tail and the port engine while the other upper gunner kept firing. He saw a line of holes appear in his wing but then he was past the formation and climbing.

"You got him skipper, he's going down," said his wing man over a crackling radio.

From above Debrody led the squadron in a slow climbing turn in order to make another run at the bombers. He could see the plane he had hit burning and falling away while another aircraft trailed smoke.

"I've got to head home Skipper. One of their gunners has hit the coolant system and my engine is overheating," said the pilot of red two.

"Off you go red two, red one you better go with him," Debrody ordered.

That left him with four fighters. He considered a single frontal attack but as he was almost behind the Soviets decided on a fast diving pass. He would come up under the enemy bombers. At least this way his flight would only face a single gunner from each Russian plane.

They dived and then dipped under the TU 2's. Debrody opened fire at two hundred metres and saw his cannon shells tear pieces from the belly of the plane. The gunner fired short burst at him and he saw two holes appear in his engine. Then the enemy bomber exploded and he was pulling back hard on the stick in order to miss the debris. His engine coughed and spluttered and Debrody checked his surrounding as the smoke cleared.

"You are on fire skipper. Get out!" yelled a voice.

He saw smoke pouring from one of the holes in the engine as he levelled out and noticed the hits around his cockpit. Thinking quickly Debrody realised that they were behind the German front lines and he was safe from being captured. He attempted to open the canopy intending to bail out but it wouldn't budge. Fear rippled through him and he swore. He hammered at the glass above his head but without effect. Smoke started to enter the cockpit, however his pilot's mask stopped him from breathing in the toxic fumes. Then he noticed the flames around his feet.

"God I don't want to burn to death," he screamed.

He unfastened his straps and turned the aircraft over. Pulling his pistol from his holster Debrody fired at the realise leaver and almost succeeded in hitting himself with a ricochet. He kicked at the canopy as the smoke thickened around him. Suddenly the glass and steel cage that was keeping him in the cockpit dropped free and he fell with it. His head snapped back as the pilot's mask was ripped from his face and he flew past the tail of his Fiat. Debrody spun for a second feeling the cold air on his skin. Reaching for his rip cord he pulled. Hearing the rush of the material of his parachute opening and then the snap as it deployed he looked up and saw the chute billow out, and then he saw the holes. The fire in the cockpit had damaged the silk and he noticed one of the tears growing. He glanced down and estimated the ground was still five hundred metres below him. For a moment the material held and the ground approached. Debrody willed the fabric to not rip but it wasn't to be. With a splitting sound the chute folded and he dropped. He said a prayer and waited for the impact that would kill him. The pine tree branches smacked past his face and he yelled in pain before plunging into a snow drift. He felt his arm jerk as the remains of his chute caught in the tree and then he was still.

Debrody felt sore all over. He realised he was on the ground and alive. He laughed with relief and stood. His ankle went from under him and he felt pain. Staggering out of the drift he waved at three circling planes. One of them waggled its wings and then flew over him at low altitude.

About an hour later a German patrol found him. They were mounted on horses and dressed in sheep skin coats. A sergeant had to assist him onto one of the animals. His ankle was throbbing and he was cold but Gyorgy Debrody couldn't stop grinning.

v

The 1st SS Panzer Division was under strength and its men exhausted and yet they were being asked to attack. Hauptsturmführer Wolfgang Fischer stood before his panzer four with an officer from the 1st motorised battalion. The Obersturmführer was younger than he was and sported a bandage around his forehead.

"It's the bosses order actually. He said to gather the villages and march them through the area where we thought the mine field was. The pioneers are otherwise engaged and Meyer wants us attacking Monakovo by noon."

Fischer thought on the force of six panzer fours and four hundred soldiers that would be attacking and wondered if it would be enough. He knew the other kampfgruppe was a little stronger but if the Russians were dug in and in strength then it would be a tough fight. They were only sixty five kilometres from the outskirts of Moscow but the late November weather and the deterioration of the army and the supply situation was making life very hard for the German forces. Many of the French half-tracks and citrons were broken down between Smolensk and the Polish border but the spares built in Germany helped keep the English Bedfords going and they were reliable. Even the infantry divisions still had a few. The fact that the QL series was four wheel drive was an added advantage.

The villagers shuffled into view swathed in blankets and coats. It was bitterly cold with the wind whipping up granules of frozen snow which stung exposed skin. He saw the dull eyes of men in their forties and fifties and women as old as his mother. Then he saw the children and young girls between twelve and eighteen.

"We are using Children?" he asked the Obersturmführer.

"Meyer said to use them all. They're all heavy enough to set off a mine and I would prefer it was them rather than us sir."

The officer gave Fischer a quizzical look so he started to walk back to his panzer. As he did his gaze caught the eye of a young girl. She couldn't have been more than twelve or thirteen years old. Her large blue eyes held his as though pleading and Fischer froze. Her look said why? Why are you going to kill me? What have I done? He tore his eyes from her and climbed into his cupola. She turned and looked at him again before a rifle butt pushed her along.

The first line of villagers formed up and was directed forward with shoves and bayonet points. One of the soldiers shouted a few words of Russian at them and they started walking slowly. For one hundred meters they trudged on and then a second line was sent forward. The girl he was watching was pushed into a third line. After the villagers had moved one hundred and fifty metres Fischer started to hope that there was no minefield. Then there was a flash and a flat boom. A body was hurled into the air and fell as bloody lump back to the earth. A few soldiers laughed

and the Obersturmführer yelled out, "and there it is!"

A few seconds later there was another explosion and

another figure was torn apart. The villagers stopped and one

started to wail. The Obersturmfuhrer gave an order and a soldier

fired a burst from his MP 40 near one of the men. Again the

Russians started to move. Some of them were crying and then a boy

broke from the third line and tried to run away. Two troopers

turned and shot him with their rifles before he had gone a dozen

paces. The villager cried and shouted but they kept going through

the mine field. One of them made it to the forest and called out in

relief. There were more explosions and additional people were torn

to pieces but a few survived. The second line hit more mines. Two

of the boys decided to run across to the forest, as though their

speed would somehow assist them. The first one hit a mine near

the edge of the woods and his pace caused it to explode a little

behind him. He was lifted from his feet and thrown to the edge of

the trees where he lay moaning. The other boy stopped when he saw his friends' fate. He took a couple a shuffling steps and then disappeared in a flash of fire.

Fischer watched the girl as she stumbled across the snow covered field. She was crying and sobbing. One of the woman stopped and refused to go any further so the Obersturmführer had a rifle man shoot her in the back. More villagers died but the girl with the blue eyes was still alive. He willed her to survive. A boy of sixteen made it and whooped with joy. Fischer thought the girl would make it when she disappeared in an eruption of fire and earth. He watched her body come apart and felt shock hit him. It was like a blow and his eyes filled with tears.

"Alright boys, let's go, but be careful. There still might be a few mines that the Russki's missed," said the Obersturmführer.

"Remember to shoot any of the villagers we find."

Fischer couldn't believe his ears. They had driven these people through a mine field and now they were going to massacre the survivors. A trooper seemed to feel the same way.

"Sir, that's a bit rough. A mean they made it!"

"Do you think they're going to thank us for that? They'll hate us more than they already do! Remember trooper what they did in East Prussia. Now follow your orders!"

The soldier grimaced but didn't object.

Fischer wiped the tears from his eyes before anyone spotted them and quietly ordered the panzer four to advance. Overhead German guns fired at distant Russian targets and somewhere close by a machine gun fired. He sighed and readied himself for battle.

v

It was strange watching the T34 moving past him. The Italian markings were clearly painted on the turret and its commander gave him a weary smile as he passed. Leutnant Hals Osser, newly promoted, coughed on the dust thrown up by the wide tracks. He was pleased their allies now had some decent armour even if it wasn't of their own design. It was said the Italians were now making at least two decent fighters and some of their infantry divisions were using ninety mm guns in the same way that the Germans used the eighty eight. He walked back to the half-track and joined the squad of men clustered in the shade.

Since the destruction of the reconnaissance battalion Hals had been transferred to the 125th motorized regiment under Major Hans von Luck. His company were in reserve near El Alamein tucked in behind the Ruweisat Ridge line. Antitank guns were dug into the other side of the gentle rise. The division had received some replacements in terms of men and equipment but they were still at only seventy percent of their supposedly established strength. The panzer fours and Marders were welcome, as were the men. The problem was that most of the youngsters were straight from the training grounds of Germany. Few veterans had made it back across the Nile. Ramcke's paratroopers had arrived safely from the Sudanese border but the infantry of the 90th light division had been hit hard.

The Commonwealth forces had gathered before them and if it hadn't been for the arrival of two French divisions from Algeria they would have already broken through. There was no doubt that the French colonial troops were tough but their equipment left a lot to be desired. Their anti-tank guns were weak and the artillery not much better. At least the two French fighter squadrons and the light bombers were proving useful.

Aircraft appeared overhead and soon black puffs exploded around them. B25 Mitchells he thought before jumping into a fox hole. The bombs fell along the ridge exploding among the positions of the French troops. Soon a plane dropped out of formation and fell away in flames. Hals smiled at the victory but he knew the enemy had many planes to replace it with. More aircraft arrived and bombs were falling everywhere. They crashed into the ground exploding not far from his deep hole. He could hear some of the new recruits screaming in terror. Hals understood that the bombers were directing their attack on the units along the high ground but enough were overshooting to make life uncomfortable for his unit.

A half-track was hit and disintegrated throwing pieces of iron and steel high into the air. He was finding it hard to breath and wondered how the enemy pilots could see their target. He supposed they didn't care. They probably relied on the weight of the bombardment to do their work for them.

Eventually the attack ended and the dust slowly settled. French ambulances were soon driving quickly to their battered units but as they arrived the artillery started. Shells screamed down onto the ridge and Hals huddled deeper into his hole. The enemy pounded the whole area now with his company also receiving its fair share of punishment. Hals was covered in dirt and he covered his ears against the noise. He believed that a bombardment of this magnitude must be the precursor to a major attack. He hoped his raw troopers would be able to stop them.

The shelling stopped and he was able to raise his head. Miraculously only one half-track had been hit. He called for his company to form up and did a quick count of heads. Three men were wounded and two missing, presumed dead. A shell had landed in their foxhole and nothing could be found of the troopers. He sighed and looked around for his Feldwebel. He tried to remember the man's name and failed. Hals spotted a Gefreiter carrying an MG 42.

"Get everyone ready to move. After that pounding the enemy will attack and I doubt if our French allies will hold the enemy armour with their 47mm guns. Tell the commander of the two Marders that are with us we will probably be called up to support the men on the ridge shortly. We'll need their guns."

As the men collected equipment and started the half-track Hals wiped his brow. He was so tired. Everyone he had served with was dead or wounded and the situation of the army was deteriorating. He wondered why he was still fighting. The war didn't seem any closer to finishing than when he was riding on a motor cycle through France. At least his brother was still alive and hopefully his position training pilots would keep him safe. If the news was to be believed the German army was winning in Russia and holding on in England but that meant nothing to him. He tried to fight off a feeling of impending doom. Hals believed he was on borrowed time. Sighing again he clambered up into the half-track and went to the radio operator.

"The Commonwealth are attacking with armour and troops against the ridge but there is a flanking move sir."

"Do we have orders?" Hals asked.

"We are to wait for now."

He grunted and drank some warm water from his canteen. At least the weather wasn't as hot at this time of the year. Hals wished some of the rations they had captured in Cairo were still available. He was already sick of the tinned meat and hard tack and would have killed for some Australian tuna or Weet-bix. He lit a cigarette and stared out over the gently sloping dirt and rocks.

Overhead Macchi fighters duelled with Kittyhawks. The Italians seemed to be getting the better of the fight with two of the enemy planes spiralling down towards the ground. It was heartening that their allies were performing better now they had decent equipment. Hals had seen the sleek Italian fighters at an airfield where his command had been collecting fuel and had been impressed by their business like appearance.

"Orders sir. We are to support the French and the AT battery we lent them."

"Alright let's move out. We'll skirt the ridge line until we are near the southern end and then find out what the situation is."

They had only gone a kilometre when four Hurricanes appeared skimming low over the desert. They opened fire with a single machine gun in each wing. These seemed to be used for aiming purposes as heavy forty millimetre cannons soon barked from under each wing. The half-track in front of them was hit in the engine and through the side armour. It ground to a halt with smoke pouring from the interior. Another vehicle was hit with tracks flying apart and a running wheel disintegrating. His command halted and men spilled onto the ground throwing themselves down. Hals got behind one of the MG 42's and fired short bursts at the planes as they flashed by. He didn't hit anything and noted the planes were climbing away. Overhead the Italian still duelled with the P40's but

two had seen the attack and dived on the Hurricanes. He lost track

of the air combat and glanced around at his company. At least

another four men were dead with more wounded. He loaded the

injured onto a kublerwagon and sent them back to the field hospital

and then the line of vehicles started moving once again.

He found the first French unit in full retreat as he reached

the half way point along the ridge. They were fleeing on foot but

keeping good order. Hals stopped an officer and tried his school boy

French.

"Stop butchering my language," growled the tall soldier.

"We are retreating because all our guns were knocked out. Your

PAK 40's destroyed a number of the new Commonwealth tanks but

there weren't enough of them. Our 47mm guns just tickled their

tanks."

Hals was impressed by the Captain's German which had the

accent of Alsace or Lorraine.

"We tried to hold on but their infantry are cooperating well with the armour," the captain continued.

Who says the enemy can't learn thought Kurt.

"You cannot stop them with this," the Frenchman waved at the line of half-tracks and Marders.

The French continued to fall back as Hals radioed in the situation. As he did four enemy tanks came over a low hill and started firing. They were a type he'd seen once before and he believed they were called Shermans. The Marders fired back and one of the enemy tanks ground to a halt spewing smoke. Then another one lost a track. His men had jumped from their SDkfz 251s and fanned out. One of the Marders blew up suddenly throwing its gun end over end. More Shermans arrived with infantry. The enemy seemed to be in small groups hugging the ground. His men started shooting at the approaching troops while the Shermans fired high explosive rounds at his vehicles. His command was in a poor position, not properly dispersed, or in ground of their choosing. Hals was about to order their retreat when the second

Marder was hit. The AT shell wrecked the gun and shield but the vehicle could still move. It was useless in terms of fighting the Shermans so Hals issued the order for his men to turn around. Shells were exploding all around them and Hals expected to be hit at any moment. Then a Sherman caught fire. Another stopped and its crew hurriedly abandoned their tank. Hals stared south and noticed eight strange tanks sitting among low hillocks firing at the Commonwealth forces.

A gefreiter stood next to him and pointed. "What are they sir?"

"Italian KV1s I think. I know we gave our allies about a dozen of them as well as one hundred or so T34s."

The Shermans started to fire back but at the range they were firing their 75mm shells broke up on the thick armour. The Italians were firing rebored 76mm guns which knocked out the Shermans easily. Eventually the Commonwealth tanks were forced back after losing at least twenty of their number. Hals thought they had won the day when the artillery started. He screamed at his men to mount up and watched as many were cut down on the open ground. The half-tracks turned back the way they had come followed by the surviving Italian tanks. Kittyhawks attacked them and then they were back behind the third defensive line. His troops dismounted and hid in trenches as Bf 109s clashed overhead with the enemy. Kurt looked around at his company and realised that they had lost at least half their vehicles and he probably had enough men to form an over strength platoon. At this rate his company wouldn't exist in another two days.

v

Speer sat with Kesselring in plush leather chairs. A glass of schnapps was near a bottle in the middle of a low table. They had been discussing the continued Japanese advances in the Pacific but Speer wanted to know about the Mediterranean.

"So they held the line in Africa?" he said.

"Just," answered Kesselring. "The Italians fought well and the Russian armour we gave them gave a good account of itself. Their air force also put up a credible performance too."

"But the Commonwealth will attack again and there is no hope of retaking Egypt?" asked Speer.

"Correct. We predict that the enemy will rebuild and try again in January."

"Luckily England is quiet," said Speer.

"Yes but with Rommel sick I don't know if Paulus will be up to the job," said Kesselring. "Everything depends on us taking Moscow."

Speer grimaced. He believed Rommel's plan to take Leningrad had been more practical given the exhaustion of the army. "At least the operations in the Ukraine have been successful."

"The Russians gave ground rather than try and fight but we still took another one hundred thousand prisoners. We might even take Rostov."

"Ever the optimist my dear Kesselring," said Speer.

The head of the Luftwaffe smiled. "And why not? In May we were looking at the possible destruction of Germany. Now we are forty kilometres from the outskirts of Moscow."

"Do you think that we will be able to take the capital before winter hits with its full force?"

"I think so. Let's hope this winter is not as bad as last year's eh. That was one of the worst in living memory."

"Well at least the troops have warm uniforms and anti-freeze," said Speer.

"Yes but we need more of everything to keep them going. You have worked wonders with production but now supplies are no longer coming from South America there must be problems?"

Speer nodded. "Fuel is always an issue but a new coal liquefaction plant just came on line. That increased output by another three percent. Everything else has increased too though we are falling short on trucks. I can keep the British one's going but can't make more of them. I have tried to compensate by building extra Opals but it's at the expense of half –track and armoured car production. Fighter aircraft output is improving and your insistence on maintaining and expanding pilot schools means we will have the men to fly them."

"I've seen the figures and am happy with them but I worry about new types," said Kesselring.

"The latest American fighters are a match for ours and will only continue to improve. The P38 is a good plane by all accounts, as is the new Spitfire."

Speer took a sip of his drink. "There are the jets."

Kesselring snorted. "The engines still give trouble though I suppose they are a little improved. I can't see them in service in any numbers before early 1944. No, we must be careful not to put all our eggs in that basket. The narrowing of aircraft types has helped production but development of new types is still all over the place.

There is a new type of FW 190 that is under development but the first proto types won't be ready until spring of next year."

"I believe the Italians are finally flying some decent fighters. I was loath to let them have any of our engines but now the investment is paying dividends. The new Fiat is supposed to be very good."

"The Hungarians are flying them and the Finns are trying to get some. They are the equal of the latest 109G," said Kesselring.

"I heard they may be a little better," said Speer.

Kesselring shrugged and took a sip of his drink.

"Anyway what else can I do to help you to increase production?" asked Kesselring.

"Encourage our leader to keep the Russian prisoners alive, I could use them."

Kesselring nodded.

Chapter Eight: December 1942

"By God it's cold," said Gefreiter Paul Becker.

"Stop your whining and look," said Feldwebel Neuman. "I'm sure I saw movement."

Paul peered through the gloom. The other side of the Muis River was a frozen waste land dotted with white pines. To the north the Russians held a bridgehead in an area of low hills and trees. Their company had attacked it two days ago and been driven back by mortar fire. Now both sides watched each other.

"It's almost dark and I can't see shit," said Paul.

Nueman continued to stare. "I swear they are up to something," muttered his Feldwebel.

Paul grunted and started to apply anti-freeze on the firing

mechanism of the MG 38. His old MP 28 lay next to him in the

snow. It was cold and his teeth chattered. If it wasn't for the gloves

and the newspaper in his boots his extremities would have

frostbite. His face was covered by a white ski mask and he wore a

white sheet over his thick grey coat. He thanked supply for planning

for winter because if the thicker uniforms and other items hadn't

arrived he believed that his unit would be dead.

The 15th Panzer's charge through the Ukraine had been

facilitated by reinforcements and the collapse in Russian morale. As

they had advanced whole units had sometimes surrendered to

them. He could still see the line of trucks pulling 76mm guns driving

up under a white flag. It seemed the battery had received little fuel

recently but had not been given any ammunition or food for weeks.

The Romanians had taken possession of most of the prisoners, and

the guns. He had to admit their allies' cavalry divisions had proved

useful covering the 15th's flanks and scouting for possible danger.

The Romanian armoured division with its British crusader

tanks had also shown their worth. He had heard tales of their crews waiting until T34's were within two hundred metres before springing ambushes or opening fire. That took guts. The 57mm guns managed to penetrate at the close ranges and usually the Russian crews were outfought by the Romanians whose experience was growing by the month.

"We'll go off watch soon," said Nueman sliding back into the trench.

"Just as well," said Paul. "Much longer and my balls will drop off."

Nueman grinned, "Never thought a smelly dugout warmed by a leaky stove would be so inviting."

The company held five hundred meters of trench line that had been blasted out of the frozen earth with grenades and explosives. In some places they had lit fires so as to thaw the soil in order to allow the men to dig.

"Don't think we'll make Rostov," said Neuman.

239

"Pity," said Paul. "Those buildings would have provided some warmth."

"Everyone's exhausted," said The Feldwebel. "The Bren carriers are just about worn out, units are at 50% of their strength. I heard the division's only got twenty tanks that are runners, another sixty are all under repair. No spares as all the supply effort went into getting the warmer clothes to us."

"I suppose something had to give," said Paul.

"Well, we've done better than most. Our carriers did get the odd spare and we got some replacements."

"Kids wet behind the ears," snorted Paul.

"They can point a gun and we were all rookies at some stage."

Paul finished with the MG 38 and handed it to his Feldwebel. "All done, I'm going to get us some coffee."

"There's some left?"

"Only the fake stuff," said Paul.

Neuman sighed and then exploded into movement. He pushed Paul aside and brought the machine gun to his hip firing a short burst. A figure in white clothing tumbled from the lip of the trench landing among some empty boxes. It was now dark and the flash of the gun's muzzle almost blinded Paul. He heard more than saw other figures slide into the trench around them. He managed a single blast from his machine pistol before a rifle butt knocked it from his hand. A man had reeled away clutching at his throat but another replaced him. The rifle butt caught him on the side of the helmet sending Paul spinning to the earth. He could hear Neuman swearing and yelling as he tried to pull himself to his feet.

Nearby Wolf and Christian appeared. Somewhere a grenade went off showering Paul with dirt. A Russian dived at him through the melee, a bayonet gripped in his right hand. He snatched at his Webley revolver in his belt and fired a shot into the man's chest. Another Soviet grabbed him from behind in a head lock. Paul accidently dropped his gun and pulled at the arm but it felt as though he was caught in a vice. He felt consciousness start to slip

and he his bladder emptied. Then the man was gone. He turned and

saw a figure in a white uniform on the ground with Wolf. Paul

pulled himself from the trench with arms like jelly. His eyes were

round and he wanted to run but his legs failed to obey. Rolling over

the sand bags on the upper lip of the fortifications he pulled a

grenade from his belt. Without thinking he pulled the cord and

dropped the stick grenade into the trench. Paul then pulled another

one from his boot and followed the procedure. There were two

explosions. Men screamed. He knelt and pulled a spare Luger from

inside his coat. Paul fired into the bodies below until the magazine

was empty. Then fell back onto the ground panting.

Further down the trench he could hear fighting. Voices

called out in Russian and German, men screamed and machine

pistols fired. Paul couldn't move. The thought of what he had just

done seared into his brain. His squad had been in the trench when

he threw the grenades. Christian, Wolf and Neuman had been

fighting the Soviets and now they were all dead. In his fear he had killed everybody. Tears racked his body as the noise of battle started to ebb. The Soviets melted away back to their own lines while Paul cried as he never had before.

v

The Russian breakthrough had been shallow but concentrated. Wolfgang Fischer had been glad Luftwaffe reconnaissance had given the army a couple of days warning of what was coming. The 1st SS division had been resting when the news came to move. The division was at sixty percent of its strength at best and been carrying out some much needed maintenance. Now the Hauptsturmführer sat in his panzer four watching the tree line ahead. So far the Soviets had thrown back the German Army by an average of forty kilometres; though in some places it was worse than this, in other places less. In the north and south Russian attacks had even been held, though at a cost. They had got to fifty kilometres from the centre of Moscow. Now the line was barely holding at Kubinka. The division still held the airbase and the military test range for Soviet tanks. Indeed the Luftwaffe was still flying missions from the airstrip even though it was now inside Russian artillery range.

A number of captured Russian guns, including some 85mm weapons had been dragged to the edge of the forest. A few prisoners had been forced to give instruction on how they worked, after being provided with the appropriate motivation. Three Soviets were shot before the others agreed to help. Wolfgang remembered turning away as the first man was killed. He knew they were just Russians but every time he saw an unarmed man gunned down something twisted inside him. He wondered if he was weak, or a poor Nazi.

The T34's could be heard well before they burst from the forest. Cavalry accompanied them riding next to the tanks. The horses churned through the snow throwing up a white mist which was caught by the wind and blown sideways across the open field. Huber opened fire causing a T34 to slew sideways, smoke pouring from its hatches. Wolfgang called out a new target and another tank was hit in the front bogies losing a track and skidding to a halt.

He ordered that they move the panzer but Braun asked to put

another shot into the damaged T34.

"Make it fast," said Wolfgang. He realised the enemy would

have marked their position by now and it was best to change to

another location. He watched as a captured 85mm gun fired an

airburst above the cavalry scything men and animals down. The hull

machine gun started to scream and more horsemen and their

mounts tumbled to the snow. Then a clang rang through the panzer

four and sparks flew around the compartment. A hole appeared in

and by its light Wolfgang could see that his driver no longer had a

head.

"Out," he roared and hauled himself out of the cupola.

Huber was right behind him. Another shell hit the frontal plates of

the tank and penetrated. Kruger, the loader was out and Wolfgang

looked back into the interior of the panzer four when a sheet of

flame erupted from within. He just managed to escape being burnt

but Kohler wasn't as lucky. The man's screams clawed into

Wolfgang's skull as he dropped to the snow and rolled away. The crew man didn't get out.

"We better get clear before she blows skipper," said Huber.

Wolfgang nodded and looked around. Many Soviet tanks were burning but so were a few panzer fours. He could see cavalry fighting with the crew of an 85mm gun, their curved swords rising and falling. It seemed bizarre to think that one could die from a medieval weapon in the 20th century. He started to move towards another gun position when three horse men charged in their direction. He drew his Walther and fired into the first animal managing to pull the trigger three times before the dying creature crashed into him. Flying through the air he landed in a snow drift his gun flying from his hand. Turning on his side Wolfgang saw Huber pull out his captured TT -33 pistol and shoot the rider. The second horseman fired at him from the back of his animal with a PPS 43. The crude submachine gun was lighter than other similar Soviet weapons but it was still difficult to fire it from horse back and the bullets sprayed around Huber. The gunner dived behind a tree as a shape flew through the air and landed near the cavalry men. Kohler always kept a stick grenade sticking out of his boot. He had thrown it and this one exploded near the man with the submachine gun hurling his mount sideways. Wolfgang ran forward and kicked the wounded man as he started to rise, then he snatched up the weapon. The third rider fired his revolver at Kohler hitting the loader in the shoulder and then the neck. Wolfgang Fischer fired two quick bursts with the Soviet machine pistol, killing both the horse and the rider.

He and Huber then ran to Kohler. The man was alive though bleeding badly. Fischer pulled the man's hands away and grimaced. It was a messy wound but at least it had missed the arteries and the wind pipe.

"You're a lucky bastard Kohler, two wounds that will give you at least six months of clean sheets and good food," said Huber. The gunner then got out his medical kit and started to bandage to wounds while Wolfgang covered them. In the end they needed his kit as well in order to do the shoulder. While he worked Huber recovered a SVT -40. Wolfgang glanced at his gunner as he loaded the weapon raising an eyebrow.

"Semi-automatic rifle; always wanted one of these," grunted his gunner.

They dragged the wounded loader to the nearest entrenchment as the Soviets fell back. The countryside was littered with dead horses and men. Burning tanks lay everywhere. They had stopped the Russians here but the cost had been high.

v

Corporal Temkan had never been so cold. He was wearing three thin shirts, all of them from dead men. He had a blanket around his shoulders and straw stuffed into shoes that were at least two sizes too big for him. All of his old comrades were dead. Some had become ill, others shot for no particular reason. More were recently frozen. The Russian prisoners he had been with had been used to change the gauge of the Russian rail lines to the German gage. Then they had been put in cattle trucks and sent back to

Poland where they had repaired roads. Now something was changing. All of the prisoners were being gathered together and some decent food had been supplied.

Standing shivering in the snow he slowly ate the bread he had been given. It was a little stale but was dipped in lard. For Sergi it was the best meal he had tasted in months.

"Looks like you're enjoying that," said a voice.

Sergi turned and saw a tall rangy man smiling at him. It took him a while to recognise Junior Sergeant Sokolov. The man was worn thin but still had the same bright blue eyes. Sergi felt a wave of euphoria. He had been so alone and now here was a familiar face.

"Sergeant!" he exclaimed wrapping the surprised man in a bear hug.

Sokolov laughed and patted him on the back. "It is good to see you too comrade."

The non-commissioned officers had been separated from the rank and file soon after they had been captured with the officers being taken away immediately. Commissars had been shot. Sergi remembered thinking it was no wonder that Volkov had not wanted to surrender.

"It seems that we are becoming mixed up with the junior ranks again. Many of us died but recently the Germans have started to take a little more care with our lives," said Sokolov.

"Do we know why?" asked Sergi.

"Well, they have shipped at least a thousand of us to the west in the last few days. They even gave me this old coat."

Sergi looked at the ripped and stained German army great coat with envy.

"Nearly all of the army that attacked into Poland was killed or captured and I don't think the Germans knew what to do with us so we starved or froze," continued Sokolov. "Now our enemy has changed their attitude. It's still no holiday camp and I will never forget how they let us die but at least now we have a chance."

Sergi stayed with his old sergeant and they gradually regained some strength as they were served vegetable soup and old bread. Occasionally the Germans threw a few pieces of pork or mutton into the pot and on these days Sergi felt a little energy return. He was given a thick shirt and a coat that must have belonged to someone very fat. It smelt of mould and urine but he didn't care. It kept him warm.

One morning they were all lined up and pushed through a barn where old German soldiers threw delousing powder on them. They were then issued with a variety of footwear and rags to wrap around their feet. Some new clothes were given out and Sergi managed to grab a woollen hat which he could pull down over his ears. He was glad he wouldn't have to tie dead men's shirts around his head anymore.

They were herded into cattle trucks attached to a locomotive and given a piece of bread and an old rind of cheese. The Russians were jammed together until the trucks were full and the train headed west. They weren't fed for another two days and the only water they received was snow melt pulled from the roof of the carriages. Men pissed through the slats in the wagon and went to the toilet in bucket which had to be emptied through the bars when it was full. The prisoners soon learnt to only tip it out when the train wasn't moving so it didn't splatter the side of the wagon and cover the prisoners as the shit splashed through the slats. As it was they all stank by the time the Germans off loaded the men somewhere in Northern Germany. Someone said they were at Kiel but Sergi wasn't sure.

There was a long harbour and he could see cranes and ships near a water front.

The prisoners were unloaded and paraded before a group of Germans who wrinkled their noses and had the Russians put in an old Navy barracks. A group of older men in the uniform of the Kriegsmarine shepherded them through the showers and Sergi luxuriated in the warm water. Then they were given grey overalls and new underwear. Sergi wondered what the Germans were up to. They were fed again and allowed to rest for two days.

It was snowing lightly when the Germans ordered the prisoners to parade in the area before the wooden barracks. A small man in a long trench coat stood on the back of the tray of a truck. His neck was wrapped in a grey scarf and he had leather gloves on to protect his hands against the cold. Next to him stood a man with a thin pinched face. This individual wore a dark blue uniform covered by a long blue German coat similar to those worn by the navy men who stood nearby carrying MP35s and rifles.

The short German spoke to the man next to him who turned to address the Russian prisoners. Sergi strained to hear.

"You have been fed, cleaned and housed. Now you will be given the chance to pay for the good treatment you have received," said the thin faced man. He turned to listen to the short German again.

"You are to work for the victory of Germany in order to pay for the attack you have made on the Greater German nation."

The man's Russian was excellent and Sergi thought he was probably a native of Leningrad by his accent.

"You will work here at the ship yard building weapons and munitions that will support Germany's war effort."

Some prisoners started to mutter and one stood forward. "We will not support our enemy in any way," yelled the man.

The short German nodded at two men in black uniforms Sergi hadn't spotted before as they had stood behind the truck. One of them pulled out a luger and shot the prisoner twice in the chest. The muttering stopped.

The thin faced man started to speak once more. "This is not a choice, nor a rest camp. You will work hard and you will be fed. If not you will die. Germany will not feed useless mouths. Choose now."

Three brave men walked from the line where they were grabbed by the Kriegsmarine soldiers and hustled away. Sergi knew they would never be seen again. He thought of joining them but then realised his commitment to the Soviet cause was not as strong

as it once was. He still loved Russia but the Soviets were another

matter. They had attacked the Germans and had been beaten. The

communists had executed the innocent and attacked an enemy that

was more organised and professional than they were. If the

Germans wanted him to help build their ships and shells then he

would. Besides the German navy would mainly be fighting the

Americans and British so why should he care. He looked at Sokolov

and gave a small nod. The man frowned but he didn't leave the line.

v

The figures for the year were better than Speer had hoped

for. The Luftwaffe had reached 18 000 of all types of aircraft and

though losses had been high new pilots and the extra aircraft meant

that the German air force could now put five thousand serviceable

frontline planes into the air every day. The Hungarians could field

about 200 planes and the Romanians about 300, all of which were

of modern standard. The Italians had, by all accounts, 1800

serviceable planes, nearly half of them modern Macchi 205's or Fiat

G55's. 50 000 trucks had been made, 7000 tanks, assault guns and tank destroyers had been delivered as well as 3000 armoured personnel carriers. He hoped to more than double production in everything over the next year. The prisoners were now working at the different factories and some on farmland. Speer had tried to ensure they were properly fed but he didn't always have the control he needed over the different factory complexes.

The Russians working in the SS factories were treated worse than those working at the docks. Those mining probably had the hardest time with the causality rate being unacceptably high. He sighed. It was impossible to have control over everything.

Speer had brought the factories in Poland under his dominion. Most of them made ammunition and had been captured by the Russians during their advance. Now Warsaw was back under German control those complexes were operating again. The Soviets hadn't had the time to blow them up so it had only taken a small amount of effort to restart production. It would have been the same at Krakow but Kaltunbruner had given the SS free rein.

Thousands of Jews had been shot and the work force for the local

munitions industry decimated. Speer had complained to Goering.

The Fuhrer had done nothing at the time but had pulled

Kaltenbruner aside later and warned him that any other 'cleansing

operations' had to be cleared by him in person. The head of the SS

was not pleased and pleaded that German's internal enemies had

to be dealt with. Goering had persisted with his position that the

war needed to be won first and the Jews were not currently a

threat. Speer put forward that they were a resource and that killing

the young and the old was a waste of German soldiers and railway

stock that were badly needed elsewhere. Speer wasn't sure how

long he could keep the Jews alive and he knew that those in the

Russian occupied territories, as well as in the Ukraine had been shot

in the thousands. It was a criminal waste of human capital as well as

a misuse of German man power as far as he was concerned.

Christmas had brought more victories in the Pacific and

Australian and Indian division had been withdrawn from the Middle

East and North Africa to stop the Japanese advance. It looked as though Singapore would fall as well as the Philippines. Their ally had taken heavy loses with the Americans pouring aircraft into the region. The Australians had sent their only carrier home, intelligence had confirmed that. Commonwealth fighter squadrons were also disappearing from the Mediterranean theatre. Speer chuckled when he heard of the Japanese's copy of the Junker 88 making attacks on Darwin from Timor. Germany's ally had not copied the BF 109 but were experimenting with a fighter that used the same engine. The Damiel Benz 605 had been delivered to Japan in August of 1942 and was being placed in the Ki 61. The new plane was probably still six months from being given to front line units but stories like this made Speer smile.

The front in North Africa hadn't moved but everything pointed to an imminent offensive in England. More American divisions had been reported as well as a build-up of aircraft. The British were using an improved Spitfire and the P38 was giving a good account of itself. Another American fighter had made an appearance as well. The P47 was a huge fighter by all accounts but it was fast, well-armed and could soak up a lot of punishment.

Speer sighed. He had warned Goering that the enemy's aircraft

development wouldn't stand still. The jet was still a year away as

was the latest FW190. For the year of 1943 the Luftwaffe would

have to make do with the fighters it had as all they would get were

improvements on older models.

The Heer was luckier. A new tank, the panzer five would be

ready by September, or maybe August. Nicknamed the Panther its

sloped armour and new 75mm L60 gun would be able to destroy all

current enemy tanks out to two thousand metres. More Tigers were

being made and the efforts to improve the huge tanks reliability

had born some fruit. The T34 and KV 1 were now vulnerable to

every German gun being used and a few panzer fours were even

being delivered to the best Hungarian and Romanian units. Then

there was the Skoda panzer. This cheaper tank would soon be ready

for production for Germany's allies.

Heavy bomber manufacture had stalled and Speer didn't

know how he felt about that. The JU 290 was a popular aircraft with the navy wanting it to patrol the Atlantic and attack enemy shipping and the Luftwaffe needing it to reequip the transport gruppen. Yet Speer could see that Russian industry could only be hit by the heavy bombers. The few experimental raids had been very successful with the Soviets having little in the way of effective air defence over their relocated factories however the fuel consumption of the big planes was a problem. At the moment only sixty of the heavy bombers were operational and they bombed Moscow by night from an airfield near Smolensk. Fifty others worked in the Atlantic and about one hundred more operated next to the Junker 52s and ME 323 Giants. He was torn on whether he should increase production of the big bombers or not.

The navy had increased construction of U boats and was repairing the ships damaged in the recent battles. Another carrier was in training though it only had a capacity of forty aircraft. No more battleships were being built as German industry was hard pressed to supply the army and Luftwaffe its needs and Russia was a land war. Admiral Raeder was quick to point out that the entry of

America into the war changed that dynamic but the entrance of

Japan into the conflict tended to lead those in power to believe that

US planners would be forced to divert resources to the Pacific

Ocean. Speer hoped his leaders were correct but he wasn't sure.

America's industrial capacity was almost legendary. He was coming

to think that if Russia wasn't knocked out of the war in 1943 then

German was in real danger of being swamped.

Part Two: 1943

Chapter Nine: January

The Luftwaffe no longer had any operational bases in England. They were just too vulnerable. Leutnant Kurt Osser lifted off from the airstrip at Desvres and turned towards the English Channel. He flew a new A5 FW190 as his old plane had been destroyed on the ground back in Britain. The Gruppe was up in strength today as radar was tracking multiple bombers heading towards the transport airfield at Juvincourt. The big ME 323s and the JU 290s and JU 52s left from the airfield every evening, flying by night to British airfields near Dover. It was a ripe target for the enemy as military stores were kept close by the bases for ease of loading into the transports. The big planes themselves flew in from Germany in the late afternoon so the enemy raid was timed to catch them as they started to touch down.

Kurt took his hat off to the men who flew the transports as the British and Americans tried to make their life as hard as possible. Flak lanes had been set up around the Dover airstrips and Bf 110 night fighters patrolled the skies trying to protect the vulnerable planes. It was fortunate that the enemy had not created an effective night fighter force of their own yet. The English had Beaufighters but the German occupation until recently meant they only had about thirty. The 110's were a match for these heavy machines and generally kept the enemy at bay. A number of P38s had tried their luck over the Dover airstrips on clear nights, the pilots trusting their eyesight. They had managed a few successes but the heavy flak had shot some of the intruders down.

Twenty four FW190s climbed inland clawing for altitude. During the briefing they had been told that Bf 109s from Holland were also racing to intercept the bombers. They had been told to be careful not to shoot any of their countrymen down. Twelve more FWs joined them as they continued to strain for height and Kurt felt a sense of growing security. Today the Luftwaffe would strike back.

The enemy bombers would be escorted but surely with so many German fighters in the air some would be able to force their way through to strike at the heavies. Warning on the radio directed them away from an enemy fighter sweep. The way the planes flew on the tracking screens suggested they weren't bombers so Luftwaffe planes steered clear of them. The targets were the bombers.

Bf 109s radioed their positions and Kurt glanced to his three o'clock high. Silver light glinted off the wings and he was pleased that the formation with which he flew had top cover. They cruised towards the enemy for ten minutes before the Gruppe commander radioed the enemy were in sight.

The Bf 109s dived on a formation of P47 thunderbolts as the FW190s of JG 26 lined up on the bombers. The stubby fighters throttled back a little in order to reduce the closing speed.

"Remember, you will only get a couple of quick bursts. Make them count and don't pull away too early," said Major Becker.

Or too late, thought Kurt. If they broke off their attacks a second or two after they needed to then a collision would occur between fighter and bomber. You would drop the enemy plane, but at the expense of your own life.

The bombers were B25 Mitchells and there were about one hundred and forty of them. The Messerschmitt's duelled over head with the Thunderbolts.

Then he was flying straight at a group of enemy bombers. Traces arched towards him from the single frontal gun of the B25s. He picked out a machine on the edge of the formation, and ignoring the enemy gunner's efforts, held his fire until the B25 filled his sights, then he held down the button for his four twenty millimetre cannons and two rifle calibre machine guns. He fired a two second burst into the front of the enemy machine seeing pieces fly off around the cockpit and wing root. He eased up on the stick and flashed over the enemy formation with his rotte. All four of his flight were unharmed. He pulled back on the stick his plane climbing slightly. At least two bombers fell away in flames while the machine he hit spiralled towards the ground, smoke pouring from its port engine. He could only imagine the carnage his cannon shells had caused in the cockpit and in the front of the B25

Some of the Fw190s had half rolled and dived away after making their attacks.

"He blew up sir!" yelled his wingman.

"Watch out for enemy fighters," he said calmly by way of acknowledgement.

"P38s chasing some of boys down," said Sergeant Hestler in Red Three.

"Let's see if we can make another run," Kurt suggested. "There are two stragglers at the rear of the enemy formation, both which look damaged. Stay close," he ordered.

The four planes half rolled and came at the damaged B25s from behind. The top gunner of the trailing machine seemed to be out of action but the rear gunner was firing wildly in their direction. As the closing speed was slower now Kurt lined up on the tail of the enemy machine and destroyed the rear gunner's position and chewed the tail off. His wing man followed up with a burst that tore into the starboard engine. The B25 started to burn and some Americans very quickly bailed out. As Kurt climbed away he counted three chutes. The other two FW190s both hit the other enemy bomber in the fuselage causing the rear of the aircraft to catch fire. A few seconds later there was a huge explosion which threw wreckage in all directions.

"Good shooting team," Kurt said.

"P38's diving from nine o'clock," said Hestler.

"Turn into them," ordered Kurt.

Eight twin engined P38 Lightnings came at them from head on and Kurt wondered if his decision had been wise. Both his fighters and the enemies had heavy armaments. Tracers flashed his way but the Americans had panicked and opened fire too soon. He fired at a plane but it wasn't lined up on him and he got the angle wrong and his burst went high. Then his wingman screamed and he saw a blossom of fire in his rear view mirror. A twisted P38 was intertwined with the tumbling wreckage of a FW190. The two groups flashed through each other with another P38 trailing smoke and a second FW190 pilot immediately bailing out as his shattered engine caught fire. The two groups then turned towards each other again. Six vs two, not good odds thought Kurt. The Fw190s were still climbing and Kurt ordered that they half roll and turn into the enemy. The P38s turned towards them bleeding off speed in their tight turns as they pulled around but the German fighters were inside them and used another roll to cut inside the American's turn. Kurt had pulled Hestler into the position of his now dead wingman as they angled in on the last machine in the formation.

The first burst from the FW190s guns went in front of the enemy plane and its pilot turned away from the fire, and out of formation. Kurt felt as though he was going to overshoot but Hestler was now in the right location for a deflection shot. The young sergeant's burst shredded the P38's port engine which immediately burst into flame. The pilot threw open his canopy and jumped just as the wing came apart. You got out just in time, thought Kurt. He wished the man well and hoped one day the Gods would also let him get free of a burning aircraft.

He ordered Hestler to dive away with him as they were now both low on ammunition. When they landed and taxied to the dispersal area where they were met by smiling mechanics.

"Why the happy faces?" he asked one as the man opened his canopy.

"All the reports suggest we have won a victory today sir. Thirty or more enemy bombers fell into French field and another sixteen enemy fighters were shot down. The French attacked with their own Dewoitine 551's. They pounced on the American fighters and though they don't pack the type of punch our aircraft do they drew them off. Then our fighters had a free run. Our transport airfields in French territory were hardly touched."

Kurt smiled, but he knew the Americans would return, and maybe next time in the Flying Fortress heavy bomber he heard about. If they did though maybe the French air force would attack them again. He wondered if the Petain government would have been so supportive if Germany had continued to occupy more than the twenty kilometre wide coastal strip along the Atlantic sea board.

v

The new panzer had left him awe struck. SS-Hauptsturmführer Wolfgang Fischer stood before the Tiger and marvelled. The gun alone reminded him of a pine tree. This one was covered in white wash and stood with six others. There were more but the other Tigers were back being repaired. Maintenance was supposed to be an on ongoing issue with the massive panzer but he didn't care. He was now part of the 13th Company of the Panzer Regiment with a new crew, all survivors from other tanks. He wished they had time to train on the beast but other than Otto, the driver, all of them had been given a quick explanation and then told to take their panzers forward. The Russians were still attacking but the line seemed to be holding. Just.

270

SS-Oberschütze Otto Lange started the Tiger and it rumbled into life. The huge panzer clanked out onto the dirt road and led four more towards the distant sound of fighting. One wouldn't go and had to be left behind. SS-Oberschütze Franz Kruger the Gunner started to examine the sights and whistled in appreciation.

"How are you finding her?" Wolfgang asked the driver.

"An easy beast to drive Sir, though I have to watch the revs. They say the Tiger can do 3000 but I've been told not to go over 2600."

"What about the gun Franz?" he said.

"The turret turns slowly but if I can line up a target I won't miss. Rate of fire will not be as fast as the panzer four but what it hits will never move again."

It all sounded promising but Wolfgang was worried about the lack of training. He knew things were desperate never the less it was important to have a clear understanding of a new weapon system.

They stopped at the edge of a forest where infantry were gathering. Ahead there was a rise in the land. Two small hills joined by a low ridge sat covered in thick woods. Open country covered in snow surrounded them.

An SS-Sturmbannführer with the infantry stopped him and climbed up on the turret.

"The edge of the woods are covered by anti-tank guns, Fischer. There are also dug in T34's. Soviet Infantry are dug in as well. We have hit them with mortars and the 105's worked them over for twenty minutes but they are still there in numbers. We are hoping your monsters can dig them out," said the officer.

"We'll do our best Sir," answered Wolfgang.

"The infantry will support you but the 105's have limited ammo and so will be saved for other missions," said the senior officer.

Wolfgang just nodded. He understood the supply situation was precarious.

The five Tigers stopped at the edge of the forest and waited. Wolfgang sat low in the cupola watching the trees across the open field. The snow was hard packed though it blew in waves across the field. The heater warmed the tank and Wolfgang thought about buttoning up inside the vehicle and watching the action through viewing slits as his neck and head were freezing. He felt for the accompanying infantry. In the end he decided he wanted a good view of the surrounding land scape. He hoped the enemy didn't have any snipers but decided the risk was worth it.

The Tigers moved forward in a line, infantry clustered behind them like pale grapes. They hadn't gone more than one hundred metres when an antitank shell hit the ground next to them before bouncing off the snow and continuing on into the woods. Wolfgang ordered the Tiger to stop. He had seen the muzzle flash on the slope and directed the gunner to its location using his binoculars to zero in. "It's near the fallen tree by the boulders," he said.

It took a while for Franz to locate the gun then he confirmed he had found it. "Got it sir," he mumbled.

A second shell tore through the air above the Tiger taking the top off a pine tree behind them. The boom of the eighty eight caused Wolfgang to jump but then he heard the soft grunt of satisfaction from his gunner.

They advanced another one hundred metres while the other Tigers fired. Mushrooms of earth and snow appeared amongst the trees and the winking lights of machine guns turned on and off. The whine and patter of bullets rattled off the armour causing Wolfgang to hunch lower into his cupola. Then there was a clang on the gun mantle that left his ears ringing. He shook his head and asked the crew if there was any damage. All reported in the negative. Wolfgang smiled. He had seen the thickness of the Tiger's armour but until it was put to the test he hadn't known for sure if it would hold.

"Dug in T34 nine hundred metres, near the gun we destroyed but a little further up the slope," he told his gunner.

Franz found this target quickly and fired. He swore as the high explosive round hit the enemy turret but failed to destroy the tank.

"Armour Piercing Karl," growled Wolfgang.

The loader apologised and placed another shell in the breech. This one tore the T34's turret off.

Another shell broke up on the Tiger's frontal armour and again Wolfgang located the culprit and destroyed the gun with a high explosive shell. When they had got to within six hundred metres of the Soviet trenches the Tigers stopped and fired their hull machine guns at the enemy infantry. The Russian anti-tank guns were silent and a score of dug in tanks had been destroyed. Not a single Tiger had been knocked out but one had lost a track to a lucky shot. Its crew had stayed with the vehicle and kept firing. They would never have chosen such a course of action if it had been a panzer four.

Soon the infantry were storming forwards. The enemy trenches were over run and the Russians fled. Wolfgang took his Tiger up the small rise along a narrow forest track and witnessed the damage the panzers had created. The eighty eight millimetre

shells had blown the Soviet guns apart. Event near misses had

scythed down crews. The T34s were complete wrecks and even a

single KV 1 was missing it turret. He looked at the destruction and

patted the top of his tank. With this monster he couldn't be

stopped.

v

The bombardment thundered down on the German

positions. Tom derrick crouched with Lieutenant Harry Breman near

the village of Nutley in a patch of woodland on the Crowborough

road. The German positions were only three hundred metres away.

Once past the fields and forests that dotted the area the Australians

would hit an area of heath land. Bare trees with interwoven

branches lined the road where the company was hidden. Four

Sentinel tanks armed with twenty five pound guns sat with them,

ready to advance. The air was cold and everyone wore their great

coats. Tom glanced around him noting the new faces. He fingered

his MP 40 and looked at the other veterans who also carried a variety of captured German equipment. Snowy had returned to them, his wounds being superficial, after walking out of the hospital. He had found another MG 42, swearing by the weapon. A number of the new privates now carried extra belts of ammo for the weapon, Snowy having convinced them of its value. He had scoured a neighbouring unit for extra rounds and now had over five thousand bullets for the weapon. Harry smiled and said that would last him one day of fighting. Snowy had shrugged. He was confident he would find more.

The 2/48 battalion was again at full strength having received reinforcements since Christmas the previous year. Tom found it hard to believe that it was 1943. He had heard the news that the Japanese were sweeping through the Pacific and worried about his home. There was a whisper that the 6th Division and the 7th Division had been pulled from Africa and sent back to Australia but this couldn't be confirmed. He knew that the Australian armoured division was in Egypt because of articles in Blighty. It seemed they had been there for a while. He wondered how the African front would be effected by the removal of the two veteran divisions and supposed others would have to be moved to India.

Overhead Beaufighters attacked German positions. As soon as they departed B25's dropped their bombs on the enemy. The noise rolled on like a storm that didn't end. Then the Sentinels were moving and Harry was ordering the company to its feet. They advanced through the forest as the tanks knocked down the smaller trees in their path. As the men emerged from the woods they saw a ruined farm house in front of them. It was surrounded by a small glade which had been ripped up by artillery and bombs. The trees in the area had been destroyed and some still burned. A few dead Germans lay in the wreckage of the house but it looked as though the enemy had recently fled. Ahead through a thin line of trees stood more open ground but Harry led the company further to the west through a narrow area of forest. They had only gone another sixty yards when enemy machine guns opened fire scything down four men.

The Australians hit the ground and stared throwing smoke grenades. The weather was misty and cold and the smoke thickened and provided some cover. Tom could tell by the scream of the guns that they were facing MG 42's. There seemed to be a pair of them with interlocking fire that had been placed here by the Germans to block any flanking move. Unfortunately the armour had gone in a different direction and was supporting another company's attack on a farm house on the edge of the open country. The rest of the battalion was pushing straight down the main road. Harry Breman quickly organised some covering fire and more smoke grenades were thrown. A man was wounded as the Germans sprayed the woods in front of them but the Australians closed on the enemy positions and deluged them with high explosive grenades before rushing them with automatic weapons. Tom found himself in the forefront of such an attack. He fired short burst at the German machine guns with his MP 40 while the grenades burst around the enemy. At the second position the Germans tried to surrender when the Australians closed in. One of the new men,

Tommy Tomlinson, or T.T as he was known, gunned them down with two bursts from his Owen gun.

The company moved on using the woods as cover until they were forced to turn east. Two more farm houses stood near a ruined wind mill. The closer of them was protected by at least a platoon judging by the amount of fire the German defenders were directing to the south. The German defence seemed to be centred around a number of fortified farm houses from which supporting fire came. All of the buildings had been destroyed by the bombardment of the artillery and the bombers but trenches and deep cellars meant there were plenty of German survivors.

Harry lay at the edge of the forest and watched the enemy positions for a moment.

"We'll need support to blow the Huns from their rat holes he muttered. Get HQ on the blower," he said to Tom. The sergeant scurried off to find the radio man and soon discovered him near a shattered oak tree.

"Come with me Trev," he said to the large man.

The corporal nodded and followed him back to the Lieutenant.

"That beast working Trev?" asked Harry.

"For the moment. I managed to get the Major before."

"We need you to get on to the Artillery. I've got a target for them."

The large corporal started twiddling dials and muttering into the microphone of the set 108. Tom knew that radio was low powered with frequency stability problems that usually drove Corporal Trevor Makenzie quietly crazy.

"Got em Harry," said the radio man after five minutes.

The Lieutenant gave the coordinates after consulting a small map and soon twenty five pounders were smashing into the nearest farm house. This continued on for a couple of minutes before the fire lifted to the further buildings. The company crossed the open ground while the Germans were still recovering and stormed the enemy fox holes and positions in a rush. A few of the enemy staggered forward with their hands in the air but the Australians didn't take any prisoners. Tom fired a burst into a young German as he limped towards him not liking the experience. Guilt twisted inside him and he tried to force the feeling away.

They took the windmill and another farm house but then German infantry and armour emerged from the woods to the north. Harry managed to warn Head Quarters of the German attack but then the Radio failed. Trevor cursed the machine in the bluest language and tried to establish contact once more, but without luck. Panzer threes and German troops fired at the Australians forcing them back from the Wind Mill and across the open ground into the forest from which they had recently advanced. A number of soldiers were cut down as they ran and Tom had difficulty rallying the company when they reached the trees. The six pounders caught up to them at this point and started to unlimber from their Bren carriers. One was spotted and blown apart by a 50 mm shell but the others were manoeuvred into position and soon a panzer was smoking at the edge of the forest. The Germans seemed to hold back at that point and Tom knew what was about to happen.

"Dig!" he screamed as he pulled his spade off his back. The soil was hard but not frozen and his frantic effort had scraped a two foot deep hole in a record period by the time the first shells started to fall. He has only managed to make an extra foot by the time he was forced to give up. Other men had not been so quick to follow his lead and were caught with little cover as the German 105 mm artillery shells found their range. He could hear the screaming of men above the explosions as the shells thundered around him. Trees came apart adding deadly splinters of wood to the flying shrapnel. Tom scrapped at the soil with his hands as he tried to burrow deeper. He wasn't sure how long the bombardment went for but the shells swept over their position and then back again before finally coming to a halt.

When he lifted his head he saw burning trees and the bodies of mangled comrades. A Bren carrier had taken a direct hit twisting it out of all recognition. Men crawled away from smoking shell holes, their life blood staining the ground behind them. His company had retreated or lay dead in this small wood.

He heard German voices and then the clanking of tank tracks. Nearby a six pound gun lay unattended. Some of its crew were dead near the Bren carrier, the rest scattered in the flattened bracken. Snowy popped his head out of a shallow hole and called to him.

"Glad I'm not alone," Tom said.

He looked at the approaching tanks and made a decision. "Help me with the gun Snowy."

Without waiting for an answer he crawled and then ran hunched over to the six pounder. Snowy joined him, his MG 42 over his shoulder.

"That chainsaw won't stop a Panzer," said Tom pointing at the machine gun.

"There's plenty of infantry out there too Sarge. Anyway, I couldn't leave the little beauty behind."

Tom grunted and then pointed at a box of shells. "Pass me one."

Snowy grabbed a shell and Tom put it in the breech and rammed it closed. He then swivelled the gun and stared through the sights.

"Do you know what you're doin' Sarge?"

"Did a course on 2 pounders a while back. These are nearly the same, just bigger."

The panzer three was only two hundred yards away; its hull machine gun shooting at some unseen target. Tom fired and was pleased to see a small hole appear in the front of the enemy tank just next to the driver's viewing port. The panzer's hatches flew open and four men rapidly left the vehicle. A second panzer came around the side of its wrecked partner, its turret machine gun firing. He took another shell off Snowy and reloaded the weapon. Bullets rattled of the gun shield. Snowy swore and threw himself behind the mangled Bren carrier. The panzer was charging straight at him and Tom let it fill his sights. Then he fired. The shell penetrated at the turret ring causing an immediate fire in the panzer. The vehicle slewed to one side hitting a large pine tree and stopping dead. The driver and radio operator scrambled from the hatches in the main hull just before an explosion sent flames pouring from the commander's cupola.

Snowy appeared next to him as German infantry came out of the smoke billowing from the burning panzer. His MG 42 tore off a burst, sounding like a buzz saw at a wood mill. Two men spun away and others started firing with rifles at their position. Puffs of dirt came up around him and Snowy rolled into a hollow. Tom noticed a box of six shells to the right of the gun near the body of the loader. They had a yellow band painted on them and he remembered from his training what that meant. High explosive shells were in very short supply for the six pound gun but they were out there. This gun crew had been supplied with at least one box of them.

He dashed the few yards to where they lay and grabbed two before diving back behind the gun shield. A bullet whined passed his ear and another tinged off the metal shield. Snowy was still pinned down so Tom loaded the gun himself and took aim at a knot of German infantry. He fired and the gun rocked back. A small explosion ripped up the earth just to the right of the group of grey clad soldiers. Two screamed and fell, while the others dropped to the ground. Tom loaded again and fired at three Germans endeavouring to set up a machine gun. The shell hit a tree next to them scything them down with razor sharp splinters.

Bullets started hitting his gun shield like hail and he was forced to hug the earth. It would only be a matter of time before a grenade sailed into his position and there was very little he could do about it. Snowy was also in a similar situation.

Then there was firing from behind him. The steady rattle of a Bren gun followed by the sound of Owen and Tommy guns. Garands added to the noise and soon the Germans were falling back. Tom found that he could move so he loaded the six pounder with an H.E. round and fired at the fleeing figures. When he had used all of the four remaining shells he loaded an anti-tank round and waited.

His lieutenant appeared next to him grinning.

"Thought you Dingoes had all forgotten me," said Tom.

"Never! A thin streak of pelican shit like you just doesn't go away," said Harry.

"Well I'm glad you showed up."

Harry looked around at the carnage in front of the gun as Snowy walked over.

"Amazing work Tom, you two held them just long enough for me to rally the boys. I recon you're both up for a gong for this."

Tom was so tired he just didn't care if he got a Victoria Cross. When he received that exact medal four months later he was left speechless.

V

288

The FW190 skimmed above the ocean surrounded by almost forty other aircraft. Kurt Osser kept a careful eye on the altimeter. Flying at this height was nerve wracking. One pause in concentration and the plane could plough into the sea.

The Luftwaffe was mounting a full scale effort to support the German Army of England. Briefings had reported that the counter attacks by the 23rd Panzer division had stopped first the Australians, and then the Canadians, though they had taken heavy casualties in doing so. The 503rd Heavy Tiger battalion had supported one of the motorized divisions and given the British a bloody nose and then attacked one of the American spearheads. The other thrust by the US army had been slowed but not stopped. The American 2nd Armoured Division was still pushing forward and unless it was halted might split the German lodgement in two.

Overhead one hundred Junker 88's and another eighty Heinkel 111's were trying to force their way through the Allied fighter screen. At least two hundred fighters were trying to protect them. Kurt didn't think they had a chance. The Allies had too many fighters and would be guided by radar onto the attacking German bombers.

He didn't think much of his wings chances either. Forty Jabos trying to sneak under the chaotic air battles in order to hit the 2nd Armoured division was a long shot. Each aircraft was carrying a single 250 kilo bomb. This impaired the aircrafts speed but could be jettisoned if the FW 190s were attacked. The problem was if they were caught they would lose the advantage of altitude and be at a severe disadvantage. Kurt thought the idea was crazy. The only thing that was in there favour was the weather. There was complete cloud cover until ten kilometres from the English coast where it broke up gradually. London was supposed to be completely clear, not that they would be going that far. The target was supposed to be just north of the High Weald.

He hated ground attack missions. It was true that the FW190 was more suited to the task than the Bf109 but this variety of 190 was supposed to be an interceptor and didn't carry the thicker belly armour that would help protect it from ground fire.

Jagdgeschwader 26 flashed over the white cliffs of the coast and headed inland. Now was the time the wing was most in danger. The cloud cover was thinning and a sharp eyed American or British pilot could radio their position and bring a swarm of P38's or maybe even the newer P47s down on them. The minutes drifted away and the dappled English countryside rolled beneath them.

Slowly the wing gained altitude until a pilot from the seventh staffel called in the target. Kurt had climbed to one thousand metres and turned towards a line of traffic that was jammed up on one of the narrow English roads. He didn't know it but the 26th Jagdgeschwader had arrived at the worst time possible for the spearhead of the 2nd Armoured Division. A tank had just broken down at the front of the column and the line had bunched. Even as the FW190s swooped American officers were running down the line of vehicles trying to order them to spread out or drive off the road into cover. It was too late.

The tenth squadron had already attacked hitting trucks and half-tracks at the rear of the column destroying at least four vehicles. Smoke rolled up into the winter sky, thick and oily. Kurt led

his flight in at a shallow angle lining up on a group of three trucks

near the front of the line. Tracers curled up towards his plane but

they were inaccurate and the weight of fire seemed low. He

released his bomb and heard it detonate as he climbed away. Kurt

wasn't to know that his bomb hit the road and bounced into the

rear of an American truck. The 250 kilo weapon exploded when the

warhead connected with the rear axle. The vehicle disintegrated in

a flash of metal and fire. The driver and his passenger ceased to

exist. A corporal running for cover twenty metres away was hit by a

flying tyre and killed instantly when struck on the head.

Kurt pulled away with his new wingman Oberfahnrich

Stephen Hessler. The man was new to the wing and had only flown

twenty hours on the FW190. He wanted to keep the young man

close and alive.

They circled around the burning column, Kurt determined to

rake it with cannon shells before heading home. He took his rotte in

behind four other FW190s. Diving in behind them he watched the schwarm fire at some half-tracks and jeeps. From amongst the

vehicles a number of fifty calibre machine guns were firing. The last

FW190 staggered under the impact of multiple hits, its engine

bursting into flames. The plane continued on its course smashing

into a pair of jeeps before exploding. Kurt strafed the halftracks

seeing his shells walk over the last in the line. Pieces flew off and

the engine caught fire before he pulled away.

"Enemy fighter's sir," radioed Hessler.

"Call in their position," snapped Kurt.

"Three O'clock low sir. American Thunderbolts, eight of

them."

The kids got sharp eyes, thought Kurt. He heard other pilots

responding and some turned in the direction of the threat. Luckily

there weren't many of the enemy at the moment. The order to

withdraw was given and the wing headed back to France. Behind

them the American had stopped to sort out the mess. While they

did the German line solidified. Later Kurt heard that there had been a huge air battle over the English Channel. The German bombers had taken heavy losses as had their escort. Sixty four aircraft had been lost for only twenty five enemy claimed. Yet their sacrifice had not been in vain. The Allies had been sucked into the air battle allowing the jabos to slip through at low level. The American Army had been forced to look up.

V

"So our leader has decided that England isn't worth the effort?" asked Speer.

"Yes," said Kesselring.

"But we stopped their latest offensive!"

"Just," said Kesselring. "We were also forced back towards the Channel by an average of fifteen kilometres."

"Into prepared positions," said Speer.

The leader of the Luftwaffe shrugged. "We need the troops elsewhere and it is the opinion of OKW we need them in Russia.

There is no way the Allies will be able to mount an attack across the Channel for at least eighteen months, perhaps longer."

"So where will they be used?" asked Speer.

"Sebastopol, maybe Leningrad. We aren't sure yet. Rommel wants a crack at the northern city, he won't be returning to England, and Manstein wants to attack the southern port in the Crimea. Both might get their chance and we might use those monstrous railway guns."

Speer frowned at the thought. The resources used to create the huge artillery pieces had been astronomical but at least he had managed to limit them to three.

"And Africa?" he said.

Kesselring shrugged. "The French have stepped up and with the PAK 40s we have given them as well as the Marders. They are doing alright. The Italians are now making their own copy of the T34 equipped with our 75mm L43 gun and a commander's cupola, though in small numbers. Finally they have listened to us and they are also making the Czech light machine gun. Their factories are still terribly inefficient but at least they have been free in the last two years to make equipment clear of any bombing. Only their navy remains useless."

"And what does the Herr and Luftwaffe want from me?"

"More of the same."

"I will not be able to keep the infantry as mobile. I just don't have the trucks anymore," said Speer.

"Just do your best."

"Now that the Hungarians and Romanian can't buy the British equipment off us I have to supply them as well."

Kesselring frowned. "That is a pity. Their armoured and motorised divisions have been useful; sort of their Nations elite. What are you giving them?"

"StuGs and Marders, though not many of them. I believe they are trying to set up their own factories. We are helping but have insisted that they use our designs. We don't want them spending a year developing a new tank just to find out that it is useless. I must admit that I did give twelve of the new Nashorns to the Hungarians."

Kesselring raised an eyebrow. "That was generous."

"There is one exception and it may be a saviour eventually for the panzer divisions. The Skoda T 25 is almost ready and will be a good alternative to the panzer four. It will have an L48 75mm gun for now. An automatic loading system is envisaged but has given teething problems."

"It sounds promising," said Kesselring.

Speer nodded and then added. "And there are also these extra SS divisions to equip. Seven extra divisions! Six of them eastern volunteers. The German Youth division will get the best equipment, the others will need to make do. None of them will be ready until early 1944 anyway and I hope to have more than doubled production by that stage."

Kesselring shook his head. "If we haven't knocked Russia out of the war by then we will need them. If the USSR is still fighting us in 44 then the best we can hope for is a draw and that exhaustion forces them to the negotiating table."

"By then the Americans will be a real factor," said Speer.

"I know,' said the head of the Luftwaffe. "That is what we are all afraid of. Soon their heavy bombers will be an issue."

Chapter Ten: February 1943

Leuntnant Kurt Osser flew over the English Channel in the dark. He was flying by instruments alone covering the evacuation of the Army of England. This was the second evening of the operation and so far everything was going well. He didn't know the elaborate preparations that had taken place in order to allow front line units to fall back on Dover, Folkestone, Hastings and Ramsgate. His squadron couldn't see the barges carrying the men and equipment of the various divisions back across the channel, nor did they know the location of the myriad of transport aircraft carrying out soldiers and Luftwaffe personnel. Kurt couldn't see the rifles and machine guns rigged to fire the odd burst of fire at enemy trenches. He knew that London had been pounded by heavy and medium bombers for the last few nights. This was supposed to keep the enemy distracted.

As was his mission. His squadron was to fly over to Portsmouth, drop their bombs and return home. Kurt realised that it would be a miracle if they hit anything of worth but it was all part of the distraction techniques to throw the enemy off balance.

The clouds parted above the harbour and Kurt dove down on an area near the water's edge releasing his bombs at one thousand metres. He heard explosions and then the crump of flak exploding. His squadron streaked away from the area before climbing back to four thousand metres. Kurt wasn't sure if he hit anything but at least the bombs had landed in the rough area of the docks.

They were crossing the French coast when Oberfahnrich Stephen Hessler spoke calmly over the radio. "Two aircraft one o'clock low. Unknown type."

God, the kid has good eyes, thought Kurt. "Friend or Foe?" he asked.

"Not sure. They are twin engined, that's for sure."

"As we don't have IFF Let's go take a look," said Kurt.

They angled down behind the two aircraft, both of which seemed to be climbing.

"They're not P38s," said Hessler.

"Bf 110s?" asked Kurt.

"Possibly, I'll know more if I can get directly above them," said his wing man.

"Beaufighters," said Hessler and Kurt almost simultaneously.

The shorter nose and the shape of the wings denoted that it wasn't a German plane and the bright winter moon helped.

Both FW190s dropped down behind the British night fighters and closed to within firing range. Kurt opened up first, his twenty millimetre shells ripping the port wing to shreds and causing the engine to explode. The plane came apart in a spray of fire and metal falling down into the water far below. Hessler's target had a second warning and dove away turning as it did. The Fw190 followed the turn and managed to hit the tail and the outer wing of the enemy machine. Kurt could barely see the two planes but Hessler seemed to have latched on the Beaufighter and the next burst must have hit a fuel tank as suddenly a sheet of flame

301

outlined the diving aircraft. His wing man then poured a long burst into the stricken machine and it blew up just over the French coast.

"Kill number three," said Hessler quietly. Kurt knew his wing man had lost his brother in England when the British first attacked. The Great Stab in the Back, Goering had called it, and Hessler had taken the words to heart. He had painted a dripping dagger under his cockpit and seemed to have a strong desire to kill as many Englishmen as he could. As he flew back to his airstrip he wondered how his brother was doing in Africa. He too faced the same enemy.

v

The Germans had tipped them out of their beds in the middle of the night kicking them and screaming at them as they did so. Corporal Temkan was disorientated and cold. He pulled his blanket around his shoulders and glanced at a groggy Sokolov.

"What's going on?" he asked and received a backhanded blow from a guard for talking. He fell heavily and his Sergeant helped him up.

The Russian prisoners were hustled out into the glare of lights. They stood on frosty cobble stones in boots without the benefit of socks, such had been the rush to get them outside. Before them stood the translator in the blue coat and next to him was the little German who ran the factory complex next to the docks where they made twenty millimetre shells. Instead of the old navy guard who usually looked after them were men in black uniforms with the twin lightning flash on their shoulders.

"SS," hissed Sokolov. "What are those bastards doing here?"

The Prisoners formed up and then the translator began. "We have fed you, given you beds and shelter and yet sabotage has been attempted. You are here to serve Greater Germany after your country's unprovoked attack on our borders and yet now some of you have put everyone at risk."

A tall SS officer strode forward in his long leather trench coat and pointed at three men randomly and then other SS soldiers ran forward and dragged these men from the line.

He then spoke to the translator who nodded.

"You are to give up the men who tried to start the fire at our factory. One man will be shot every five minutes until you do," said the man in the blue coat. "Starting now."

The German officer pulled out a Walther PPK and shot the first man between the eyes. Temkan jumped at the noise. He was feeling wide awake now.

"Stupid Raztoritz and his friends. They have put us all at risk," said Sokolov.

"I thought the committee said not to do anything. We were going to see if it was possible to steal a boat and slip across to Sweden," said Sergi.

"Little chance of that now. Not sure how realistic the idea was anyway but any thoughts of escape are dead. The guards will be watching us like hawks."

"What can we do?" Sergi asked.

"I'm not dying for a bunch of party men," said Sergeant Sokolov.

Sergi knew there was a small group of communist party members who had hidden that fact from the Germans. They had called the Prisoners Committee a bunch of cowards and stated it was their duty to strike at the enemy. Numbers had prevailed and this group had been out voted. It now looked as though they had decided to act independently.

"If you hand them over then you will be branded a traitor," whispered Malikov. The thin man had stepped close to him without being heard. Solokov turned and stared at him. "If I do nothing then you might be next."

Yet Sokolov didn't say anything and for ten minutes they stood there waiting. Eventually the SS officer stepped forward and shot another man before going inside a nearby building. This happened again and another three men were chosen.

"This will go on until the culprits are found," said the translator.

Six more were shot and yet no one stepped forward. "You would think that Raztoritz would admit what he had done to save lives," said Malikov.

"The communists are just as bad as the SS," said Sokolov. He then stepped forward.

The SS took him to the room where the officer was keeping warm and they soon returned to the courtyard. Sokolov pointed out the three men who had tried to set the fire and was cursed by them.

"You are a traitor to Russia," screamed Raztoritz.

"I will not die so that you can feel good about yourself. It's typical of you communists that you are willing to let us all die for your cause."

"It is our cause," yelled the man.

"I don't remember being asked," said Sokolov.

The three men were dragged away and never seen again.

The Australians advanced slowly. No fire came from the enemy trenches but Tom was cautious. It would be just like the Germans to tempt them forward then blast his platoon at point blank range and yet it remained quiet. His squad reached a sand bagged fox hole partially camouflaged by branches.

"Look at this Sarge," said Snowy.

The blond haired man pointed at two machine guns linked by rope to a tin filled with water. Another tin was suspended above them with a small hole drilled in the bottom. Tom relaxed.

"The Jerries are gone."

"How do you know?" asked Freddy Macklin, one of the new boys.

"We used this trick when we left Gallipoli. Water drips down from the top tin slowly filling the bottom one until the weight pulls the trigger."

"Yeh," said Snowy, "but why two guns?"

Tom scratched his head. "Against the Turks we mainly used rifles for this trick. Maybe the Germans thought two separate bursts would be more convincing."

Lieutenant Harry Breman approached them. "It's like this everywhere. It looks like the Jerries are leaving. I just got a message from HQ. Other units are having the same experience."

"What's Ming the Merciless want us to do?' asked Snowy referring to their divisional commander.

"Push on, but watch out for mines."

The battalion advanced from Uckfield to Polegate before a German machine gun post opened up on the lead elements. The position was quickly flanked and the enemy chose to surrender rather than be killed. There were only six of then led by a Corporal, and all were wounded in some way.

Harry Breman questioned the prisoners but they refused to talk even when Snowy threatened them with his machine gun.

"Leave 'em mate," said Tom. "We know what's going on anyway."

It had become clear the Germans had, or were in the process of, leaving England. All along the line the Americans and Canadians had reported empty trenches. A few positions had been heavily mined and small groups of German soldiers had sprung ambushes. In the main though the Germans looked like they had gone. English civilians filled in the missing pieces. They had been told there was a curfew two days ago and anyone found outside would be shot. Many had watched as silent lines of German soldiers marched towards the coast in the dark. Vehicles without lights had driven slowly passed houses and it hadn't taken the civilians long to work out what was happening. Small groups of the SS had kept them pinned inside their homes until most of the enemy was gone.

"They did this well," said Harry Breman. "The Luftwaffe hammered London and Jabos harassed our lines. Hell even their arty was really active until three days ago. Some of the other officers thought the Germans might be getting ready for a local offensive."

"What about radio traffic, or the air boys? Didn't they spot anything?" asked Tom.

"They were all busy with the renewed Luftwaffe effort. Also I guess the Jerries did most of this at night."

Tom shook his head. The Germans had played them for fools.

They reached the coast at Norman's Bay where German resistance increased. That night the allies attacked everywhere in force and punched through to the outskirts of Hastings. The Canadians and Americans got to within six miles of Folkstone and Dover respectively. Allied aircraft swarmed over the channel and Pt boats attacked barges and other small German craft. Many on both sides died as the belated attempted to interfere with the withdrawal took hold, but it was too late. The majority of the enemy were gone. Thirty thousand Germans surrendered the following day, most near the small British channel ports. A battalion fought on in the streets of Ramsgate for another day but gave up when they ran low on ammunition.

Tom Derrick walked with Snowy and his squad through the street of Hastings on that late February day. He could see the grey water of the channel glinting in weak sunlight. A cold breeze blew from the north and dark clouds seemed to build.

"Looks like a storm," said Snowy.

Just then there was an enormous explosion. Tom watched as the White Rock Theatre disappeared. Flame and brick flew up into the air with pieces flying across the road to land in the sea. The screaming started and Tom saw men down. Australians who had been looking at the sights and English civilians lay where they had fallen.

"Bloody Jerries have left time bombs," yelled Harry Breman as he ran passed them towards the wounded. Tom could see a small child lying near her mother. Both were twisted and bent. Fire sent plumes of dark smoke from the wreckage.

"We need to check the town," he whispered. "And we shouldn't risk any of our men in doing so." He put his idea to Hammer Heathcote the battalion commander the next day. By lunch time German prisoners were being sent into all of the important buildings to check for bombs. To make sure they were thorough the enemy prisoners were forced to sleep in the suspect buildings making it in their own best interest to report anything suspicious. One group of Germans did just that, but the Hammer made them diffuse the bomb themselves. They weren't successful and their bodies were later dug out of the ruins of the Hastings Railway station.

v

Smolensk was four hundred kilometres from the centre of Moscow and three hundred from the frontline. The last days of February were bitterly cold but at least the Russians had stopped attacking. Hauptsturmführer Wolfgang Fischer was finally getting a break from the fighting. The 1st SS had been withdrawn many hundreds of kilometres into reserve. The division was a shell of its former self being at only forty percent of its strength. It had just forty tanks left and half of those were operational. Two Tigers remained and the division was waiting for more.

Franz and Otto were with him as was Karl and Hans. His crew had decided to accompany him to the comforts of Smolensk. Not that there was much to do here. The city was badly damaged and the population unfriendly. They all wore side arms in case of trouble with Otto even carrying an MP 40, just in case. Some of the buildings were undamaged but others were burnt out or collapsed. The streets had been cleared and the rail line was running. There was plenty of food here and the crew ate well at the mess every night. Wolfgang thought he had finally put some weight back on and felt rested. He slept warm on a mattress and was clean. The lice had been combed from his beard and his clothes washed by grim Russian washer women who frowned whenever he met their grey eyes.

The boys went to a state run brothel in the evenings but Wolfgang didn't go with them. He wasn't sure if it was his strict up bringing or the thought of the dead eyes of the women who serviced the needs of the soldiers of the Reich. He had gone once, a year ago in Poland, and sworn never to do it again. He was happy to sleep, eat, read and stay warm.

In the evening he built up the fire in a metal hearth inside the apartment they had been allocated and let the heat fill the small room. Then he would read his copy of All Quiet on the Western Front and science fiction novels by Alfred Doblin. Both were banned but he didn't care. He also read the Blood and Soil novels the Nazis liked to push but found them to lack subtlety. He kept the banned books well hidden but trusted his crew and would read them in front of them. Sometimes he would read Steppenwolf by Herman Hesse and his crew would listen with rapt attention. The tension would drain from them and the warmth of the room plus the tone of his voice would often cause Otto to fall asleep. They would tease the short balding man when he woke but he would just smile lazily at them.

The streets were covered with snow as Wolfgang walked with his men towards the make shift theatre. It was cold but at least there was no wind. They watched 'The Golden City' but Wolfgang found it depressing and didn't understand why the lead actress had to die.

"She slept with a Czech so she paid for her sin," said Big Karl, scratching at his thin beard.

Wolfgang snorted, "So says the man who has recently bedded a Russian."

"But it is different for women, different rules," said Otto.

Wolfgang nodded as this was true. Men had their needs and women had a place within the family that shouldn't be sullied.

There was noise around the corner. Boots thudded and orders barked. Wolfgang and his crew wandered around the bend and saw two trucks parked in the street. SS soldiers carrying rifles and sub machine guns were lining up a group of civilians. An Oberscharführer was laughing as a woman was pulled towards him.

One of his men slapped her and then ripped her top open tearing away a bra and parts of her dress. Wolfgang saw her milky white breasts and knew what would happen if he didn't step forward. He should have walked on but maybe it was the fate of the woman in the movie that caused him to step forward.

"What is going on here Oberscharführer?" he asked.

The man turned and the saluted. "Sorry Hauptsturmführer, didn't see you sir."

"I asked you a question."

The older man's eyes narrowed but Wolfgang heard his crew move in behind him.

"Bandits sir. We find 'em and then we shoot them."

Wolfgang gestured at the young woman who hung between the two SS soldiers. "So what are you doing with the woman?"

The Oberscharführer's eyes darted away. "Just questioning her sir."

"Really, it looked as though you were getting ready to rape her."

The older man looked straight at him. "The boys were just going to have a bit of fun first sir."

Wolfgang shook his head. "I don't think so. I think I'll question her and then take the prisoner to the proper authorities tomorrow."

The Oberscharführer frowned. "On what authority sir? I mean we are tasked with cleaning this town of Jews and communists. This is the territory of Einsatzgruppen A not the Leibstandarte."

Wolfgang put steel in his voice. "Does a part time non-commissioned officer dare to tell a holder of the iron cross and a Hauptsturmführer in the premier division of the Third Reich that this is his territory. You part time soldiers may be SS but to me you are like cleaning maids. You drag these 'bandits' out and kill them, an important job maybe, but do you ever face a man with a gun in his hand. Do not question me again! Now hand her over."

The Oberscharführer nodded to his men and they dropped the young woman at his feet. Wolfgang signalled Otto and Karl who lifted her to her feet.

"This isn't finished," said the older man.

"This isn't finished Sir!" snapped Wolfgang. He stepped forward and slapped the man hard before staring into his face. "I have rank," he growled.

He gestured at his crew and they started to move away. The woman howled and pointed at two older figures in the line.

"She wants her mother and father," said Otto, who spoke Russian.

The Oberscharführer smiled and barked an order. Rifles and sub machine guns flamed in the dark and people screamed before falling in ragged heaps onto the snow. It was over quickly and soon the only sound was the young woman sobbing.

Wolfgang and his crew led her away. He wrapped the woman in his coat and supported her along the snow cover street to their lodgings. When they approached the building where they had been saying. Karl spoke up. "Sir, what are we going to do with her?"

Wolfgang shrugged. "I have no idea."

That night he spoke to the young woman through Otto who told him that her name was Larisa and her parents had been minor officials in the Communist party. She wasn't a member and was officially a widow, her young husband having being killed in Poland. Larisa said she was nineteen years old and her marriage had lasted only three months.

"She doesn't seem very threatening," said Wolfgang gesturing at the dark haired woman.

They had found her a shirt and she had curled up in front of the fire after eating some cheese that Hans had found for her and now slept.

"She is just another victim in this war. No family, no husband and the Einsatzgruppen will come for her tomorrow. That non-com will go to some high up and that will be it," said Kurt.

"We could hide her," said Otto.

"And then what?" asked Hans.

"Keep her as a cleaner and general worker," said Kurt. "There are plenty of Hiwi's working for us now."

"She is a pretty young woman," said Otto. "Stunning actually," he said leaning closer to her prone form.

"Easy, soldier," said Wolfgang with a grin. "I think we can make Kurt's idea work. We'll hide her and keep her with us until a way can be found to get her to Germany. Then we can put her with one of our families. While she is with us we'll make her look unattractive in shapeless clothes. We can let it be known she is under my protection and then we'll find the papers we need and put her on a train to the Fatherland."

The next morning when the Oberscharführer showed up at their lodgings waving a piece of paper demanding the girl be handed over Wolfgang explained that she had escaped during the night. The man threatened further action but nothing came of it and two days later the crew smuggled Larisa into a train with them heading for Minsk where the 1st SS division had travelled to retrain and reequip before being hurled back into the maelstrom of the Eastern Front.

Chapter Eleven: March 1943

Speer stood before the new tank smiling and shaking hands. The officials at Skoda had shown him around the plant and he admitted he was quietly impressed. The plan was to produce one hundred machines a month with another factory starting production soon. Eventually the aim was around two hundred a month with some being converted to tank destroyers carrying 75mm L70 guns.

The T-25 or Cheetah as it was now called was a fast medium battle tank with sloped armour and an L48 75mm gun. It was cheaper to make than a panzer four and was being produced to equip Germany's allies. Speer knew the first fifty were going to Finland. The Finns already had fourteen pre-production machines which they were using for training. They were the price of gaining their allies cooperation in the upcoming offensive on Leningrad, that and forty Junker 88's. The Finns had plenty of high quality Italian fighters but they were short on ground support planes.

The Skoda tank had been proposed as an answer to the T34 but Goering had opted for a heavy more powerful, and more expensive option. The Panther would be ready for action in August or September. It was a powerful weapon system but not without its problems. The engine in particular was prone to fires and overheating. Speer glanced at the row of T25's. At least their engines were reliable. The automatic gun was still being developed and the panzer had needed to use the L48 cannon for now but eventually they would work out the bugs and then they would have a tank that could fire so quickly it could overwhelm their enemy by sheer weight of fire. Of course that would lead to the crew exhausting their ammunition quickly but eventually they would find a solution to that problem as well.

He had supported Skoda. It was ridiculous that every weapon system Germany developed seemed to have to be more complex and expensive than their enemies. Speer had secretly commissioned the construction of another Skoda factory in Southern Poland to build the Cheetah for the German army as well.

The camera flashed and he shook some more hands before fleeing to his car.

That evening he met Kesselring for dinner. They ate alone, watched from a distance by a guard of tough paratroopers, a reminder that the Czech capital was not Germany and there were still people in Prague who would who would gladly see them dead.

"How did your opening go today?" Speer asked the head of the Luftwaffe.

Kesselring shrugged, "The Junker 188 plant will provide torpedo bombers for the Mediterranean and the Arctic. The plane is not much of an improvement over the 88 but its extra range, or larger bomb load is useful."

"So again we have no real improvement on our aircraft performance this year," said Speer.

"Not really," said Kesselring. "We have abandoned the HE 177 project because of the engines and the Junker 288 because of the undercarriage difficulties. Oh, the Junkers 252 is now replacing

324

the old 52 and we have managed to slightly increase the output of the Junkers 290."

"So basically we wait until 1944 and the jet."

"The first Gruppe of Messerschmitt 262's is expected to become operational in January of that year with the Ardo bombers coming into use a month later."

"What of our enemies? Do we know what they are developing?"

Kesselring snorted. "Our intelligence services have proved to be disappointing. Their latest types have been worrying enough. The P38 is fast and well-armed, the P47 is tough and packs an amazing punch and the latest Spitfire is a match for any of our fighters. The Bf and the FW are not out classed but they are not superior to the American and British planes. Then there are the improvements the Russians have made. The Yak 9 and the LA 5N are also a match for our fighters, though not without their problems. The main factor that separates us on the Russian front is training."

"If we win the war this year then I suppose none of it will matter," said Speer.

The usually optimistic Kesselring shook his head. "We are stretched too thin. Maybe we could defeat the Russians if the Western allies did nothing, but that won't happen. A negotiated settlement with the Soviet Union might allow us enough time to turn and give the West a bloody nose but our fearless leader is angry. He remembers that first Russia and then the west stabbed us in the back."

Speer took a mouthful of his red wine before answering. "We invaded Poland, which was when it all started."

"Hitler attacked Poland, Goering believes we won and Churchill couldn't accept the results."

"The war with the Commonwealth never stopped. When we sunk those American destroyers, well, they seized the chance to attack us," said Speer.

326

Kesselring waved his hand. "War with America was always inevitable, now or in five years. They would never have just stood by as we dominated Europe. I wish we could have dealt with Russia first but..." he trailed away. "Anyway Goering wants to humiliate Russia if not destroy it. He wants Stalin's head."

"So the war will continue," sighed Speer. "Then we will need those Baltic SS divisions."

"Yes and the Galician one. Also there have been moves to create a Western Ukrainian force. Talks are underway to make a semi automatous state based on Kiev and covering mainly territory on the western side of the Dnieper. If that happens we might be able to create another two or three SS divisions, and the new country will be allowed a small army of its own."

"Which we will have to equip," growled Speer.

Kesselring laughed. "We need the men. Look on the bright side my friend. Remember my earlier statement of how thin Germany is on the ground."

"I suppose you are right, I just don't know how much more I can squeeze out of our country."

"You have worked wonders! The Luftwaffe will reach an operation strength of six thousand aircraft by the end of 1943 if the schools keep producing the pilots, and you make the planes. In 1944, with the jets, we will end it," said Kesselring.

"There is another issue," said Speer.

"Let me guess," said Kesselring. "The Jews?"

Speer grimaced. "Kaltenbruner wants to get rid of them, all of them, and is pressuring Goering to give him the resources to do so."

"You can't blame him. After what they did to our country they deserve little sympathy."

"I understand they are our enemy but at this time they are not a priority. Dachau was expanded and the Jews have been purged from the Fatherland. Kaltenbruner has slaughtered them in the Ukraine, Belarus and occupied Russia. Men that should be at the front drive around shooting communists and killing Jews! Those men are needed at the front."

"Some say they do valuable work," said Kesselring. "Besides I have heard the extent of the killing is exaggerated."

"I've looked into it and it is actually more extensive than we have been led to believe."

Kesselring shrugged and looked uncomfortable.

"Now Kaltenbruner wants to 'organise' the process. He wants to empty the ghettos in Poland."

The head of the Luftwaffe shrugged.

"This will use rolling stock, steel, concrete, timber and valuable man power. Besides the Jews in Poland are valuable labour. I would keep them alive and use them."

There was still little response from Kesselring.

"It will impact production, maybe even aircraft production. The Jews need to wait until after the war," said Speer.

Finally Kesselring sighed. "I'll do what I can. I can't stop what is happening in Russia, but that is close to being finished anyway. I can talk to our fearless leader and warn him about the loss of production. That might sway him. If Hitler was still alive then we wouldn't have a chance but Goering, though he sees the Jews as the enemy, he is not as passionate on the subject. I don't like what is happening personally and find the killing of woman and children distasteful. I will do what I can."

Chapter Twelve: 1943 April

In war lulls can occur that allow both sides to catch their breath or to concentrate on a specific task. Goering knew that the thaw would soon end in Russia and the Western Allies would strike, whether that would be in Africa or somewhere else he wasn't sure. For now he just wanted to enjoy his hunting lodge in Bavaria. Nobody was allowed in the park without his permission so the bison, bear and wolves he had brought into the region were for him and his party to hunt alone.

The day was spent hunting deer and bear but only the former crossed the group's path. The group shot a couple of stags and a doe before coming across a few lowland bison. He always cursed the fact that the forest cousin of this magnificent animal was now extinct. They had enough meat for the day so left the large animals alone and returned to the hunting lodge set at the foot of the Alps. Goering loved it here but he also was creating another larger reserve at the Białowieża forest in Poland. Game keepers had already moved into the area and local farms or villages in the proposed boundaries of the new Polish game reserve destroyed. The Poles that had lived there had been dumped near Cracow and had to fend for themselves.

The lodge itself was a camouflaged mansion with hidden Flak positions sitting on nearby hills. Underground bunkers had been created with a small centre of communications positioned one hundred metres from the residence. As yet the Allies hadn't made many attacks on Germany with heavy bombers and those raids that had occurred were directed at the Ruhr and the Atlantic coast.

As his little convoy of hunters pulled up Goering noticed a small group of staff cars parked nearby. As he left his kublerwagon he saw Keitel and Kesselring standing on the porch. He hoped that the news was good and the French hadn't changed sides or Mussolini had a heart attack.

"Good hunting my Fuhrer?" asked the head of the Luftwaffe.

"Yes, we have meat for the table and a nice rack of antlers. Since I created the park the number of animals has increased, but you are not here for small talk."

Both of the men glanced at each other.

"Let us retire to the Smoking room. I feel the need for some refreshments," said Goering.

He sat with the other men on plush leather couches while sipping real coffee.

"What has happened?" he asked.

Kesselring smiled and waved his hand at Keitel. "It was the army's victory."

The general nodded. "Sebastopol has fallen. The Crimea is ours. We destroyed the Russian bridge head as well and chased the Russians from Kerch."

"Marvellous," said Goering. "This is the area I wanted for Germany. Western Poland and the Crimea will be our living space. The Baltic States, Belarus and the Ukraine can be buffer states and the rest of Russia can be sliced up into different districts. Of course we will need the oil in the Caucuses too. The Borders of what is left of Poland will move east."

"It is about the summer campaign we have come," said Kesselring. "We were wondering if you have made a decision but your previous statement suggests to me that you have."

"Yes, we leave Moscow for now. We need the oil if there is to be any chance of matching the Americans. They have Texas and the Middle East. We have the Romanians and some oil in Hungary, but it is not enough."

"What about Leningrad?" asked General Keitel.

"Rommel gets his chance," said Goering. "He has a month to take the city, or completely cut it off. In June we go south."

"And if the Allies land somewhere?" said Kesselring.

"Albert, we have reserves now. Six infantry, one panzer grenadier, as they are now called, and one panzer division sit in the Low Countries, rested and ready. Rommel has the 16th army with ten divisions and two panzer divisions. Von Kuchler will screen the city with his six divisions and Hoepner will protect the southern flank of the thrust with his five divisions. Now that the Finns have agreed to assist us we have a real chance of finishing off operations on the northern flank of Russia. I think there is little chance of reaching the White Sea but if we can meet the Finns on the other side of Lake Ladoga we will have Leningrad."

"The Russians will counter attack," said Keitel.

"I'm counting on it," said Goering. "A mobile operation, even with infantry, brings out the best in Erwin. As long as Hoepner protects his flank then I have every faith in him."

Kesselring shrugged and then smiled. "Even if he fails he draws Soviet attention north. The real game is in the south during high summer."

Goering raised a glass. "Let's drink to German forces on the Caspian Sea in autumn."

The head of the Luftwaffe and the supreme commander of OKW

raised their glasses.

Chapter Thirteen: May 1943

The skies were clear and the forest alive with insects. The German thrust filled the fifty kilometre gap between Neva and Volkhov rivers. The Eighteenth army had reached Lake Ladoga but then been thrown back by a vigorous Soviet counter attack. The way to Leningrad for the Russians was still open though nobody thought the situation would last for much longer.

Geifreiter Paul Becker was back with a new division in a different part of the front after two months in hospital. After the attack near the Mius River where he had blown up his own comrades as well as the attacking Russians Paul had been catatonic. He had lain in a bed needing to be fed and cleaned until life had started to return. First he had cringed when touched and then he just cried. Eventually Paul started talking to one of the young doctors who had spent time at the front himself.

It had helped to talk and the doctor had shielded him from the authorities for as long as possible. Then the doctor had been transferred and Paul moved back to a new division. The 11th infantry division had served in northern Russia since moving from East Prussia at the start of the great offensive that had destroyed most of the best Russian troops in Poland. Now Paul had been placed in an ordinary company and was trying to avoid the responsibility the young Leutnant tried to send his way. The best way of doing this, he found, was by pretending to be a sniper. He had acquired a Mosin–Nagant rifle with a scope from a dead Russian and had used it since his arrival with his new unit at the start of May. Rommel's offensive had started three days later.

Now he watched the Russian lines from a well camouflaged position slightly back from the river bank. The armour was pushing between the two rivers for the lake after the initial repulse but the 11th Infantry had been given the task of creating a bridge head on the east bank but at the moment his division was waiting for landing craft and a bridging detachment. He had slipped away from his company and watched for a target. Paul was being very cautious as he knew that the Russians had some of the best snipers in the world, many of them women. He wondered if the task he had taken on was foolish. It was likely to get him killed. Yet at least death would be a release from his dreams.

He kept waking at least once a night with his dead friends asking him why he was killing them. Paul often dozed during the day and these short naps kept him going. There was something about sleeping in short snatches that protected him from the dreams.

Paul spotted movement and crawled very slowly forward in his hide. Back from the river someone was very carefully clearing some scrub, probably so they had a better field of fire. He checked the angle of the sun so it wouldn't glint from his sights and took aim. He had to be careful in case the movement was bait to get him to expose his position. The branches were bent slowly away and through his sights he made out a young man. Behind him there was another soldier crouched behind a DP. The flat round magazine and the flared barrel could just be glimpsed. Aiming carefully he squeezed the trigger. The sound of the rifle barking was loud in his ears but he saw the gunner slump sideways. The loader dived for cover as Paul worked the bolt but his legs were still exposed. The next bullet hit the Soviet soldier just below the knee. The man screamed and sat up grasping the wound. The next shot took the soldier in the throat.

Immediately retreating from his position Paul wriggled deeper into the forest. Soon mortar shells hit the western side of the river to be answered by German shells. This continued for about ten minutes before both sides decided they had used enough ammunition. By this time Paul was back in a fox hole well away from the action. Later he claimed his kills though they remained unconfirmed as he insisted t he worked alone. He didn't care. The company commander Hauptman Rainer Klein believed him and left him alone and that was all that mattered.

V

The first Gruppe of JG26 had moved with its FW190s to

Northern Russia in April. The tenth staffle with its jabos were also

present. Kurt Osser had hated the deployment at first but Narva,

where they were based was surprisingly friendly. The range from

the Estonian city to Leningrad was only 160 kilometres, well within

the 250 kilometre circle that the Gruppe liked to operate in.

The other bonus was that the Russians were easier to shoot

down. Since he had arrived Kurt had added another twenty kills to

his tally and now had fifty five bars painted on the tail of his aircraft.

The LA5N was supposed to be a difficult opponent but having flown

a captured one when he first arrived in the east he wasn't

impressed. All the engine controls had different levers so to get

optimum performance from the plane constant tinkering was

necessary. This wasn't something a pilot wanted to be

concentrating on during a dogfight. The other opponent he had met

was the P39, not an aircraft to be underestimated. Down low it

could turn with a Bf 109 and you didn't want to get hit by its 37mm

gun. The plane seemed to be able to swat German bombers from the sky. Yet Kurt believed the FW190 was more than a match for the Iron dog, as the Russians called the plane.

He led his squadron north east for a sweep over the German advance. He had been briefed that the 254th infantry division had reached the Narva River to the east of the city and had been attacked by P40 fighter bombers. Kurt sighed thinking of the western equipment that was still making its way to Russia via Murmansk. The naval battles the previous year had only stopped the supply of equipment temporarily.

His wingman called over the radio. "Bandits three o'clock low. More above them. Two lots of twelve by the look of it."

Hessler was right and it looked as though the Russians hadn't seen them. The area was dotted with towering strata cumulus clouds which seemed to grow as time passed. Kurt guessed there would be thunderstorms later.

"Blue flight wait until we are past this large cloud then dive straight through it on an intercept course for the P40s. Red and

Green flight will curve with me around the cloud and come down on the P39s. We have surprise so let's not waste it."

They curved around the back of the towering cloud and Kurt felt how small he was. He wondered if he would survive the war and if it mattered. At least his brother was safe for now. Paul was wounded and back in Rome in a nice cosy hospital. Both of his legs had been broken in a car accident of all things and he would be out of action for at least three months. Maybe one of the family would make it through the war alive.

The FW190s had height and surprise. Blue flight fell on the enemy fighter bombers scattering them and forcing the Russians to drop their bombs. Two planes curved away trailing smoke and Kurt was fairly sure they weren't Germans. The Airacobras dived to help their stricken brethren, not seeing the trap Kurt had set. His two flights bounced them from out of the sun.

Kurt lined up the diving FW on the enemy plane and then shifted the stick slightly settling his sights behind the Russian pilot. He had just remembered the P39 had its engine behind the cockpit.

He was the first of his squadron to fire and the Russian plane staggered and then came apart as twenty millimetre cannon shells tore into the wing root. Enemy planes then broke in all directions but his wing man, Oberfahnrich Hessler had made a kill with the Russian plane pouring smoke and flames from a shattered engine. Then there were aircraft everywhere and Kurt had to manoeuvre quickly to avoid collision. A P39 tried to dive away but his plane was faster. He settled in behind the enemy machine as his speed built up and fired a burst that went high. The P39 just kept diving in a straight line towards the forest. Kurt's next burst tore into the enemy's tail and bits of the rudder came away, then the wing was hit. Finally the P39 took evasive action and pulled into a turn to the right. Kurt cut inside and fired in front of the enemy aircraft. It flew straight through the stream of fire. Pieces flew off around the cockpit and nose. The Russian then flipped slowly over with smoke coming from the engine. The aircraft started to spin in lazy circles until it hit the ground near a wide river. Kurt eased back on the stick using the momentum of the dive to regain altitude. Looking around him he saw, that except for Hessler, the sky was empty. Below him the German army pushed on towards Lake Ladoga.

v

Paul had heard over dinner that the 1st Panzer division had reached the lake at Novaya and the 36th Panzer Grenadier were fighting at Gorgola, five kilometres from the water. Leningrad was cut off but the city had access to the outside world via boats. None of this mattered to Paul though, his division was fighting to hold a ten kilometre long bridgehead over the Volkhov River from a shattered monastery on the west bank down to the small town of Volkhov itself. The Spanish Blue division had crossed with them making divisional frontage manageable. The shallow penetration only took the Germans a few kilometres into the forest meaning that every metre of the line was subject to fierce artillery bombardment. The Russians definitely wanted them back on the western side of the river and were doing all in their power to throw them into the water.

Paul didn't know it but the 78th Sturm division and the 61st division were assaulting the southern suburbs of Leningrad. His division and the blue division were a diversion on the river and Rommel was going to put his main effort into the two mobile formations next to the lake. Then it was a sixty kilometre push towards the Svir River along one of the few roads in the area and a link up with the Finns. Germany's northern ally was also supporting the effort by attacking south west to meet Rommel's forces using the new T25's from the Skoda factories. These attempts were diverting more Soviets away from the main effort, and there was still a chance that the ever adaptable Rommel would choose to use their bridgehead on the eastern side of the river as the focus of the attack east if the panzers got into trouble by the lake.

It was dark but the thunderstorms had cleared and a bright moon shone above the forest. Paul decided to see if he could scrounge some more food and walked slowly towards the food wagon. He heard a sound through the trees like a strong breeze and stopped. There was no wind.

"Night Witches," he screamed. The PO 2 came gliding out of the night as Paul sprinted to an unmanned anti-aircraft position. He jumped over the sand bags and cocked the MG 42 swinging it round to open fire. Men were scurrying for cover as small fifty kilo bombs dropped free of the biplane. To Paul the aircraft looked like a relic from world war one but he knew the sneak raids by these old bombers killed men every night. His first burst went high as the Soviet pilot started the plane's engine. The next burst went into the fuselage and then the plane was pulling away over the trees. He heard the bombs exploding as he sent a final long rush of fire at the plane. Over the noise of a man screaming he heard the sound of the engine falter and splutter. Then the plane disappeared to be followed by the crash of splintering wood and shattering metal. He snatched up his rifle and ran in the direction of the plane.

The aircraft had clipped the top of a tree before ploughing into the ground next to the river. Other soldiers had got there before he had and two of them held a figure between them. As he watched one of them struck and the crew member toppled to the

347

ground. Paul reached them as one of the soldiers drew his knife and sliced away the pilot's jacket. Another man pulled off the goggles allowing long hair to tumble loose.

"I shot it down, she's mine," said Paul.

The three soldiers turned and saw the sniper's rifle. One of them kicked the woman hard in the ribs but then stepped back.

"You can go first then," said the man. "Her friend isn't going to live long but we can have this one. I've hoped for some time to get a hold of one of the witches."

Paul looked at the woman as she pulled herself into a sitting position. She was young with a strong hard face. It was difficult to make out the colour of her eyes in the light provided by the moon but he could see that her hair was dark.

"They want to kill you slowly," he said to her in Russian.

"As I do them," she answered holding her ribs.

"You are in no position comrade," said Paul softly.

348

The woman grimaced and glanced at her crumpled friend. "We all die," she said.

"Indeed we do," said Paul. He lifted his rifle and worked the bolt just as his Hauptman yelled. Ignoring the voice he shot the woman through the chest. Quickly he chambered another round before putting a bullet into the wounded woman lying in the flattened grass. The round almost took her head off but at least it was a quick death. Better than she could have hoped for had he let her be taken off for questioning.

"I called for you to stop Becker," said the Hauptman.

'Sorry sir," didn't hear you in time.

"That's bullshit. I should put you on a charge. Your attitude since you arrived with the company has been shit and I'm sick of it."

A voice came from somewhere off to the left. "Sir, it was Becker who shot them down."

Paul glanced sideways and noticed a tall young man with blond red hair. The kid was skinny and looked new, but he carried a Papaha.

349

The PPsH 41 marked the man as someone who had been at the front for some time.

"I didn't ask you Hoffmann," said the Hauptman. His company commander stood with hands on hips for a second before shrugging. "Get their ID then bury them," he said to Paul. "You can help him Hoffmann."

As they dug together Stefan Hoffmann kept up a steady stream of conversation. The fact that Paul only answered with the occasional grunt didn't seem to faze him. It seemed the young Soldat had been wounded the previous year and had only recently returned to the division.

"So the T34 almost ran me down but I clambered around the side of the tank and straight into a big ugly Russian carrying this little beauty. He patted the submachine gun. "We fired at the same time but I must have got my round off a fraction before him as his burst hit me in the legs. My bullet hit him in the chest. Anyway I roll into a ditch just as a shell rips the turret of the T34. The bloody thing sails high in the air and falls over the top of the ditch covering

350

me like a huge hat! Tell you what, I needed the brown underwear after that."

Paul chuckled in spite of himself. "You were very lucky," he said.

The skinny man shrugged. "I suppose so. I reckon you have to be lucky to make it through this Hell alive. No use worrying about it though. Just keep your head down and your fingers crossed."

"Wise words," said Paul.

The following day the Russian pounded the line with artillery. The Katyushas were the worst. Paul had burrowed into his fox hole and pulled a number logs over the top to form a roof. Tree splinters had proved as dangerous as shrapnel in the previous days and a lid of some type had become essential. There was a break in the explosions and then his covering was pulled back and a smiling Hoffmann dropped in next to him.

"A bit noisy today," he said.

Paul grunted. He didn't want to encourage this young man but the kid's smiling face sparked something in him. "Kid, I'm dangerous to be around."

Just then a number of 76mm shells dropped nearby. Hoffmann looked at him and then burst out laughing. Paul couldn't help but grin. Under the present circumstances what he had just said couldn't have sounded more stupid.

v

"Leningrad is cut off," said Generalfeldmarschall Keitel. "Rommel and the Finns have linked up south west of the Svir and so far have thrown back a number of counter attacks. The city is on borrowed time."

Goering smiled and clapped his hands together. "Great news. Make sure the ring is tight and don't go into the city. Soon we will ask them to surrender. We need to make sure they understand there will be no reprisals. Even the commissars can live, but send them to

352

the Finns. We will take the rank and file and Speer can have them. Is there any chance of an air lift to supply the city?"

"It is too big," answered Kesselring. "If the ring holds then the city will fall. They will try and fly out some important people, probably by night. To counter this we are moving night fighters to the area. Some of JG 26 have experience flying in the dark so they will also patrol the skies over Leningrad."

"Good, good," said Goering. He stood and paced the floor boards of Carinhall. "We will be able to concentrate on the Caucasus come June. Russia is still the key. If we take their oil we cripple them."

Kesselring glanced at Keitel. "Except for what is happening in North Africa. The French can't hold. They have been brave but their armed forces have been ground down at El Alamein and are now retreating with our two division and the Italians towards Tobruk. Now the Americans, British and Australians have landed in Algeria and Morocco. The question is what we should do about it."

"The French navy tried to intervene, but one battle ship and half a dozen cruisers were never going to be able to compete with the Commonwealth fleet," said Keitel.

"A pity the Italian navy didn't join them," said Goering.

"That was never going to happen," since the beatings the Italian navy received in 41 it has been loath to take any chances."

"Our aircraft have attacked with some success but we only had a few units in Sicily. The Regia Aeronautica was also caught napping but has recently sent torpedo bombers to attack. Unfortunately without fighter cover losses were heavy and only a few ships hit."

"So the French have no navy anymore and the units that were left to guard their western positions are under equipped and thin on the ground," said Goering.

"That was the price of their support in Egypt," said Kesselring.

Goering sighed. "Alright, we need to slow the allies, keep them occupied at least until autumn."

"We are sending JG77 and KG 30 to assist as well as the 22nd Air Landing Division," said Kesselring.

"I thought we needed that unit for capturing the oil fields in the Caucasus?" said Goering.

"It is only a short term measure before we can land 60th Panzer Grenadier and a battalion of Tigers. Even if we can't get them back we will still have the 1st and newly formed 2nd paratrooper divisions. Then there are the independent brigades," said Kesselring.

Goering grunted but didn't comment for a moment. "Alright, that's enough from us, what are the Italian's sending?"

"185th Airborne Division *Folgore* is being sent. This is about all they have in reserve. Two batteries with truck mounted 90mm guns are going with them but our allies have recently sent its mountain troops to Russia. The *Pistoia* division is also being sent but this division has poor anti-tank guns. We must remember that the Italians do nearly all the occupation work in Greece and this unit suffered heavy losses in 1940," said Keitel.

"Ask Speer to send them something, even if they are old Russian 76mm pieces," said Goering. "We must hold Africa for as long as possible."

The Australians were sea sick and two hours behind schedule. Not only that, they had been landed on the wrong beach.

"Trust the British to stuff it up," said Snowy.

The beach was crowded with trucks, jeeps and Bren Carriers. So far no tanks had made it ashore, a fact that worried Tom. If the landing had been opposed it would have been a massacre. Now his regiment was to drive into Algiers and bounce the French out of the city. The only thing that was on the Australians side is that the British were going to try the same stunt, except from the west. The docks were the main game as the Australians were to link up with

American rangers who had been landed by British destroyers. A few M3 halftracks equipped with baby 25 pounders were attacked to the Australian column as well as some carrying .5 calibre machine guns. Tom wasn't sure if it would be enough. The other thing working in the allies favour was that so many French divisions were in Libya and the units that were left seemed to be paralysed.

The first enemy fire hit the front vehicle as the 2/48 battalion approached a bridge over a small river. Route Nationale 5 was a wide road but it was still lined with many building, most of which in this area were warehouses. Machine gun fire lashed the leading Bren Carrier and it clattered off the bitumen and between two tall structures. Rifle fire snapped as the Australians piled out of their trucks and half-tracks and took cover. Mortar fire caused a jeep to catch fire and Brens spat defiance at the hidden French.

"Still five miles from the docks," said Lieutenant Harry Breman as he flopped down beside Tom.

"We need to get those 25 pounders to blast a way through," said Tom.

"They won't move until we can assure them that there is no AT around."

Tom grunted. The poor bloody infantry had to clear the way as usual.

"Smoke? There's no wind Harry."

The Lieutenant nodded and signalled to a radio man. Soon he was barking instructions into a microphone while staring at a map. It wasn't long before mortar shells were popping in front of them and clouds of white smoke began to form. The area was wreathed in a thick fog that both hid the Australians from the enemy but made covering fire impossible.

"Right, now we flank 'em," said Harry.

Tom smiled. While the enemy stared into the smoke and a few Australians fired through it the bulk of the men would swing around the enemy position. Of course if there were men covering the side roads then the Australians would have to try a new tactic.

As it turned out the French troops weren't present in strength and when their officer went down they either fled or surrendered.

"Senegalese troops," said Harry. "Their hearts are not in this."

Tom stared at the tall black men with their frightened eyes. They reminded him of the Aboriginals he had seen back in South Australia, not of the ones lying drunk by the Torrens River, but the football players that played for Port Adelaide. Harry Hewitt stood out in his memory from when he was a kid. The recollection gave him a powerful jolt as he imagined the roar of the crowd and the smell of spilt beer in the stands.

"We have the bridge but we're not there yet," said Harry Breman giving him a slap on the arm. Tom came out of his memories and looked out over the North African city. It was hot, but even this dry heat reminded him of home. He shook his head and trotted back to one of the Bren carriers.

So far casualties had been light but ahead the French were dug in. These were regular troops and they had built barricades and taken positions on the roof tops. Snipers had become a problem and so far three men had been picked off. Tom could hear firing further to the north west and knew that the American Rangers were in trouble.

"There's nothing for it but to use the bombers," said Harry.

Snowy nodded. "The Yanks will be dead or captured otherwise. I don't know why the Frogs just don't give up. All they have are mortars and infantry. Their big guns are all in Libya."

"They have some stuff," said Harry. "Radio says the Brits face some old tanks, Char B's I think, and the Septics got hit with 75's. We've just been lucky."

That the Americans had been hit by artillery was a surprise but the old World War One guns weren't exactly modern, though the rangers had nothing to reply with.

Commonwealth Dauntless dive bombers from the Canadian flagged

Ark Royal came screaming out of the sky and pounded the French

positions followed by Wildcats carrying one hundred pound bombs.

Long range shelling from some unseen cruisers also hit the enemy

barricades and soon the streets were burning. The 2/48th charged

forward through the dust and smoke and over ran the French. A

soldier carrying a rifle came running from a doorway and Tom cut

him down with a burst from his new Tommy gun. Snowy killed two

more men from behind with his Bren, the MG42 having being left in

the half-track due to there being no chance to find more

ammunition. Enemy soldiers had set up an old Hotchkiss machine

gun and were waiting to ambush the company. Snowy and his

squad had slipped around behind them and it was all over with two

quick bursts.

The dead civilians lay in the rubble and near the market.

Tom had seen a few such casualties in England but never like this.

Women and children lay curled together near a well. They were

riddled with bullets. It seemed the Wildcat pilots had mistaken them for enemy soldiers and strafed the group. Whole families had been killed by the heavy shelling from the cruisers and others killed in clay hovels that came apart easily when hit by a one thousand pound bomb. Tom saw the little girl lying near the shattered palm tree. At first he thought maybe she was just asleep. As he got closer he could see that her legs were twisted into an unnatural position and there was a thin line of blood on the top of her skull.

Her large brown eyes were open in shock but they didn't blink or flicker.

"Poor kid must have hit the tree," said Snowy. "Tossed into by the blast."

Tom tried to look away but the image held him. "She needs to be buried," he said.

"Where?" said Snowy gesturing at the cobble stone streets and the rock hard earth.

Harry Breman put his hand on his Sergeant's shoulder.

"We'll return later and cremate them. There's plenty of wood lying around."

That night the 2/48 gathered as much timber as they could and built pyres for the dead civilians. Palms and timber frames were collected and soon the forty dead were laid on the wood. Tom poured fuel over the dry timber and set the match. Then he walked away before he saw the little girl's body blacken. However the smell followed and stayed with him for the rest of his life.

Two days later the 9th Australian Motorised Division made a dash for the Tunisian capital. Italian paratroopers barred their way at Djefna and at Joumine. There the Australians waited for the Americans, British, and their air support to catch up.

Chapter Fourteen: June 1943

"We hold a bridgehead in Tunisia, which is all, my Fuhrer. The Australians held against our early counter attacks, despite the pounding the Luftwaffe gave them. Of the troops we hoped to send only the 22nd Air Landing Division and the Italian Paratroopers arrived before the Americans reached the coast at Hazeg. We were forced to evacuate the Afrika Corps from Tripoli as well as the Italians. Fortunately the Allies Navy isn't strong in the central Mediterranean yet, though I think that is about to change," said Keitel.

Goering put his head in his hands. "What did we save?" he asked.

"Well, the 21st Panzer got out but lost most of its tanks. Only parts of the panzer grenadier divisions got out. The Italian 132 and 133 panzer divisions were saved, without their tanks and their 101st motorised. We saved one French division and parts of another. If

Montgomery had moved faster even this wouldn't have been possible."

"So the French North African Army is gone and we lost fifty thousand troops in Libya and if we don't move quickly then we will lose two more divisions in Tunisia."

"Yes, we are just waiting on your word to pull them out, even so there will be losses," said Keitel.

The General stood in front of a large map of the central Mediterranean in a large antechamber in Carinhall. Speer, Kesselring and Grand Admiral Raeder were all there. Goering liked keeping his group of advisors small only allowing other Generals to join when specific advice was needed. In this case Generaloberst Alfred Jodl and Rommel were present to give advice on Russia.

"So we can rebuild?" said Kesselring.

Speer nodded slowly. "The divisions in the East have most of what they need. The Hungarians have just taken delivery of one hundred T25s and the Romanians have fifty five percent of the Pak 40's they ordered, though their armour is out of date now, or worn out. The Italians are making the P40 tank in numbers and have put a copy of the 75mm L43 in place of their own gun. A couple of small factories are making straight copies of the T34. Why they didn't go with this design as their main tank I don't know. At least the P40 is almost as good as a panzer four. If we slow the equipping of some of the new SS divisions we can reequip the 21st Panzer Division quickly. The army has told me they have enough troops and equipment to create a new panzer grenadier division from the other remnants from Afrika," finished Speer.

"So we have a corps reserve in the area and if we can get the 22nd out quickly it can join the other divisions," said Keitel.

"We also had the 60th panzer grenadier slated for North Africa so leave it in the region," said Goering. "The Tiger battalion can stay in Germany as a reserve to be sent in any direction. What about the Luftwaffe?"

Kesslering sat up a little straighter. "We took heavy losses but there were also some great achievements. We thought we had sunk the

Ark Royal but it was heavily damaged and is now back in England. An American heavy cruiser was destroyed as were two Commonwealth light cruisers. JG 77 shot down many British and American planes, as did Italian fighters, but our own losses are growing and the bomber force has been hit particularly hard. JG 27 is back in Greece but its third Gruppen is at Rome. This fighter group is exhausted and needs new equipment. It has about a dozen serviceable planes at Athens, and probably the same number in Italy."

"New planes are on the way," said Speer. "FW 190s for Italy and BF 109G 6s for Greece. They should be heading south by the end of the month."

Goering nodded as though satisfied. "Good, it will have to be enough for now, though we should find an infantry division from somewhere to add to the reserve, a solid formation from Northern Russia perhaps that needs a rest."

"Speaking of the East my Fuhrer," said Jodl.

Goering gestured and the General unrolled a map of Southern

Russia. "All is ready. Operation Green starts in a week," said Jodl.

"What about Leningrad?" asked Goering.

"The last counter attack was stopped and thrown back just

as it reached the point where the Volkhov river runs into Lake

Ladoga. A flanking attack by the panzers towards Tikhvin forced

them to retreat, though we failed to take the town. Leningrad has

had no supplies in a month and cannot hold much longer. I still

need all of my troops though, just in case."

"Soon the Russians will be looking south but I promise I

won't take more than a division," said Goering. "With any luck our

next attack will cripple them or knock them out of the war."

v

They had crossed the Don south of Voronezh but the high

ground and gullies to the east of the river were heavily fortified. The

Germans held the low river plain which was about a kilometre wide

but the pontoon bridges were destroyed during the day. At night the pioneers rebuilt them but as soon as the sun came up the Russians would rain artillery shells down on them and they were twisted wrecks again. The 1st SS had used counter battery fire to try and solve the problem, but with limited success. The Luftwaffe had also tried to assist but there was a patch of forest approximately 4klms square within easy artillery rang of the river. The only way to solve the situation was to break out into the flat country clear of the river valley.

The Tigers were said to be the answer. The 101st heavy tank battalion had formed a month ago though the SS divisions had been loath to give up their Tiger companies. It had been found that the heavy tank couldn't keep up with the fast moving advance of a panzer division. They had been designed as a break through tank and that's what they were to be used as on this occasion. Hauptsturmführer Wolfgang Fischer had shepherded his vehicles over the pontoon bridge during the night. He hadn't been at all confident that the bridge would carry the 56 tons of the Tiger and each had crossed individually. Once, the heavy panzer could have forded the river with a snorkel but that equipment had been removed. The Tigers had been emptied of all their ammunition and fuel before being reloaded on the other side. The Russians had got wind of the crossing and shelled the panzers as they tried to reload making the night long and dangerous. Hauptsturmführer Wittmann was supposed to bring his second company across but that proved impossible with all the delays. The rest of the battalion would instead provide what covering fire they could from the other bank.

Of his fourteen Tigers only nine had made it over the river and one of those wouldn't start. Wolfgang hoped that what he had left would be enough.

Larisa was back with the medical section and the transport platoon. Wolfgang was reasonably sure she would be safe there. A few attempts had been made to sexually harass the young woman but the crew of Tiger 305 protected her fiercely. Being away from Panzer Meyer and the bulk of the division made it easier to shield Larisa. The atmosphere in the new heavy panzer battalions were all about taking the next objective or holding Russian counter attacks.

It wasn't that the SS formation was apolitical. All of the battalion were still Nazis, it's just that their focus had shifted. The same couldn't be said for the parent division.

His crew had tried to get Larisa to Germany but so far every idea they had come up with had been deemed too risky. Sometimes Wolfgang wondered if they were just trying to hold onto her and this was partially true. The fact she didn't have papers and a check at any railway station could see her arrested was a real concern. Franz had pointed out the safest way to get her into the Fatherland was if she was accompanied by one of them while on leave. The balding gunner had also stated that to further the chance of her getting to Germany it would need to be Wolfgang who took her.

"You are a decorated officer, we are nobodies," he had said.

Wolfgang shook his head. He had no idea when he would be granted leave again. The last one hadn't even allowed him to leave Russia.

The Tigers roared into life and shook out into an arrow head formation. Infantry of the third battalion of the 2nd SS Panzergrenadier Battalion clustered behind the massive panzers while the Hummels of the 1st SS Artillery Battalion pounded the high ground. Ju87s flew passed and dived on to the small woods trying to keep the Russian artillery quiet.

The first anti-tank shell hit with a clank and shook the whole Tiger.

"Anyone see that?" asked Wolfgang.

"Negative, too much dust," said Franz.

"I can barely see the cutting we are supposed to take," said Otto.

Wolfgang wanted to stick his head outside the cupola for a better look but knew that would be extremely dangerous. Bullets were rattling off the frontal plates as it was. Another AT shell hit the ground in front of them and then skipped off the flat earth to clip the mantle next to the gun. Wolfgang's head rang with the sound of impact.

"God I hate it when that happens," said Otto.

"Better than it penetrating," said Hans.

Wolfgang had seen the flash of a gun from inside the cutting and as he stared another gun flashed.

"Untersturmführer Günther has reported his Tiger has lost a track," said Karl over the intercom.

"Tell him to stay with the vehicle and direct his fire into the left side of the cutting. I'm pretty sure there's a battery of 76mm guns there," said Wolfgang.

Fire from the other Tigers across the river was hitting the Russian infantry positions but they were too far away to properly identify the AT guns locations. Wolfgang however knew where the enemy guns were.

"On the left side of the cutting half way up you'll see some disturbed earth. Next to that is the first gun," he told Franz.

"Got it skipper," said the man. The 88 roared and a high explosive shell exploded next to the hidden gun tossing men and sand bags into the air. Tiger 311 destroyed another 76mm AT gun, even though the heavy panzer had lost its track and SS-Unterscharführer Otto Blasé in Tiger 314 blew two more apart. The panzers then rumbled into the cutting with the infantry as the Russians fled. Some threw their hands in the air but few prisoners were taken. Wolfgang took his Tiger passed an oxbow lake that once would one have been part of the river and into the draw itself. The gully itself was probably only five metres deep and tracks dipped into it before climbing back onto the plain. A nearby farm house burned and barb wire lay in tangled heaps just back from some blasted scrub land. Soviet soldiers scurried away and Karl chased them with fire from the hull machine gun. Wolfgang heard the spent shell casings ping as they hit the metal floor of the Tiger.

"Stay on the road," he ordered Otto. "Tell the others to follow," he said to Karl.

Across open fields of growing wheat he could see a patch of forest to the east. He judged it to be three to four kilometres away and knew that was where most of the Russian artillery fire had come from. The Stukas had gone and though smoke curled from the woodland it hadn't caught fire and the guns would soon be firing at the troops trying to cross the river.

Five Tigers followed him after picking up a cluster of infantry men. They moved at top speed across the open ground before dipping down into a shallow creek bed. Wolfgang used the cover to get within a kilometre of the Forest before re-emerging onto the field. He could hear artillery firing from amongst the trees and pitied the poor men at the river.

Stopping briefly to let the company of SS troopers dismount, the Tigers then advanced in a line until a group of KV1s burst from the woods. Wolfgang wouldn't find out until later that these were the S model. Faster than the original tank but made so by the sacrifice of armour.

"Halt panzer, target 900 metres, take out the KV with the man waving the flags," said Wolfgang. It still surprised him that the Soviets didn't have radios and used this archaic method to try and direct their tanks. The 88mm shell tore the turret off the KV tossing the Russian officer clear. Somehow the man lived with a broken hip and two busted ankles. He would be captured and treated at an SS medical post later in the day, while some of his companions were shot near the pontoon bridge by an angry SS officer, such were the vagaries of war.

There were fifteen enemy tanks and the Tigers made short work of them. None made it back to the forest and few of their crews survived the catastrophic impact of an 88mm AT shell.

As the Tigers charged towards the woods again Wolfgang spotted movement to his left. Trucks and jeeps were leaving the trees, many of them towing guns. The Russians were trying to save their artillery but were too late. The Tigers swung north and opened fire with high explosive shells. While the SS infantry set up their machine guns. The range was under a kilometre so Wolfgang ordered his machines to stop using their main guns. If they could capture the enemy battery it would be even better. Soon the enemy were abandoning their vehicles as tyres were shredded and radiators blown. Some trucks burned and many of the Russian gun crews ran back towards the trees. A few jeeps escaped but at least fourteen 76mm guns were captured intact. Later many of the Soviets who had hidden in the forest were captured and a few of those executed later by the river. By that time Wolfgang and his Tigers would be refuelling in the village of Boyevo twenty kilometres behind the previous Russian lines.

v

The Fiat G55 was flying at four kilometres high and was at least three hundred kilometres behind the Russian lines. This was the second week back at his unit for Captain Gyorgy Debrody and already he had another eight victories. His score now stood at sixty putting him above his friend Miklos Kenyres who had fifty eight kills. The rivalry had now gone into the Hungarian press but the stories had died down when his friend had been wounded and both of them ended up in the same hospital. Gyorgy ankle had recovered first and was now in command of Puma squadron.

This mission worried him but it was understandable that the Luftwaffe would ask his planes to run escort on this mission. The G55s were the only fighter that could make it to Stalingrad and back at the moment. Rostov had fallen and the Germans were pushing into the Don bend but it was still 350 kilometres to Stalingrad from their airstrip. Voronezh had fallen to the SS but then the Germans had attacked south east aiming at the confluence of the Don and Donets rivers. While this had happened another great thrust had come from the Muis River sweeping through Rostov on Don and meeting the SS and army formations. After Rostov had fallen the Germans had crossed the Kerch straights while another thrust charged south to meet it. The eastern thrust toward the Volga was slowing as it seemed the Germans were putting the main effort into the attempt to take the Caucuses. He supposed the northerly of the two thrusts was mainly to protect their growing southern flank.

Gyorgy had heard that the Russians had given ground and only thirty thousand prisoners had been taken when the thrusts meet at the junction of the two rivers. The attacks to the south hadn't yet met so there was no way of knowing if the result would be the same.

Below him sixty HE 111s flew over the steppe. They had just crossed the Don and in the distance the mighty Volga could be seen. Strung out along the river was the city named for the leader of the Soviet Union. The target for today was supposed to be the Tractor Factory which was turning out T34s.

He eased his plane into a gentle turn in order to better check all of the sky. You never knew which direction the enemy might attack from. He saw the enemy aircraft climbing to meet them and told his squadron to prepare for action.

"They're Mig3s, dogs down low but in their element up here. Remember they are fast but are poor at climbing and we turn better, so get them into a dogfight," said Gyorgy.

They dived on the Migs even though they were outnumbered two to one, tearing through the enemy formation before pulling up. Two Migs fell away, one burning fiercely, the other in a flat spin. None of the Fiats had been hit. They turned in a hard G circle as the Migs scattered.

"I don't think these boys have had much experience," said Senior Aircraftsman Agi Toth.

Gyorgy thought his wing man was probably correct. The enemy had climbed straight at them and then broken apart in the first attack. They had low air speed and an altitude disadvantage and should have climbed above the Fiats before trying to engage. Gyorgy latched onto one of the machines noting the long nose of the aircraft. The plane tried to turn towards him but he easily cut in side its circle and started firing short bursts with his two wing mounted 15mm guns and the two heavy machine guns mounted above the engine. He didn't want to use the engine mounted 20mm cannon just yet as they were short of ammunition for the guns at the moment and each Fiat had only sixty rounds instead of the usual two hundred and fifty. He saw pieces fly off around the Mig's tail. The third burst tore up the fuselage behind the pilot and was followed by a small explosion. An oil tank under the engine had been hit and flames quickly spread. As Gyorgy pulled up he noted that the Russian pilot had opened his canopy and was scrambling clear of his stricken fighter.

The combat below him had scattered but two Migs were trying to line up on the He111s. Gyorgy rolled the Fiat on its back and dived with his wing man to intercept. He came in behind the two planes and told Agi to take the one on the left. The two Migs never even knew they were there. Gyorgy's victim lost a wing and his wingman's kill blew up. Just then bursts of flak appeared around the bombers. They were over Stalingrad.

The bomber dived to three thousand metres and levelled out. Using there extra speed they avoided most of the flak which burst behind them. Gyorgy kept his fighters at four and a half thousand metres, above the range of the Russian guns. One of the Heinkels was hit but kept on flying. A thin line of grey smoke streamed from a damaged engine and the plane started to lose speed. It would be a close thing to get the wounded bomber back to German lines.

The German planes suddenly lurched upwards as sticks of black bombs fell away. Soon Gyorgy could see the concussion of the explosions and then watched as mushrooms of smoke and earth obscured the ground. The sound rolled like thunder and he felt for the Russian civilians who would have been near the target area.

They were lucky on the return home. Gyorgy allocated two fighters to bring the wounded bomber in but was worried for them. Any Russian fighters in more than flight strength would have swept them from the sky. As it was the bomber was forced to land in a field next to an advancing panzer column. It had been flying on one engine and losing fuel from damaged tanks. It landed on the last fumes ploughing through green wheat until coming to a stop. At least the chance of fire had been much reduced.

Puma squadron landed without any losses and with more kills to its credit but the Hungarian group's luck wasn't to last. The battle for the Caucuses was just beginning.

v

"So Leningrad has yet to surrender!" Goering was frustrated and Speer was worried. When there leader got angry he sometime made irrational decisions, like the night bombing campaign of London which had been nothing more than spite.

"It can't hold out much longer," said Kesselring. "Rommel has the noose tight and only a trickle of supplies are getting through from the air.

"I want even that stopped! Tell your fighter wings to fly at night if they have to. Attack the landing strips like the Americans tried to do to us when we were supplying our forces in Britain by air."

"We have moved the new train busting unit to the area. It will slow the supply of munitions to the forward Russian airstrips," said Kesselring soothingly.

"Good," mumbled Goering.

The Junker 88C's and P's were dedicated heavy fighters with the range and bombs to hit the Russian rail network far behind enemy lines. It also had the speed to attempt to run from Russian fighters. Yet the favoured plane was the new ME 410 which was faster but still packed a punch. The 410 has almost been overlooked in the interest of keeping the number of aircraft types down yet a replacement for the ME 110 was needed though the type was now considered multipurpose, not a just a heavy fighter.

"They will surrender," said Keitel. They stood around maps of Russia in the drawing room of Carinhall as servants brought them coffee and sandwiches. It was supposed to be a working lunch but it looked as though the meeting would go late into the afternoon.

"All counter attacks have been held, though at a cost. Rommel's flexible defence has worked and though he had a long flank the Russians were never able to keep any gains for long enough to get supplies across the lake," said Kesselring.

"Yet still they hold out," said Goering, quieter now.

"Not for long," Keitel reiterated.

"Offer them generous terms, they can surrender to the Finns for all I care," said Goering. "As long as the city is ours."

"It's going to be a lot of extra mouths to feed," said Kesselring.

"Many Russians have died in the siege so the city's population is much reduced. If we make it clear that ships laden with food are ready to feed the city then it might speed the surrender," said Goering.

"What ships?" asked Keitel.

"I didn't say it had to be true," said Goering. He took a bite from his sandwich and chewed for a while. "We should make an effort though or they might not trust us when similar situations occur. I'll ask Raeder to gather a small convoy and we will fill it with wheat and oats, maybe some potatoes. Then we will send it north. That is the carrot. The stick will be the heavy bombers. Send KG 4. It will give them a chance to get used to their new JU 290s."

The men around the room nodded and a stenographer sitting at a small table typed away.

"Now, the south. Where are we at?" asked Goering.

Keitel stood, after putting down his plate. He picking up a small stick and pointed at a map covered with small pins and pencil lines. "We are well into the bend of the Don but when our pincers snapped together the pickings were small. Few Russians were captured. The Luftwaffe has been carrying out wide spread reconnaissance and it seems they are withdrawing when threatened with being surrounded."

"So we have them on the run," said Goering.

"Perhaps," continued Keitel. "However there is no panic in their retreats so we are wary."

"They could be trading space for time, like we did in Poland."

"If I follow that logic then we should watch our flanks," said Goering.

Keitel shook his head. "Intelligence says the Russians are on their last legs in terms of reserves and equipment."

Goering snorted. "I've heard that before! If I believe the projections from the cloak and dagger boys we would already be in Siberia. I think I'll trust our eyes in the sky instead. Tell the Luftwaffe to keep looking."

Kesselring nodded.

"Anyway," continued Keitel. The Army Group A had crossed the Don and is pushing south but it is yet to link up with the forces in the Kerch Peninsular. The first Panzer army has freedom of action with enormous advances being made. Krymsk has just fallen and the Forty Sixth infantry division is just outside Novorossiysk. The Wiking Panzer division is eighty kilometres north of Krasnodar and the Luftwaffe says there is little in front of them. We suggest if we are to initiate Operation Firefly it is now. The 1st Paratrooper division needs to be dropped on the oil facilities before the Russians blow them. ME 323 are ready to fly in heavier support for the paratroopers soon after they have landed. If we don't do it now the Russians will destroy the wells."

"How long will they need to hold out for?" said Goering.

"We predict two days, three at the most," said Keitel.

"It's a risk," said Goering.

"This type of mission is exactly why we created them," sad Kesselring.

Goering thought for a moment. "Send them in. I want the oil."

Then he pointed at a smaller map of the Mediterranean. "And what are the allies doing now that they have Africa?"

"We think they are preparing an invasion of either Malta or Crete. Intelligence is not sure which one," aid Kesselring.

Goering frowned. "It would help if we could narrow it down."

Keitel nodded. "At the moment we are forced to split our reserves between the two areas. For all we know they could bypass Malta and land directly in Sicily. Air combat has been hectic in both areas as the Allies obviously want to keep us guessing."

"Losses have been heavy," added Kesselring.

"Can we reinforce the area?" asked Goering.

"If we pull JG26 from Leningrad I can send them south," said Kesselring.

Goering shook his head. "Not yet; as soon as Leningrad surrenders do so. Also send SG 2s second Gruppe as they have FW190s now. Stukas are too vulnerable to the Allies."

"The Spanish are sending a fighter wing north, maybe it could almost be a straight swap," said Kesselring.

"Speer told me that we will have to totally reequip that wing with BF 109 Gs. The Spanish are still using the old F model or out dated Russian planes. Their air force needs to be totally reequipped and their army isn't much better. The Blue Division has German equipment but the Spanish armed forces have been screaming for panzers and decent artillery and planes so they can support us in the East. A second division is in Germany but it will be a month or more before they have what is needed to face the Russians. As for the French, they have decent planes but only a small air force now, their navy is smashed and their army is a shell."

"What about the Italians?" asked Kesselring.

"They have lost heavily but now have tanks and planes that can match the allies. It's their morale that's questionable and that varies from division to division. Their air force is handy and still wants to fight. The Italian navy is another matter. We cannot count on them and they need to be watched," said Goering. "All Italian units have been withdrawn to the Mediterranean except for the Alpini Divsions. Three of these divisions are still in Russia and will be used to try and force a passage over the Caucus Mountains. The rest are in Greece, with one actually on Crete. They are high quality units, or so I am told."

"So we have the Romanians, Hungarians and the Finns in the east," said Kesselring

"Not to be sneezed at," said Goering. "Some of their better divisions have done well..."

Kesselring nodded reluctantly. He knew that it often depended on whether these units had received German equipment or not, especially AT guns.

"So now we send in the paratroopers and wait," said Keitel. The three men sat back and sipped their coffee while staring at the map of Southern Russia.

Chapter Fifteen: July 1943

As the Tigers couldn't keep up with the slashing drive south to the oil fields they were allocated to support the Sixth Army's push towards the Volga. The 101st SS Heavy Panzer Battalion wasn't the only Tiger unit in the area, the Wehrmacht also had the 503rd heavy Panzer Battalion operating with the Fourteenth Panzer Division, while Wolfgang's unit still support the 1st SS panzer division. The 5th SS, 3rd SS and 2nd SS had all headed south with the 13th panzer division and 3rd panzer division. All of the mountain divisions had fought their way from Kerch with the infantry and some independent StuG battalions and now readied themselves to assault the mountain passes. The paratroopers had taken most of oil fields around Krasnodar intact. Panzers were at Stavrapol but of course Wolfgang knew little of this. He only understood that the resistance in the Don River bend was increasing and that it was a constant battle to get resupplied.

Today they had been ordered north east to meet a counter attack from near the head waters of the Chir River. The ground here was open though cut with many creek beds and gullies. At this point the Chir ran close to the Don River, only separated from the larger water course by low hills. The Sixth Army had pushed north trying to throw the Russians back onto the other side of the Don, but lacked the strength to do so. The Soviets used the land they still held on the western bank to launch counter attacks into the northern flank of the advancing Germans. It was the job of the two Tiger battalions to help the Hungarian and German infantry hold the Russians back while the panzer and motorised divisions continued to cut east towards the Volga River.

The third company had combined with the first as each only had two working Tigers. The battalion commander SS-Obersturmbannführer Heinz von Westernhagen led the way in Tiger 007. The second company under Michael Wittmann had five tigers of its own and was attacking from further south.

The five Tigers advanced slowly along a dry creek bed towards the Chir. The sky was clear and Wolfgang sat in the cupola enjoying the breeze. The panzers were well spaced so he was clear of the dust and fumes being given off by his commander's leading panzer. Along the top of the gully ran a dust road along which a single half-track rattled. The vehicle stopped occasionally and a man would peer through his binoculars before advancing again. Enemy armour had attacked and made it as far as the Chir, before then driving straight through the shallow water and capturing a collective farm. The 101st was to take back the area and destroy the enemy armour, or at least those were the orders.

The half-track suddenly changed direction and plunged into a group of trees near a dusty crossroad. The radio then crackled into life. It seemed enemy armour was eight hundred metres away amongst the building of the farms and also in a forest a couple of kilometres further to the east across a long shallow lake formed by an old branch of the river.

"All units shake out into panzer keil. We will drive the enemy from the buildings using the smoke and structures to shield us from flanking shots from across the lake. Don't try and cross it. Reports says the water is shallow, but it's also muddy," said Obersturmbannführer Heinz von Westernhagen.

Wolfgang told the crew to close the side hatches. They groaned knowing how hot it was about to get inside the Tiger, but obeyed. He didn't button up as he wanted a good view of the enemy armour as ranges were going to be close. No infantry had been reported as yet so he felt safe from snipers. They left the cutting and charged towards the closest buildings catching the enemy by surprise. Some of the Russian tanks were maned and going while other crews were out doing routine maintenance. A few had even started to brew tea. Two men next to a T70 were cut down by machine gun fire from the commander's Tiger while another light tank was blown apart by an eighty eight millimetre shell.

The collective farm became a hornet's nest with men running everywhere and T34s driving straight at the Tigers. Wolfgang ordered Otto to halt while Franz quickly picked off the enemy tanks as they attacked singularly in small groups. T34s began to explode as turrets were shattered. Fires took hold of some of the buildings in the farm and the enemy seemed to retire into the smoke.

A Tiger stopped and its crew hurriedly took cover before the vehicle started to burn. Wolfgang ordered Otto Blase to turn Tiger 314 towards the enemy across the lake and engage them. A group of T34s sat among a thin strip of trees in the river valley firing into the flanks of the Tigers. The range was over 800 metres so the Soviets weren't all that accurate but a lucky shot into the side armour could still knock out a Tiger. Soon Blase had destroyed two tanks and the others were starting to pull back. Then Wittmann and his company crashed into the enemy's rear. It seemed the company commander had led his Tigers in a flank march using a village and patches of forest as cover to reach a position above the Russian armoured concentration. He had been slowed by a few light tanks in the village but had eventually pushed through the forest behind the T34s and was now firing at them at short range.

Heinz von Westernhagen took his Tiger slowly into the buildings. Now that his flank was secured he wanted to drive the surviving Russian armour into the open. Wolfgang advanced slowly behind tiger 007. A squat shape pulled out of the smoke and fired. His commander's tank staggered and Westernhagen managed to throw himself from the Tiger's cupola just before flames erupted from the vehicle. Brief screams were cut short as an internal explosion shook the vehicle.

"Target right," yelled Wolfgang. The enemy armoured vehicle wasn't a tank. It seemed to be some sort of self-propelled howitzer. Whatever it was it had a massive gun and looked extremely mean and ugly. Otto swung the Tiger quickly to face it and Franz fired. The eighty eight millimetre shell punched a clean hole in the middle of the AVF causing its hatches to fly open. Two men scrambled clear to be cut down by the hull machine gun before smoke started to pour from the vehicle. Westernhagen clambered up next to Wolfgang looking singed and shaken but otherwise alright.

"That bastard killed my crew," he yelled. He stood on the turret staring around wildly before nodding. "They've gone," he finally said.

Wolfgang took his Tiger through the buildings of the collective farm seeing the burning T34s and light tanks. From the east he could watch the fires Wittmann's Tigers had caused. This enemy thrust had been defeated.

He dropped his commander off with the medical section to be checked and spotted Larisa wrapping a bandage around the hand of a crew member of one of the Tigers. The man stood to salute and Wolfgang told him to relax. "Dropped a shell casing on my hand sir," but your angel here says nothing is broken," said the Oberschütze.

Larisa smiled at the description. She understood German now, though she spoke it with a terrible accent.

"That's good to hear. Alfred would be sad if you weren't there loading his gun." Wolfgang had recognised the man as a crew member from Tiger 311 in the first platoon of his company. The man stood and favoured Larisa with a smile before walking away to find his crew.

"They all have taken a shine to you," said Wolfgang.

Larisa tilted her head and looked at him, her expression unreadable. "I don't mind treating them yet it feels strange."

"Because we are German."

She nodded. "You are supposed to be my enemy."

He shrugged. "War is strange."

"Wolfy, I need to get away from here."

He looked around making sure that none of his men had heard the use of the pet name. "I know."

"If I fall into Russian hands now I'm dead. If the Gestapo find out who my parents were, I'm dead"

"I won't let that happen," said Wolfgang stepping closer to her.

She reached out and touched his arm gently. "You and the boys have been good to me and part of me would like to stay with you but it's dangerous."

He felt his pulse quicken as he did whenever she touched him and tried to push the sensation away.

"Next time I get leave to return home I promise you'll be with me."

She sighed. "I hope that happens soon. This war seems to keep dragging on and even though your armies still press east my countrymen keep attacking. I don't know if it will ever end."

He took her hand. "I'll get you to safety somehow," he promised.

She smiled and kissed him softly on the cheek.

The mountains towered to the south of him as he eased back on the stick. Below him the 13th Panzer Division was said to have captured Maysky and the 5th SS were motoring on Mozdok. Yet there were signs that Soviet resistance was stiffening. Gyorgy Debrody had heard that the German mountain troops had yet to force a passage through the mountains, though the Italians had succeeded in reaching Sochi. Puma squadron had been moved south because the Fiat G55 had a range of 1600 kilometres with the two drop tanks. This meant his Hungarian squadron could cover the 450 kilometres from their airfield at Maykop to the German spear heads and still have time to hover over the front for a time. They could also cover the captured oil fields in case the Russians decided to bomb them.

It was true that a quarter of the wells had been wrecked but the paratroopers had saved enough of them to make the high casualties of the airborne operation worthwhile. It was rumoured that a small amount of the oil was already being shipped back to the refineries in Romania on small freighters and barges. The

Soviets had tried to intervene and his squadron had helped drive off Russian fighters allowing Stukas and JU 88s to attack and sink two cruisers while damaging the battleship The Sevastopol. A type 2 U boat had then finished it off with a torpedo.

Grozny was still however over a hundred kilometres away and even though Gyorgy knew German and even Italian transport planes were making herculean efforts to supply the panzer spear heads it was a difficult task to keep them going. Even if they took Grozny the Soviets would probably blow it up. Gyorgy had heard the German paratroopers had taken a battering so it was unlikely they could be used again. At least the Russians wouldn't be able to use the oil.

Below a river snaked east with Mozok siting on its northern bank. The SS Regiment Germania was only two kilometres from the town but had been held up by dug in Russian infantry. The 13th Panzer Division was closer to the mountains at Terek and the 3rd SS division was somewhere to the north at Kurskaya waiting for fuel.

Russian planes had been few and far between until yesterday when

he had shot down a PE2. Now however a big bulky group of single

engined fighters approached from the east at the same altitude.

"What the Hell are they?" asked his wingman Agi Toth.

"I think I know," answered Gyorgy. "I saw a picture of a

wrecked one in the German magazine Signal. They must be P47

Thunderbolts. All I know about them is that they have eight wing

mounted 13mm machine guns so don't go head on."

Gyorgy ordered his squadron to drop their extra fuel tanks.

The big fighters turned towards them but he instructed Puma

squadron to climb towards a bank of cloud to the south.

Thunderheads were building near the peaks and he decided to try

and use them to his advantage.

He led the Fiat G55s back and around the thunderhead

climbing away from the P47s before turning around the rear of the

cloud to hopefully come onto the enemy's tail. As Puma squadron curved passed the cloud into a dive they searched the sky for the Thunderbolts without luck.

"Where are they skipper," asked Agi.

Gyorgy glanced into his mirror and caught a flash of metal in the sunlight. "They're behind," us he yelled. Turn into them."

His squadron followed and they all pulled around in a high G turn to face the now diving P47s.

"I thought this wasn't a good idea Skipper," said Agi.

"They have out foxed me. We have no choice."

Gyorgy realised that the Russian commander had known what he was up to so had climbed *into* the cloud and then half rolled out of it when the time was right. If the P47s could have climbed faster then there would have been no time to even turn into them. He lined up on the second machine as tracers raced towards his plane. The Russians had opened fire too soon and he waited until the enemy aircraft filled his sights. He felt his plane shudder as bullets tore into the wing and then fired himself. The area around the P47's cockpit tore open with the impact of twenty millimetre shells. Then his squadron was through. Planes went in all directions but at least one Fiat was on fire. A P47 was in a flat spin, probably the one he had hit, and another was turning away with a thin stream of grey smoke coming from the engine.

His plane was vibrating and bucking. Gyorgy glanced at his port wing and noted the profusion of fist sized holes. His wing gun had been hit and was twisted up through the aluminium skin. He knew he only had seconds before the wing folded up on itself or tore off. Gyorgy eased the throttle back and headed west. The vibrations grew as he tried to calculate whether he was over German lines or not. In the end he realised he couldn't wait. Hauling back the canopy Gyorgy radioed that he was bailing out. He pulled off his mask as the wind whipped around him and was half out of the cockpit when the wing gave way. Thinking he had left it too late Gyorgy fought against the force of the now spinning plane that seemed to be unwilling to let him go. His back was pushed into the frame of the cockpit but the top half of his body was free, though being mercilessly battered by the wind. The world was appearing at crazy angles as the ruined aircraft spiralled. Eventually he got his foot on the back of his seat and pushed with all his strength.

Then he was free. Missing the tail of the Fiat by centimetres he rocket passed into the sky. Scrabbling around with his right hand he found the rip cord of his parachute. He hopped it was undamaged this time as there were no trees or snow to break his fall. The silk snapped open above him and Gyorgy breathed a sigh of relief. The Thunderbolts and Fiats had all disappeared and he was alone floating in the sky.

Below he noticed a vehicle, a half-track by the look of it, speeding to where he would land. Before he knew it the earth was rushing up to meet him and Gyorgy was readying himself to roll like they had taught him. The ground still hit hard and he managed to graze his cheek as he tumbled. There was little breeze so he pulled the chute to him and then undid the buckles. Pulling out his pistol he ran for a clump of trees but was cut off by the half-track. It was

German and carried the black shield and crooked cross of the 5th SS Panzer Division.

Gyorgy stood tall and waved. "I'm happy to see you," he said in broken German as a big man strode towards him frowning. The blow from the rifle butt took him by surprise and everything went black.

He woke in a thin cot with a thick bandage on his head. An SS Obergruppenfuhrer stood next to him. With him was another man in SS uniform. The high ranking officer spoke and then the other man translated.

"Obergruppenfuhrer Felix Steiner apologises for his men. They mistook you for a Soviet and acted accordingly," said the younger man.

Gyorgy touched his bandages and nodded, but immediately regretted the action.

"The doctor has told us that no permanent damage has been done but you will need a few days rest before you can return to flying," the man continued to translate.

"The commander says in the meantime the Wiking Division is honoured to play host to such a famous ace and can confirm your kill of the P47. We have heard that takes your total to seventy. The commander has a gift to commemorate the milestone."

The smiling officer then placed a large bottle of Champagne on his cot. Gyorgy wondered where he had got the French alcohol from. There was plenty of vodka to be had and a little schnapps in Russia but never anything else. He thanked the commander of the SS division profusely and planned on sharing the bottle with his pilots when he returned to the airfield. In the meantime he would enjoy about a week of no flying as it was a long drive to return him to his unit.

v

Goering was positively skipping with joy. Speer watched his leader and noted the smile didn't leave his face. July 31 had been the day that Leningrad had finally surrendered. The Soviets were in the process of laying down their arms and German troops were at the Winter Palace. Even the news that nearly all the Russian ships had scuttled themselves had not dampened the occasion. Only two modern destroyers had gone over to the Finns but Goering didn't care. He didn't mind that at least half of the three hundred thousand enemy soldiers had preferred to give themselves up to Finnish troops.

A small convoy of ships carrying food would enter the harbour tomorrow and begin unloading. The Soviets had left a small area of the port undamaged so that this could occur, such was the plight of the city's remaining civilians. Goering had insisted on a price for the food and his demand had been met. The two tank factories hadn't been blown up and Speer was glad about this. The machine tools and even some of the steel needed was still present and soon T34s would roll from the plant to be sent to panzer divisions that were kept in reserve to fight the western allies. Cupolas would be added and the guns would be rebored to take German 75mm shells but that had been done before.

They stood on the platform drinking white wine and watching the ME 262 go through its paces. The jet was performing well and Speer was sure he would have at least a gruppe operating by the end of December.

"It needs a name," said Goering.

"I think it looks like a shark," said Kesselring.

"To nautical," said Goering. "The navy would claim it as one of their own," he said laughing.

"I think it looks like a swallow," said Speer.

Goering stroked his chin. "Yes, I can see it in the wings, but a swallow is not exactly ferocious. The jets will sweep the sky clear like a storm! That's it! I'll call it a Stormbird."

Speer nodded. It wasn't a bad name.

They left the air base and returned by car to Goering's hunting lodge in Bavaria. As they arrived a messenger ran out from the radio room waving a message. The Russians had blown the oil fields at Groznoy just as the 3rd SS and 5th SS had reached within ten kilometres of the town.

Goering shrugged at the news. "We didn't have the paratroopers to take it. I would have done the same thing if I was the Russians."

Speer didn't feel that blasé about it. He could have used that oil. Synthetic production had halved the short fall in oil to 1million barrels a month but juggling production was always difficult and corners had to be cut. Maikop produced 19 million barrels annually according to before the war data. Already half a million had been transported to Romania for processing. It was a pity that there was no refinery at Maikop but you couldn't have everything. As it was Speer was frantically looking for shipping to move the oil across the Black Sea. The rail network was also another way to move the precious liquid but this was damaged and only good enough to get

411

the oil to the small ports in the area. The rail links were a priority and he had Organisation Todt working on it. There was only a single line running to Rostov and it would need a lot of work.

"Soviet resistance is stiffening," said Kesselring as the small group gathered around the map table. "Even though the Alpini crossed the mountain and Sochi has fallen the Russians have kept us penned in the small area of Abkhazain region. Further east the mountain divisions have not taken the high passes," Keitel said. The general had been waiting for them when they got back from the airfield. "It is just proving impossible to supply them with what they needed. Nearer the ports on the Black Sea things are better. The Luftwaffe had been amazing with what it has delivered but it can't be everywhere."

"I suggest we concentrate on the mobile divisions," said Kesselring. "We need to hold Grozny and reach the Caspian Sea. Aerial reconnaissance has shown us the main route for American equipment to the area comes via roads running along the coast from Persia. The Russians use railways to move the equipment through the mountains then they drive it to Stalingrad after following the Volga."

"I want the Volga route cut and I agree with Albert," said Goering. "Priority is to go to the mobile units. Get to the Caspian and then turn north east. The mountains can form our southern front for now. Maintain the pressure near Sochi but that is all."

"The good news is that the 1st Hungarian panzer division has received one hundred and twenty five T25s and is back protecting the Sixth Army's flank. This has given us a chance to rest the 1st SS. The Romanians are in the process of getting fifty T25s for their panzer division and have passed their remaining Marders and Crusaders on to support the cavalry divisions which are deep in the central Caucuses. We are currently reequipping the 24th panzer division with fifty T25s as well. They can't keep using the old 38Ts forever. The 37mm gun on the old Czech tank is useless. The 24th will be sent to the northern Don front as soon as possible."

Goering pushed himself back in his chair. "Gentleman the Russians are on the brink. They are not beaten as the still hold their capital and it might be another year before we force them to give

up but without oil they're in trouble. The question is what the allies

will do about it."

Chapter Sixteen: August 1943

Tom couldn't believe he was in sunny Spain. The Australian 9th Division had motored from the Portuguese port of Portimao with extreme haste and had relieved the British paratroopers who had taken the Spanish border town of Isla Christiana. Now they were back on the main highway bypassing the large town of Cartaya.

The Allies had come ashore in Portugal two days ago and had stormed quickly across the Spanish border. They had been welcomed in Lisbon and assisted in getting into Spain as quickly as possible by the Portuguese authorities. Fleets of aircraft had attacked the Spanish navy and air force and the enemy had been taken completely by surprise. There had even been an attack from Gibraltar which had forced the Spanish back ten miles. British forces had reached Estacion and the Canas River. Unfortunately they hadn't been able to clear the Bay of Gibraltar as yet so the British couldn't use their harbour but there were plenty of places for the Allies to land in Lisbon so that wasn't an issue.

None of this concerned Tom. He had been surprised that they were going into Spain, yet he supposed that the Spanish were fighting the Russians, and Uncle Joe was on their side and needed help. He didn't realise that the level of Spanish assistance to the Germans had been growing and the Soviet Union was screaming for the Allies to do something to take the pressure off them. He did know that the Americans were now sending bombers into Germany but that obviously wasn't enough.

Landings also took place at Pedro Valiente in order to attack Algeciras from behind and secure the Bay of Gibraltar. It was the only opposed landing of the campaign and though it would take the Spanish by surprise, the mountain ranges that dominated the area would lock the Americans and British into a bridgehead ten kilometres deep by about the same width until Allied forces broke out a month later. The huge stockpile of ammunition and stores at the Gibraltar sustained the forces in the area until the bay was secure.

Meanwhile the Americans were advancing on Salamanca and the Eight Army under Montgomery was moving north east from Merida towards Toledo. Smaller forces attacked north from Portugal into Basque country but the main thrust was from the Americans as it was the shortest route to Madrid.

The first serious resistance to the Australians occurred at the crossing of the Odiel River near Los Almendros. The bridge had been blown but the river was running low with large sand banks and weed beds showing that it was possible to wade across. The problem was the countryside was flat and extremely open. There were olive groves and patches of scrub hundreds of yards beyond the river but even that gave little shelter. It was almost a mile before the Australians would reach any decent cover and that's where the enemy was likely to be thickest on the ground. The big advantage they had was complete dominance of the air.

As Tom watched Kittyhawks and Hurricanes plastered all of the areas where the enemy could be hiding then the artillery worked the area over. Mortars then laid down smoke and the 2/48th was jumping from the scrubby forest on the western bank of the river into the water. Smoke obscured the flat country beyond and the fire that came from the Spanish machine guns was wild and ineffective. Tom found the water refreshing as the weather was hot. As he watched the southerly wind from the Sahara Desert picked up scattering the smoke and exposing the battalion just as it left the water. Tom immediately ran for the ruins of the bridge with Snowy and Harry Breman following him.

Spanish Browning machine guns firing from hidden positions cut down Australians who were too slow to get into cover and soon Brens were firing back. Recently promoted Captain Harry Breman pulled a radio operator over to him only to find that the unreliable British set wasn't working.

"I wish they would give us some of those Handie Talkies the Yanks are using," the captain said.

It didn't matter in the end because 'The Hammer', their company commander, spotted the problem and ordered the mortars to switch to high explosives. He then directed their fire himself from the scrub at the edge of the river. Soon the Australians were up and running for the small forest at the top of a low hill. More men fell to rifle fire but groups of men cut down the Spanish in their fox holes with automatic fire. The Australians had begged, stolen or taken every quick firing weapon they could find but the Garand was still kept in large numbers and remained a favourite with the troops. The captain sprayed retreating Spaniards with his Owen sub machine gun and a man fell clutching his back. Snowy cut down the other two firing his Bren from the hip, the MG42 still being in storage.

Seventy five millimetre shells from old French guns fell amongst the Australians briefly causing a few casualties before counter battery fire from 25 pounders forced them to cease fire. Tom and Snowy were soon amongst the shattered pine trees. Burning wood and smouldering trucks stood in what was left of the small wood land. Machine gun nests had been destroyed and the remains of Spanish soldiers littered the area.

"It looks like Hell." muttered Snowy.

A Spanish officer, his arm shredded and his face blackened staggered towards them muttering. In his left hand he held a German luger. Snowy casually killed him with a quick burst before collecting the gun. Tom frowned at him.

"What? This will earn me some good coin from the Yanks. They love these type of souvenirs," said Snowy.

"Our boy scout doesn't approve," said Harry. He smiled to take the sting out of the words but Tom ignored him. After three years of war he was used to his platoon robbing the dead. He had done it himself a few times though he hated himself afterwards.

After they had fired the green and orange flares from the top of the hill a group of Sentinel tanks and M3 half-tracks drove into the water and out the other side. The blowing of the bridge wouldn't slow them unless it rained and that was looking unlikely.

The advance would continue and soon the Australian 9th Division and the Canadians would be outside Seville.

v

Goering wasn't celebrating anymore. The panzers had taken Grozny but it was a ruin with burning oil wells darkening the sky. The 3rd SS was pushing for the Caspian Sea but had again been forced to stop due to lack of fuel and persistent counter attacks. The Don bend had been cleared but the bridge head created by the 14th panzer division on the eastern bank had been evacuated due to a shortage of ammunition and massive counter attacks. The Russians had even tried to recross the Don themselves but Hungarian T25s had thrown them back.

And then there was Spain. Goering screamed abuse at the intelligence services and replaced Vice Admiral Wilhelm Canaris as head of the Abwehr after hearing of the invasion. He replaced him with Gruppenfuhrer Walter Schellenburg and then spent two days shooting in his Bavarian park before speaking to anyone. "Do what you will," he told Keitel and Kesselring who immediately took

Goering on his word.

The 22nd Air Landing, which was fast becoming a fire brigade

unit, was rushed into Spain along with the 11th Infantry division

which had been withdrawn from the Leningrad front and brought

up to strength. The new 2nd Parachute Division was sent south

along with the 9th SS Herman Goering Panzer Division. The 23rd

Panzer and the reconstituted 21st Panzer Division would also be put

on trains to Madrid soon. The 25th Panzer Grenadier Division was

also being pulled from theatre reserve near Smolensk and sent to

help. Keitel wasn't sure if seven divisions would be enough and

tried to get the Italians or Vichy French to send troops. Neither

would, though the Italians sent eighty Macchi 205s as well as

twenty of the new Reggiane 2005 high altitude fighters. Kesselring

sent a gruppe of forty FW190 ground attack aircraft as well as all of

JG 77 with one hundred BF 109 G6s.

It didn't look like it was enough. Spain, though mountainous

in some area, was a wide theatre with many plains. The allies, particularly the Americans under General Patton, had advanced quickly and now stood twenty kilometres west of Salamanca and two hundred kilometres from Madrid. The British under Montgomery had only reached Caceres. Seville had fallen to the Australians and the Bay of Gibraltar had just been cleared so the British could again use it.

Goering had ordered that the traitors in Lisbon be bombed but the Allies were ready for the Luftwaffe and the two night raids had been disasters. Radar had been placed around the capital city of Portugal and British night fighters had savaged the He 111s sent to attack the port. It seemed a new plane called the Mosquito was being used by the British and it was very effective. The Heinkels had been withdrawn.

The Spanish army had crumbled quickly in the face of the massive allied onslaught. The fact they had only twenty panzer fours and an equal number of StuG threes contributed to the problem. The Spaniards had no decent antitank guns and their air force had only twenty BF 109 Gs. It didn't help that their two best divisions were in Russia. The Blue Corps had only just reached Madrid and were marching to stop Montgomery. Keitel hopped these veterans with their German equipment would at least slow the British. The 22nd Air Landing Division and the 11th Infantry had gone south to fight the British First Army near Gibraltar. The 9th SS, and parts of the 21st panzer division had advanced to take on Patton. Other divisions would be fed into the front as they arrived.

The new front meant more resources would need to be pulled from Russia as important mines were at risk, particularly those that provided tungsten. Newly promoted Field Marshal Erwin Rommel, victor of Leningrad had been placed in command and was already calling for more divisions. Already the 3rd Mountain Division was being looked at to be plucked from Norway and the 30th Infantry Division was also slated to be moved from northern Russia, though neither unit had yet received its orders. The 117 Jaeger division had however received its orders and was getting ready to leave Greece. So Rommel would soon have twelve quality divisions, including the Spanish Blue Corps. Keitel warned that eventually they would have to find at least another six divisions. Kesselring was confident the Spanish could take up some of the slack once their army had some decent equipment. The same went for their air force. That's where Speer came in and the Minister of Armaments was already complaining about the extra strain it was placing on German resources.

v

The mountains were covered in a thin forest giving Paul Becker some protection from the blazing sun. He thought the Los Alcornocales Mountains with their cork oaks and holly trees very beautiful. It was a pity he had to kill men while admiring the view. The British First Army was still trying to force its way out of the southern corner of Spain. Their aim was obviously to link up with the Canadians and Australians who were currently stuck along the line of the Guadalquivir River. The Canadians were still clearing the last suburbs of Seville where the poorly armed Spanish were putting up a brave fight. Still, it was only one hundred kilometres between the two allied armies so it was only a matter of time before the Axis troops were forced back to the north he supposed.

Soldat Stephan Hoffmann crouched down with him watching the road. From the rocky spur on which they sat they could make out most of the river valley below. He could not see the Mediterranean any more but he believed there were positions from which the Germans could still see the Bay of Gibraltar. Long range artillery could just make the distance but the divisions 105s were out of range. Even the 150mm howitzer's shells fell just short of the water. The valley they were protecting ran north south and his battalion was at its northern entrance. The road below continued on before twisting with the valley like a dog leg towards the west and the open country around Tahivilla.

"They are creeping closer," whispered Stephan.

Paul was forward of the platoon hiding beneath an earth coloured tarpaulin. His uniform was patterned with the latest camouflage as was Stephan's but Paul wasn't completely happy with it as the Spanish countryside was a little lighter in its shading. Still, it broke

426

up his outline and that was more than the rest of his company had. The rest of the division had to make do with the uniforms put aside for the Tunisian campaign.

"Who are they?" said Paul quietly.

"I can just catch some colours on their shoulder patch. I can see yellow and red so probably the British 4th Infantry," answered Stephan.

Paul eased the Mauser to his shoulder, the Russian sniper's weapon having run short of ammunition. The 98K was exceptionally accurate and with the anti-slip butt and the Zeiss telescopic sight it was a great weapon. The man leading the group was young and had blond hair. Paul adjusted the sight for bullet drop as the range was eight hundred metres. Shooting downhill made it even more difficult. Paul eased his aim to the man's shoulder and squeezed the trigger. The British corporal spun around with a yell and tumbled into a patch of scrub. The enemy squad picked up their leader and scuttled back down the slope.

"Aimed for the wound again did you?" said Stephan as he and Paul eased back into a hollow.

Paul gave a small shrug. "I really don't like killing people."

Stephan smiled. "I get it. I don't particularly enjoy it either, but I don't think we'll tell the Hauptman, he wouldn't understand.

Paul grinned back at his friend. He hadn't wanted to get close to anyone after killing his squad in southern Russia but Stephan hadn't let him alone. The fact his friend was popular with the rest of the platoon meant that Paul had slowly become accepted by the group. They also appreciated his growing ability as a sniper. Stephan had dragged Paul along to the night clubs and flesh pots in both Cherbourg, where the division had first been placed, and then in Madrid. At first Paul had refused but he found Stephan's unfailing optimism and friendliness infectious. He found himself loosening up and enjoying the company of young women again, even if it was paid for.

One night in Madrid Stephan had sat with him on a balcony overlooking the city. The air raid sirens had not sounded and it looked as though the sky would be free of B25s tonight. The Americans generally sent a few squadrons over the city just to annoy the population. It was dark due to the blackout restrictions but both men sat on an old bench at the front of the two storey inn enjoying the balmy night air.

"Paul, if I die I don't want you to go back to the wreck you were before," said his friend.

Paul had been stunned and just looked at him.

"I mean there is a good chance one of us will die or be badly wounded but it doesn't mean the other man has to give up," continued Stephan.

Paul shook his head. "It's more than that. I changed because of a mistake."

"Yeh, the boys guessed as much but truth be told you're not the first soldier who has killed a friend and you won't be the last. Under extreme pressure we make mistakes."

"I killed most of my squad," whispered Paul.

For a moment Stephan was quiet but then he shrugged. "An FW190 attacked the company not long before you joined. It gunned down two men and then returned and killed four more with a bomb. When we first entered Russia the mortar squad killed three men by accident. War is shit and we do our best to survive."

"But I dropped grenades on my own people!" said Paul.

"The platoon doesn't care. We all know it could have been us doing the same thing," said Stephan.

Paul stared into the dregs of his beer as his friend left to get more drinks. When he returned he had two Spanish women with long dark hair in tow.

They watched Italian fighters duel with British Spitfires the next day and from what they could work out the combat was a draw with both sides losing two planes. Later Kittyhawks flew north escorted by more Spitfires. This time they were unopposed.

"I'm guessing the air boys are outnumbered," said Stephan.

"A bit different to Russia where we seemed to dominate the sky," said Paul.

"I was speaking to a wounded Soldat from the 21st Panzer in Madrid. They were some of the first boys to go up against the Americans, anyway he said the Yanks had just about everything that opens and closes. They have coffee, jam and cigarettes that are so smooth. Then there's the support they get from their artillery and air force. He told me the only thing that helps when fighting them is the lack of experience. It seems they have only bought a couple of veteran divisions over from England and Africa. It looks like they are blooding new troops."

Paul grunted, "Great, when they send the ones over with

experience then we will really be in the shit."

"It looks as though it's going to be a long war," said Stephan.

Historical Notes

1. Assassination attempt: Johann Georg Esler did attempt to blow

up Adolf Hitler and other high ranking Nazis on November 8 1939.

Hitler, for various reasons, cut his speech short and left the beer

hall a mere thirteen minutes before the bomb exploded.

2. Goering and the Jews: Goering did believe much of the propaganda about the Jews but he wasn't fanatical in his hatred of them and was known to protect the odd Jew on his staff.

3. Note on equipment: Every item used in this novel was either on the drawing board or actually used. The only aircraft that has been shifted substantially in its development is the Me155. Here I decided that an increased interest in naval aviation by the Germans would advance perhaps at least one German planes development.

4. The Jets: It is now common historical opinion that the real factor which delayed the development of the ME262 was the engines. I believe with everything going right the very earliest they could have introduced them was at the start of 1944.

5. The Defeat of England: This was possible in 1940, probably if an invasion was launched in late August/ early September, and if the British defeat at Dunkirk had been catastrophic. Even then it would have been a close run thing.

6. Russia invading: This was discussed at length by the Russian leadership. In this time line Stalin tries to take advantage of what he believes is weak German leadership.

7. Spain: This attempt to get the Allies back into Europe is my Sledgehammer. This operation was to be an invasion of France if it looked like the Soviet Union was going to fall. In this time line common sense prevails, Portugal is bought off and Spain, which has been more involved in the fighting against Russia than it was in the real time line, is invaded. It was also chosen instead of Sicily as the Axis hold Malta, and though Greece was a possibility the Americans would never have agreed to an attack so far from France. Hence Spain is the compromise.

In book two some characters will remain a focus, new ones will be brought in and others left to make their own way in the war without the writer's attention.

Made in the USA
San Bernardino, CA
02 January 2018